C000245360

COURAGE
for the
HOME FRONT
GIRLS

BOOKS BY SUSANNA BAVIN

COURAGE
for the
HOME FRONT
GIRLS

SUSANNA BAVIN

bookouture

Published by Bookouture in 2024

An imprint of Storyfire Ltd.
Carmelite House
50 Victoria Embankment
London EC4Y 0DZ

www.bookouture.com

ISBN: 978-1-83790-788-5
eBook ISBN: 978-1-83790-787-8

In memory of Benjamin
And also to his parents, Annette and Trevor

CHAPTER ONE

OCTOBER 1940

Betty was dragged back to consciousness as the all too familiar sound of the air-raid siren penetrated her deep sleep. When the raids had begun back in the summer, she had sat bolt upright in bed, instantly awake, each time the siren commenced its wailing. These days, or rather these nights, she was more likely to take some seconds to surface. Was that because everyone was so accustomed to the raids by this time? Or was it a simple matter of sleep deprivation? Night after night the Luftwaffe crossed the English Channel on its deadly mission, set upon causing as much destruction as possible. Night after night the civilians of Britain stayed in a state of readiness in their voluntary capacities – fire-watchers, first-aiders, rescue squads, gas, electricity and water engineers, the ARP ready to shepherd folk to public shelters, the women of the WVS ready with their tea urns and blankets.

Betty's voluntary night-time work was as a fire-watcher, which she did regularly alongside her friend and colleague, the newly married Sally Henshaw, on the roof of the local salvage depot. But tonight Betty and Sally weren't on duty.

Switching on her bedside lamp, Betty swung her feet out of

bed. She always pulled the chair where she left her clothes near to the bed last thing at night, so she could stand on the bedside mat while she flung her clothes on, to save her bare feet from having to cross the cold floor. After quickly dressing, she turned off the lamp, then removed the lightweight frame covered in blackout material from the window, and finally opened the curtains. This was so that, should an incendiary penetrate the roof-tiles and end up in her room, the flames would be seen from outside.

Snatching up her handbag, she hurried to help the other residents of Star House to prepare the place. There were three of them here tonight: herself and Mrs Beaumont, the landlady, and Mary, another of the billetees. The other two, Lottie and Stella, were out on first-aid duty.

The preparations didn't take long. As well as opening the curtains, the water, gas and electricity needed to be switched off, and the buckets of sand and water that stood all day in the hallway had to be placed outside the front door. While the girls saw to this, Mrs Beaumont prepared hot-water bottles and a Thermos flask of tea before checking the contents of the air-raid box. Most households had one of these. They were meant to contain important papers like birth certificates and insurance details. Mrs Beaumont, who had been a theatrical landlady before the war, also kept in hers treasured photographs of the stars of the music hall such as Vesta Victoria, Marie Kendall and Charles Penrose – otherwise known as the Laughing Policeman.

'All done?' asked Mrs Beaumont, opening the back door.

With the sound of enemy engines droning overhead, they made their way down the garden by the light of tissue-dimmed torches. Betty, the last in line, took one final glance upwards at the starry sky before carefully descending the steep steps into the cold, damp air of the Anderson shelter. Mary put down the biscuit tin, the full kettle, tea-caddy and milk jug. Then she took the candle off the little wooden shelf, as Mrs Beaumont took the box of matches from her pocket. There was a brief *fzzz* sound as she struck the match, then she put the flame to the wick, holding it there until it caught.

'There you are.' She handed the candle to Betty. 'Let's see if this works.'

'Fingers crossed it's going to make the Andy a bit more comfy,' said Mary, her blue eyes shining in the candlelight's golden glow.

'Let's hope so,' agreed Betty.

It was an idea she had come across in *Vera's Voice*, which, like all the women's magazines, published ideas every week to help families make the best of living in wartime conditions.

Earlier that evening, Betty and Mary had lugged two large terracotta flowerpots out of the garden shed and into the shelter. Now Betty stood the candle in the base of one of the flowerpots and then Mary helped her to upend the other pot on the top of it, making sure both were steady.

'Ta da!' sang Betty. 'Our very own flowerpot stove.'

'Apparently, it'll heat up really well,' Mary told Mrs Beaumont.

'Put the kettle on top of it,' said Mrs Beaumont. 'Let's see if we can keep it boiling.'

'I don't know about boiling,' said Betty, 'but it'll certainly keep it hot.'

The three of them settled down to wait out the raid. Mrs Beaumont reclined in the striped deckchair, her black hair curled around rollers and covered by a hairnet. Betty and Mary sat on folding chairs and played cards. All three of them smoked, Mrs Beaumont with her cigarette in a long holder.

She smiled at her lodgers. 'Rollers and a cigarette-holder: the height of sophistication.'

It was a long raid. They had been summoned from their beds at two o'clock and the all-clear didn't sound until seven.

Seven! Usually raids ended during the night and you had the chance to slip back into bed to grab some decent shut-eye, but not this time.

Sleeping on the bunks in the Andy was never a comfortable experience, but at least Betty had a day off work to look forward to, unlike Mary, who had to get ready for a ten-hour shift at the munitions, where Lottie and Stella also worked.

The three of them had recently told Mrs Beaumont they were looking for a billet closer to Trafford Park, where the munitions factory was. Betty had been sorry to hear it. She liked the other three and would miss them, let alone she felt she had been through enough upheaval since the summer.

The thought of upheaval brought Grace instantly to mind. Grace, her stepmother, the woman who had been all too obviously on the lookout for a husband and who had bagged Betty's beloved dad while he was a relatively new widower. He and Grace had got married before Mum had been gone even a year, which had caused many a sharp glance and a critical murmur among the neighbours, but it hadn't been long before Grace had worked her charms on everyone and those same neighbours had ended up telling Betty that her dear mum would have been pleased to know her dad was being properly looked after.

That was the thing about Grace. She always got things to go her way. Just look at how she'd eased Betty out of her lifelong home. Grace had not only arranged for her to leave but had sent her all the way to the other end of Manchester. And it had all been achieved with a smile and a trilling laugh that had left everybody convinced that Grace Hughes had done her very best for her stepdaughter. Everybody except Betty. Betty knew that Grace had wanted to get rid of her.

Thank goodness for Mrs Beaumont. She had her rules, of course, but as long as you stuck to them she was good humour itself, and she liked nothing better than to serve one of her delicious meals in the dining room, then light up a cigarette and sit

'Oh, now, steady on,' said Dad, raising an eyebrow at Grace.

'It's all right, Dad,' said Betty, even though it wasn't. 'I'm happy for Sally to be the new manager. She deserves it. She got the post because of her hard work and initiative.'

She prattled on, praising her friend. Her voice sounded cheerful but really she felt humiliated. Wasn't it enough that Grace had succeeded in ousting her from her own home? Was she now trying to drive a wedge between her and Dad too?

CHAPTER TWO

The girls took turns to work on Saturdays at the salvage depot and today was Sally's day. Eagerness expanded inside her chest at the thought of becoming the manager when Mr Overton took up his new position in the Town Hall. He used to be the local bank manager, which had made him a person of standing in the local community here in Chorlton, and he had come out of retirement to run the depot. But he had been unhappy there, never making any secret of how he considered salvage to be women's work and therefore detrimental to his reputation and his masculinity.

Sally smiled to herself as she got on with her work. Detrimental to his masculinity! That made him sound like a handsome film star like Errol Flynn or James Stewart. Mr Overton definitely didn't fit into the category. He had an ample tummy and a round face, with deep-set eyes beneath bushy eyebrows. No, he definitely wasn't film-star material!

He had been happier since he had secured his new post. Sally had herself worked in the Town Hall before she'd come to the salvage depot. She had been a clerk in the Food Office, a job she had loved and taken great pride in doing to the best of her ability. Now she applied that same attitude to her salvage work, and had made a point of researching all the different uses to which the salvage was put, such as newspapers being turned into shell-caps, envelopes into cartridge wads and soap powder boxes into aero-engine caskets.

She was proud to be a salvage girl. She wished her parents could feel the same but they, especially her mother, thought that salvage was a come-down from the office-based job she had been in before. Fortunately her new husband, Andrew, and his mother saw things differently and admired her for the dedication she had developed to her salvage work.

A shiver of delight ran through Sally as Andrew popped into her mind. He was everything she had ever dreamed of, and more. He had a tall, athletic figure and a narrow face with a firm jawline. His warm brown eyes were kind and intelligent and his way of looking people straight in the eyes spoke of the honesty and integrity of his character.

The day that Dad had written his letter of consent to her marriage – without which Sally and Andrew couldn't have married, with Sally being under twenty-one – had been one of the happiest of her life, and her wedding day just one week ago had been the absolute happiest, not least because Mum, in spite of all her early reservations, had thrown herself into making the occasion as memorable as she could. With her new friend Betty and her oldest friend Deborah as her bridesmaids, Sally had felt supported and special.

She laughed at herself, comparing the thought of her in her forget-me-not-blue suit on her wedding day with the way she looked today at the depot. Salvage wasn't the cleanest of jobs and she wore dungarees with her hair protected by a headscarf tied underneath the back of her hair. She had heavy-duty gloves as well.

Much as Sally loved working alongside Betty and truly enjoyed her company, she didn't at all mind being on her own.

She worked steadily at the daily tasks, starting with emptying the sacks of mixed salvage and putting all the various types – tin, rubber, string, paper and so on – into the correct places around the salvage yard for them to be collected and taken away. Ugh – some animal bones had ended up in one of the sacks. They ought to have gone into one of the bone-baskets that were attached to lamp-posts. Bones were used to make explosives, fertiliser, glue and even soap.

They were past the middle of October now and autumn was well and truly here. Gold and red leaves were starting to fall, swirling in the breeze and collecting in the gutters. The days were drawing in, but no welcoming light spilled out from windows at dusk because the blackout rules were strictly enforced and hefty fines were imposed on householders who transgressed. Some people didn't like it when an ARP warden ticked them off for letting a tiny sliver of light show, but Sally's darling dad was an ARP warden, so she was firmly on their side.

She kept herself busy all day, though as the afternoon wore on she thought more and more about going home and being with Andrew. Neither of them was on duty tonight, and they were going out this evening. Sally's voluntary night-time work was fire-watching, while Andrew worked in light rescue – as opposed to heavy rescue, which involved the use of machinery – helping get people out of ruined buildings during and after air raids.

Sally was looking forward to dancing at the Ritz in the middle of Manchester. It was one of her favourite ballrooms, with its pillars and art deco features, and the balcony from where you could sit at the tables and look down onto the ballroom floor. The Ritz had two orchestras and, when one was coming to the end of its set, the famous revolving stage would begin to turn and the other orchestra would come into view, playing the same music so that the dancing didn't stop.

At the end of the day Sally changed out of her dungarees

and back into her own clothes before heading home for tea. She and Andrew lived with his mother. Mrs Henshaw was a sensible woman whose austere features belied her kind heart. She had made Sally welcome from the first, which was a lot more than could be said for the way Sally's mother had initially felt towards Andrew.

Sally had lived in the Henshaw household for some weeks before she and Andrew got married. Andrew had given up his bedroom to her and had slept downstairs. Now that they were man and wife, they had the double bedroom that had previously been Mrs Henshaw's and she had moved into the smaller bedroom.

When Sally arrived home, she opened the front door onto the aroma of cooking.

'It's only me,' she called as she removed her outdoor things.

Smoothing her fair hair, she went into the kitchen, where Mrs Henshaw was busy at the gas-stove. Because Sally worked long hours at the salvage depot, Mrs Henshaw did almost all the cooking. It had been easy for Sally to fall in with this, though the wish to cook for her husband was starting to niggle a little.

Mrs Henshaw angled her cheek to receive Sally's kiss.

'That smells good,' Sally commented. 'What are we having?'

'Baked vegetable roll with jacket potatoes.'

'I love jacket potatoes,' Sally said at once.

Mrs Henshaw laughed. 'Oh, you! I've yet to find a way of cooking potatoes that you don't like.'

'Don't mock,' Sally retorted good-naturedly. 'Just think how easy I am to feed.'

'Then you'll be delighted to know that the vegetable roll is made with potato pastry.'

Sally's heart gave a happy little bump as the front door opened. She went eagerly into the hallway as Andrew walked inside, but the greeting on her lips gave way to an exclamation of surprise and concern.

'Andrew! Are you all right?'

He was covered in dust – his clothes, his face, his hair.

Mrs Henshaw appeared at Sally's side. She too exclaimed in shock.

Andrew's familiar smile appeared through the dust. 'Not to worry. I'm fine. Let's just say that today's training day turned out to be rather more realistic than anticipated.'

Sally hurried to him, wanting to wrap her arms round him, but then she stopped short because of the thick layer of dust.

'What happened?' she asked.

'A wall came down. No one was hurt.'

Mrs Henshaw took over. She bustled forward, spreading newspaper on the floor. 'Jacket, shirt and trousers on there now. Sally can take them outside and give them a good go with the carpet-beater while you have a strip-wash.'

'Mum,' Andrew protested, laughing, 'I'm not going to take my trousers off here.'

'Well, it's either here or outside,' his mother retorted. 'I'm not having that dust walked through the house, thank you.'

She withdrew into the kitchen while Andrew complied. Sally took the filthy garments into the back garden and draped them over the washing-line before administering a thorough beating, which brought forth grey clouds that made her cough. Andrew might be making light of what had taken place, but he had clearly been very close to it.

She grinned at her mother-in-law as she walked back through the scullery and the kitchen. 'No one warned me about this sort of thing before I got married.'

Soon they were all seated at the table, tucking into the baked vegetable roll and jacket potato.

'Tell us what happened at the light rescue training day,' said Mrs Henshaw.

'We went to a bomb site to practise safe methods of shifting rubble,' Andrew began. 'It all went according to plan. The site was beside a house that had been bombed out, but its shell was still standing. There we were, working away, when there was a tremendous noise. Before any of us had time to work out what it was or where it was coming from, the side of the bombed-out house collapsed.'

'No,' breathed Sally.

'It's a good job nobody was beside it or they'd have bought it outright,' said Andrew, looking serious. 'As it was, we all headed for home looking like we'd spent the day rolling about in brick dust.'

'I'm very glad that no one was hurt,' said Mrs Henshaw.

'What about your day, Mum?' Andrew asked. 'You had a WVS committee meeting this morning, didn't you?'

'We've decided to set up a "shop day" once a week,' said Mrs Henshaw. 'We need to collect second-hand goods of all kinds that we can sell on. The idea is to raise money to buy Christmas presents for children.'

'That's a lovely idea,' said Sally, touched.

'One of the committee members has a fur coat that she wants to donate,' said Mrs Henshaw. 'I've seen the coat and it's a good one.'

'It doesn't sound like the normal sort of thing you'd find in a second-hand shop,' Andrew commented.

'It isn't,' his mother agreed. 'The East Didsbury WVS are holding an auction later this month, so we're going to ask them if they'll sell it for us. We hope to raise quite a sum.'

They finished the first course and Mrs Henshaw removed the plates. She had made a steamed date pudding. She placed the cream-jug on the table.

'That's never cream, is it?' Andrew asked.

'Try it and see,' said his mother. 'It's what they're calling mock-cream. It's made with milk, margarine, water and some of our precious sugar ration.'

After tea, Sally washed up and Mrs Henshaw dried while Andrew read the newspaper, then the three of them sat chatting and smoking over a cup of tea.

'Are you going to listen to something while we're out?' Sally asked her mother-in-law. She picked up their copy of the *Radio Times*, which had on its cover a pretty photograph of the Princess Elizabeth fussing a corgi, together with the announcement: *HRH Princess Elizabeth will broadcast to the children of the Empire on Sunday.* That had taken place last weekend. This Saturday was the last day of the week's information.

'There's *Star Time* later on,' said Mrs Henshaw, 'with Henry Hall and his orchestra, though it doesn't say which stars will be appearing. Before that, there's *Garrison Theatre.* Jack Warner is on it this evening. I like him.'

Andrew smiled at Sally, his brown eyes softening. 'Time for you to go and get ready, young Mrs Henshaw.'

Sally ran upstairs. She put on a pretty dress with lightly padded shoulders, a sweetheart neckline and a nipped-in waist above a skirt that would flare nicely when she danced in Andrew's arms.

She tidied her fair hair, fluffing out the waves. Her chum Betty called her a dark-blonde, a description Sally loved. It was far more flattering than being called a dirty-blonde, which was what her mum had always said.

The best moment of the whole day came when she returned to the parlour and saw the look on Andrew's face – delighted and proud. More than that, she had obviously taken his breath away. His startled look made her feel beautiful.

He stood up and kissed her, but only on the cheek because his mother was there.

'You'll be the loveliest girl on the dance-floor,' he told her.

'Let me look at you. Do a twirl,' said Mrs Henshaw as Andrew disappeared to get changed.

Andrew reappeared presently, wearing his suit. Sally hoped the way she looked at him made him feel as attractive and confident as his admiration for her had made her feel, though the truth was that she didn't mind what he wore. He always looked handsome in her eyes.

But before they could leave the house the air-raid siren went off, filling the darkness with its mournful wailing. Quickly the three of them got the house ready, and then hurried to their Anderson shelter.

'What a shame you didn't get your night out together,' said Mrs Henshaw when they'd been in the shelter for nearly two hours. 'And you looked so pretty in that dress, Sally.' She smiled ruefully. 'Or you did before you had to smother it with a warm overcoat.'

'Never mind,' said Andrew. 'There'll be other dances. I'm just not sure when. It seems to be air raids more or less every night at the moment.'

They played a few hands of whist, then Sally and Mrs Henshaw brought out their knitting.

'What are you making?' Andrew asked his mother.

'A cardigan for Auntie Vera. Her birthday's coming up.'

Sally nodded to herself. She had met Andrew's Auntie Vera at the wedding. She was Mrs Henshaw's sister, though you wouldn't have known it to look at them. Mrs Henshaw was tall with a slim build and her face was severe in repose. Her sister was shorter with a more rounded figure and her rosy cheeks were made for smiling.

'It's a pretty colour,' said Sally, looking at the moss-green wool.

'The wool shop is running low on supplies,' said Mrs Henshaw, 'so I had to get some of this as well.' She delved inside her work-bag and produced a ball of cream wool. 'I'm going to work a couple of stripes of this into it.'

'They're called patriotic stripes when you have to adapt your pattern like that,' said Sally.

The raid dragged on until the early hours of Sunday, but there was no point in complaining or feeling hard done by. This was wartime and it was everyone's duty to make the best of it. Sally concentrated on the good things, not just because it was in her nature to do so but also because she believed it helped Andrew's spirits. He had never again mentioned his secret wartime work, not since their emotional conversation about it earlier in the month, but Sally knew she would never forget it as long as she lived and she wanted to do everything she could to support him.

CHAPTER THREE

'I bet you can't wait for Mr Overton to leave so you can step into his shoes,' Betty said to Sally as they got on with sorting through the daily salvage sacks. 'Actually, I don't think that's the right way to put it. You'll hardly be stepping into his shoes because he's never liked being here.'

'That's true,' Sally agreed. 'I'm sure he'll be far happier in an office. He'll be in a senior position in the accounts department, which will suit him perfectly with his banking background.'

Betty nodded. Mr Overton drove her mad sometimes but at heart she was fond of him, and she liked the thought that he was moving somewhere he would be happier. 'When you're in charge, the depot will have a manager who is seriously interested in the work and who wants to make the most of it. I'm looking forward to that.'

Mr Overton came out into the yard while they were removing the inner tubes from old bicycle tyres.

'Good morning, ladies. I'm expecting a visitor shortly, a Mr Atkinson. He runs a bookshop. As well as selling new books, he deals in second-hand ones, including those that are valuable and antiquarian.'

'Good,' said Sally. 'Is he coming to look at the books we set aside in case they were worth something?'

'He is indeed,' said Mr Overton. 'Let's hope we're not wasting his time. Would you take the books to my office, please, Miss Hughes?'

'Yes, Mr Overton.'

Betty went into the building. It had been a warehouse before the war. Flat-roofed and no taller than an ordinary two-storey house, it was a bit wider than two houses joined together. Some of the depot's rooms were used for storage but quite a few of them were empty. Betty fetched the books, some of which had handsome leather covers or gilt-edged pages. She took them to Mr Overton's office on the ground floor, then went back outside into the yard, one side of which was covered over by a simple frame with a flat roof like a bike shed would be.

'I hope the books will fetch a decent sum to contribute to the war effort,' said Sally.

'I hope so too,' said Betty. 'It was your idea to see about a book expert, so it would be a big feather in your cap.'

'I wonder what he'll be like, this Mr Atkinson,' said Sally.

Betty laughed. 'He'll be an old boy with white hair and deathly-pale skin because he spends all his time with his books and doesn't see enough sunshine.'

They carried on working, breaking off to help load up a Corporation van with the latest collection of metal. Not long after it had left, a bespectacled young man walked through the gates. He was rather gangly, in a way you might expect of a tall person, but this fellow was of little more than medium height. He wore an overcoat and a trilby with a grey band. He stood for a moment, getting his bearings.

'Good morning,' Sally called. 'Can we help you? Are you Mr Atkinson?'

'Yes, I am.' He came towards them. Behind his glasses, his eyes were hazel. His lean face and straight nose made him good-looking, while a certain gentleness in his features gave an impression of modesty. Stopping, he raised his hat politely, giving the girls a shy smile. 'Good morning, ladies. S-Samuel Atkinson at your service.'

At your service, Betty thought. How old-fashioned. But she was impressed too. He had nice manners.

The moment he replaced his hat on his head, a splat of bird mess landed on it. The girls exclaimed in dismay.

'Good job you had your hat on,' said Sally.

'It's meant to be lucky, isn't it,' asked Betty, 'if a bird does it on your head?'

'I'd f-far rather it d-did it on my hat,' said Mr Atkinson.

'Give it here,' said Betty, 'and I'll wash it off while you see Mr Overton.'

'There's no need.'

'Don't be daft. It's no trouble. We can't send you on your way looking like that or you might not come back again.'

'Very well,' said Mr Atkinson. 'Thank you.'

Removing his trilby, he handed it over. His hair was dark and, although it showed signs of having been Brilliantined flat as was the custom, some stubborn curls sprang up as if he had just run his hands through it. Betty smiled. She wanted to tidy it for him.

'Mr Overton is expecting you,' Sally told Mr Atkinson. 'I'll show you to his office.'

Betty caught her eye and gave her an encouraging nod, hoping Mr Overton would invite Sally to remain while Mr Atkinson examined the books. After all, she was the person he would be dealing with in the future.

Betty followed the other two across the yard to the building, then peeled off so she could sort out Mr Atkinson's hat. She gave the stain a good rinse to get it off, knowing she mustn't rub it while it was wet because that would make it worse. When she went back into the yard, spinning the trilby deftly on her finger, she was disappointed to find Sally outside. It was typical of Mr Overton that it hadn't occurred to him to let her stay.

Sally looked at the hat. 'Success?'

'Right as ninepence,' said Betty. 'It just needs to dry off.'

'You've made a good job of it,' said Sally.

'Really it should have been left to dry and then it could have been brushed off,' said Betty, 'but I couldn't let him leave here with his hat in that state.' She chuckled. 'Nobody would have wanted to sit next to him on the bus.'

'I hope he appreciates it,' said Sally.

'I'm sure he will,' said Betty. Now why did she feel so sure of that? She remembered how he had said, 'At your service.' It seemed right that somebody who used old-fashioned courtesies would take notice of a kindness.

'He seems nice,' said Sally. 'I hope he'll come here on a regular basis.'

'We get a lot of books, so maybe he will.'

'He's good-looking,' said Sally. 'It's a shame about his stammer.'

'Oh, I don't know,' said Betty. 'I think it's sweet. He has a sense of humour too. Another chap might have blown his top about the bird mess.'

'That's true,' agreed Sally. She smiled and her fawny-hazel eyes twinkled. 'It's funny how accidents can bring people together. Look at Andrew and me. If I hadn't tripped over my feet on the stairs at the Town Hall, we'd never have met.'

Betty smiled. She was familiar with the story. 'You fell into his arms.' A dreamy sigh escaped her. 'That's so romantic. I wish something like that would happen to me.' Then she laughed at herself. 'You can't call meeting because of a dollop of bird mess romantic.'

. . .

locking the depot behind them. Betty unlocked it again when she started work at eight. The depot had a six-foot wooden fence across the front of the yard, with a big pair of gates that were bolted on the inside. Betty gained access via a separate door in the fence, stepping over the plank of wood that stood up across the bottom.

Crossing the yard, she unlocked the door to the building and went upstairs to change into her dungarees and put her hair into a turban. On went her thick gloves. No one could call salvage a glamorous job, but it made an essential contribution to the war effort. The government wanted all citizens to be salvage-minded.

Betty went back into the yard, unbolted the gates and hauled them open one at a time. They had to stand open all day in case a collection van arrived, and so that people could drop off the salvage they had collected. On Saturdays clerks sometimes popped in from local offices to hand over a week's worth of waste paper. Betty hoped there would be heaps of paper today, because that would give her a reason to light the fire in the office and keep warm while she sorted through the sheets to remove what Mr Overton called 'foreign bodies,' namely paperclips and treasury-tags, because they caused problems for the machines at the paper-mill, which was the waste paper's final destination.

Any waste paper wasn't usually brought until early afternoon because most offices stayed open until one or two o'clock on Saturdays. Betty spent the morning emptying the sacks of mixed salvage and putting the bits of rubber, metal, string and so on into the right places. She hummed popular songs to herself as she worked but when she started on 'Kiss Me Goodnight, Sergeant-Major' she forgot the humming and started singing.

When she reached the end, a man's voice behind her called, 'Bravo!'

All of a flutter, Betty turned and found herself staring at the most handsome man she'd ever seen, which only served to increase the fluttering. His blue eyes regarded her with amusement as he raised his cigarette and deposited it between his lips so he had both hands free to applaud her, one of his dark eyebrows climbing lazily up his forehead in a way that was almost but not quite mocking. The cigarette gave a little jerk as his lips twitched into a smile under a Clark Gable moustache. He wore a cloth cap, beneath which showed dark hair. His eyelashes were equally dark, making his blue eyes seem the bluest Betty had ever seen. Her heart pitter-pattered.

He grinned at her, removing the cigarette from his lips to say in a cheery voice, 'Will you give me an encore if I ask nicely?'

'I didn't know anybody was listening.'

'You've got a pretty voice,' he said.

It was impossible not to smile. 'Thanks. Have you brought some salvage?'

He looked around as if taking in his surroundings for the first time. 'This is the salvage depot, is it? I'd heard there was one hereabouts. I came in to ask for directions, actually. I'm looking for a pub called the Horse and Jockey.'

'Turn right out of the gates, left at the end of the road and you'll find it at this end of Chorlton Green,' said Betty, glad to help. 'It's Tudory-looking. You know, black and white. You can't miss it.'

'Cheers.' He seemed about to turn away, but then he added, 'I say, maybe I should come back again with some salvage as a thank-you.'

'Yes, do that,' Betty said before she could stop herself. Her chin dipped down for a moment in embarrassment. Did she sound forward?

The young man took a final drag on his cigarette, chucked it down and ground it beneath the heel of his leather shoe.

'If I ever pass this way again,' he said. He tipped his cap to her and went on his way.

Drawn by an invisible thread, Betty followed him to the entrance, and watched him walk away along the street, admiring the way he carried himself with his shoulders thrown back and a certain jaunty confidence in his step. She thought: *He's full of himself.* Then she thought: *He deserves to be, a man like that.*

Oh heavens, what on earth was she thinking, standing here gazing after him like a lovelorn maiden? What if he turned around and saw her? Feeling fluttery all over again, Betty ducked back into the yard.

But really – would it have been so bad if he had seen her?

CHAPTER FOUR

It was a beautiful day. From the hotel where she and her parents were staying, Lorna looked between the lines of anti-blast tape that criss-crossed the window at the private garden in the middle of the leafy square. Her insides felt quivery with nerves. The court case was due to begin the day after tomorrow. The thought of it filled her with unhappiness as well as nerves. It was the last thing she wanted.

A van came to a halt along the road and the driver and another man got out. From the back, they hauled out sandbag after sandbag, making a heap of them on the pavement. Then they climbed back into the van, drove round the square and formed another heap over there. For putting out incendiaries, Lorna knew.

It was very different here in London to how it was up in Lancaster, where her family lived. London was taking a hammering night after night, whereas Lancaster, for all its preparedness, had yet to be on the receiving end of Jerry's calling card.

Lorna and her parents had been in London for some weeks

in the spring and early summer and Mummy had been against returning now.

'It isn't safe,' she had declared, her eyes widening at the thought.

'There isn't a choice,' Daddy had replied in his don't-argue voice. Much of what he said was uttered in that tone. 'Lorna has to appear in court. It's required of her.'

But what if – what if the court case didn't go ahead? What if Lorna and George made up their differences before it commenced?

Those were the questions filling Lorna's mind. There had been no contact between her and George since their engagement had ended, no letters, no telephone calls, nothing. Daddy had whisked her and Mummy back to Lancaster and Lorna had hoped day after day for a letter from George, but none had arrived. Should she write to him? But pride had forbidden it. He was the one who had called it off, and she wasn't going to crawl.

Now she and her parents were back in London. The last time they had come, they'd stayed in Belgravia in a handsome house with sumptuous William Morris wallpaper, the furniture button-upholstered in printed silk. The decor and furnishings were old-fashioned and costly. It might look as if the West-Sadlers had lived there for generations but in truth Daddy had rented the house, complete with all its furnishings, china, linen, the lot. They hadn't even needed to bring their own face-flannels. Even the staff came with the house.

This time they were staying in a smart but discreet hotel tucked away in a quiet, exclusive backwater. 'Discreet' wasn't Daddy's usual style, but apparently this was what Mr Wilding, the barrister, had advised.

Turning away from the window, Lorna looked at the black marble clock on the mantelpiece, working out times in her head.

Mummy and Daddy had gone out but would want to be back before the nightly air raid started. Lorna had feigned a headache so as to be left behind. George was working dreadfully long hours at the War Office – at least, she presumed he still was – but he liked to nip home around teatime to collect his post, so this was Lorna's chance.

Was she about to make a colossal idiot of herself? In the weeks she had been in Lancaster following their separation, she had gone round and round in circles, wanting to be reunited with George, wanting never to see him again... wanting another chance while wishing that she didn't want it.

With a sigh so deep it seemed to be dredged up all the way from the soles of her shoes, she looked at her engagement ring. She had removed it when she'd gone home to Lancaster but now she was wearing it again.

She had replaced it on her finger when they arrived in London yesterday because she wanted George to see her wearing it.

'Oh, good,' Daddy had said. 'You've put your ring back on.'

'You don't mind?' Lorna had asked.

'I was going to tell you to put it on. Wilding says it'll look better in court, make you cut a sympathetic figure.'

How Lorna wished Daddy hadn't said that. Did it mean that others would assume she was wearing it to get the judge on her side? Would George think that? Oh, please let him realise she was wearing it in good faith.

The marble clock pinged the quarter-hour. It was time to get ready. A tiny shiver skittered through her. She wasn't sure if it was excitement or fear. Either way, it only served to make her all the more determined.

She had selected her midnight-blue two-piece suit, comprising a flared skirt and hip-length jacket fitted so that it went in at the waist and out at the bust, making her not-so-ample bosom look more shapely. Under it she wore a silk blouse. She dabbed some lily-of-the-valley scent on her wrists.

Perfume was something that girls were stashing away because of the inevitable shortages, though Lorna had no such worries. Daddy had presented her and Mummy with fresh bottles only last week, thanks to what he referred to as his contacts.

Blue-and-white leather slingbacks, gloves with scalloped cuffs, and a clutch-purse completed her outfit. Lorna leaned towards the mirror to check her glossy dark-brown hair. She curled it regularly and wore it drawn back over her ears, where it was held in position by pretty combs and fell in loose waves to her shoulders at the back. She curled her fringe as well, and pushed it aside to create a little froth at each temple. She put on clip-on earrings and positioned her blue felt hat with the upswept brim, giving her hair a final fluff-up. She ought to wear a coat, really, but she looked good as she was, and George liked this stylish blue ensemble.

Slipping the string of her gas-mask box over her shoulder, she left the hotel suite. She ran lightly downstairs, left the hotel and took a taxi to Mount Street, where George had his rooms in what he and his pals referred to as 'the bachelor building' because the apartments were let only to single men.

The doorman was an old boy who had emerged from retirement to take the place of the young man who had joined up. He politely touched the brim of his top hat to her as he admitted her. He followed her inside, closing the door behind them.

'Can I assist you with the lift, miss?' he enquired.

'No, thank you,' Lorna replied. 'I'll go up the stairs. I'm only going to the first floor.'

She took her time on the stairs. She didn't want to arrive looking flustered.

The hall, stairs and landing all smelled of tobacco, which made the atmosphere seem masculine and sophisticated. Lorna walked along the forest-green runner and stopped outside George's door. Her heart thumped. A faint whiff of lily-of-the-valley trembled in the air, tantalising her nostrils. Might George be tantalised too?

She knocked and waited, her heartbeat picking up speed. When George opened the door, he exclaimed 'Lorna!', startled. Then his pupils filled his eyes until there was space only for the narrowest rim of grey-blue. The breath caught in Lorna's throat and her skin tingled just the way she remembered.

She had evidently caught George in the middle of getting ready to go out. Evening dress suited him – well, actually, anything suited him, with his upright figure and his air of confidence and authority. In the single-breasted jacket, straight-cut trousers and white cotton piqué shirt, he looked immaculate, while the black-satin bow-tie made Lorna remember overhearing a titled young lady murmur to her friend that she would very much like to unfasten it for him. Lorna knew exactly how that girl had felt because she felt the same, but with the added delight of being George's fiancée.

He was everything she had ever dreamed of. His face was lean with sharp cheekbones. His eyes were more grey than blue and their intensity when he gazed at her – or rather, when he used to gaze at her – was enough to make her bones melt. The cherry on the cake – for her father, at least – had been that, when his father died, he would become a baronet, which had meant she would have been a Lady with a capital L.

'Good afternoon, George.' She kept her voice light and bright, despite the sensations that trembled inside her. 'Or should I say, "Good evening," given what you're wearing?'

'Oh – this. I've got a function to go to – air raids permitting.'

'Which means you probably won't go,' said Lorna. 'Aren't you going to invite me in?'

George frowned, his dark eyebrows drawing together. 'I'm not sure that's a good idea.'

Lorna felt as if a bucket of cold water had been thrown over her. Her dismay must have shown, because George hastened to soften the blow.

'I mean, because of the court case. We're probably not meant to see one another.'

Lorna forced a smile. 'Consorting with the enemy?'

He stood back to let her by. His flat contained old-fashioned furniture in dark wood awash with carving. Lorna had assumed it was all family heirlooms until George had told her he rented the rooms furnished.

With a gesture, he invited her to sit down and she perched on the edge of the sofa, her body at a slight angle so that her knees leaned to one side, her trim ankles to the other. It was the way she had been taught by the deportment coach at the finishing school Daddy had insisted upon.

Peeling off her gloves, she slid them into her bag. She wanted George to see she was wearing her engagement ring, but at the same time she didn't want him to see it in case wearing it was a mistake. It was a pear-shaped diamond on a slender gold band. Daddy said it must be worth a mint.

'I've seen the London air raids in the papers and on the newsreel at the cinema,' said Lorna, 'but seeing the destruction with my own eyes...'

'It's pretty bad,' George said quietly, 'but we don't let it stop us.'

He picked up the engraved silver cigarette-box from the low table in front of the fireplace, opening it as he leaned towards her. Lorna caught a breath of his cologne and her senses swam. As she helped herself to a cigarette, she brushed his hand with her fingers. Her fingertips tingled but she didn't look at him – couldn't. She mustn't give any sign that the touch might mean something.

George struck a match and held it close. Lorna let him light her cigarette, inhaling deeply to get it going. She turned her head away, lifting her chin as she exhaled a stream of smoke.

George lit his own cigarette and threw himself into an armchair.

'Sad business,' he remarked.

Sad? *Sad?* The most devastating thing that had ever happened to her in her whole life, and he called it sad?

'Still,' George went on, 'it'll be over soon.'

Lorna focused not on the words but on their delivery. George's tone was neutral. What did that mean? It was better than his sounding relieved or vexed, but nowhere near as good as sounding... No, she mustn't torture herself with thoughts like that.

'Is that what you want?' she asked. 'For it to be over?'

'Don't you?' George replied. 'I've found it... painful to have it hanging over me these past few weeks.'

Lorna leaned forward. 'So have I.' Oh, were they in agreement? Thank goodness she had come here today.

'It's been dashed awkward as well,' George added.

'Awkward?'

'Yes. Haven't you found it so?' George asked. 'The knowing glances, the sympathetic murmurs. The flash of interest that someone can't quite hide.'

A small splutter of shock burst from Lorna's lips. Just when she'd hoped for George to speak of loneliness, heartbreak, regret, what he'd found difficult was the *gossip*. Heat crept into her cheeks and she had to glance down. As if her situation wasn't bad enough without this extra humiliation. Determined to hang on to her dignity, she lifted her chin.

'Perhaps I shouldn't have come here after all,' she said.

'Why did you come?'

And that said it all, didn't it? George hadn't opened the door, taken one look at her and uttered a choked cry before he pulled her into his arms. He hadn't fallen to his knees beside her as she sat on the sofa, begging her to reconsider. He hadn't said, 'You've come... I've wished so hard for you to come.'

'Why?' She put on a breezy voice. What reason could she offer? Inspiration struck. 'I just wanted to say that I'm sorry we have to go through this horrid court appearance. I wouldn't wish that on anybody.'

George frowned, a deeper frown than his earlier one. Yes, there was confusion but there was something else too: a dark displeasure.

'What are you talking about?' he demanded crisply. 'You're the one who brought the case.'

Lorna stared. 'Don't be silly. Of course I didn't.'

'Yes, you did – unless you're suggesting it somehow burst into existence out of thin air.'

For a second, Lorna's lips tightened in annoyance. 'The court case is happening because whenever a person from a titled family is involved in a broken engagement, a breach of promise case automatically follows.'

George stared at her. 'Where on earth did you get that stupid idea?'

Offended, Lorna jerked her chin. 'Daddy told me.'

George released a mirthless laugh. 'Did he indeed?'

'What are you implying?'

'I'm not implying anything,' said George. 'I'm telling you straight that there are no circumstances in which the law requires a breach of promise case to take place automatically. The only way for such a case to be brought is if the jilted girl instigates it.'

Lorna's lips parted on a gasp. A hundred thoughts wheeled around in her mind, but no words emerged.

George shook his head. 'Or, in this case, assuming your shock is as genuine as it looks, the jilted girl's father has brought the case without telling her.' His mouth twisted in what Lorna could only think was disgust. 'I always knew you were under his thumb, Lorna, but I never realised the extent of it until this moment.'

Lorna stiffened in shock. She didn't know what to say. Could it be true? Daddy had told her that because George's family had a title, that made the breach of promise a legal inevitability, but now George was saying that...

Leaning forward, George ground out his unfinished cigarette in the ashtray, then came to his feet in a single movement. He was a tall man and his anger made him appear taller.

'I can't say it surprises me that your father is behind the court case. It ties in with everything that happened earlier in the year after you and I got engaged.'

Anger flared inside Lorna. 'The gossip, you mean. You shouldn't have listened.'

George's eyes glittered, their blue-grey turning to flint. 'When the world and his wife were freely discussing the way my fiancée's family had brought her here to London to bag a title, it was difficult not to listen. But, in any case, I didn't need to listen to gossip to work out that your family was using me, Lorna.'

'That's not true.'

'Yes, it is,' George stated flatly. 'The very first time I saw you, I was captivated. You're so beautiful and graceful and I'd never seen eyes of true green before. I couldn't wait to propose to you. It was only later that I began to see that it was all a scheme by your parents. They dangled you in front of me.'

'Don't be ridiculous,' Lorna objected.

'They used you, Lorna,' said George. 'Your father wanted to bring a title into the family—'

'No, he didn't—'

'—and it's ended up being whispered about freely all over London.'

'And you elected to listen to the whispers,' Lorna said scornfully. 'How *could* you? Didn't you know how I felt about you?'

'The honest answer to that is no, I didn't. I thought I did. I thought you truly loved me but, once your family's plan became obvious, that made me doubt your feelings.'

Resentment boiled up. 'You listened to nasty gossip. I deserve better than that from you.' Lorna stood up. 'Don't leave out your own family. They never wanted you to marry someone with a background in trade.' She could force herself to sound scornful now, but how it had hurt at the time. She would have done anything to please George's mother, but Lady Broughton had been unyielding.

'Don't attempt to divert the blame away from your father,' said George. 'He's the one who's about to drag me into court with the intention of getting a whopping great financial settlement for you. Having failed in his ambition to secure a future baronet as a son-in-law, he's now out for whatever he can get.'

'Oh!' Lorna's blood raced around her body and her muscles quivered. 'Here – you'd better have this back!'

She wrenched the diamond from her finger so violently that it almost took her knuckle with it and hurled it at him. A little flash made a brilliant arc in the air between them.

She didn't even wait for it to land. With a strangled exclamation, she grabbed her clutch-purse and gas-mask box and rushed for the door.

Please don't let Mummy and Daddy have returned to the hotel before me. The only way for Lorna to get into her bedroom was via their suite's sitting room. Pausing outside to draw a breath, she opened the door and walked in. She was unable to prevent herself stopping dead at the sight of her parents.

'You're back,' said her father. 'Good. We want to talk to you.'

Oh cripes. That was the last thing Lorna wanted but she couldn't say so to her father. Daddy hadn't got where he was today by letting people say no to him.

Mummy sat on a damask-covered sofa. Both she and Daddy were dressed for dinner, Mummy in a glorious gown of beaded velvet and Daddy in his evening suit. He couldn't carry evening dress as well as George did. Daddy was a thickset man, with strong shoulders and a heavy jawline. Dressed differently, he might have looked like a boxer. Even so, his expensively tailored clothes showed him in all his prosperousness. He was handsome in a craggy sort of way, his dark eyes forming a contrast to his iron-grey hair.

Fortunately for Lorna, she had inherited her mother's looks – 'only better,' according to Daddy, which might not be entirely flattering to Mummy but was nevertheless true. Lorna's eyes were pure green, a very unusual and rare colour, while Mummy's were greeny-hazel.

'Sit down,' said Daddy.

Lorna sank onto a plush chair.

'Darling, you look ghastly,' said Mummy. 'Does that mean it didn't go well with George?'

Lorna was startled. 'How do you know where I've been?'

'We thought that if we brought you to London in good time before the court case,' said Daddy, 'you'd probably sneak off to see him.'

Lorna's hand flew to her chest. 'D'you mean that you went out earlier on purpose so that I could...'

'Of course we did,' Daddy replied bluntly. 'The point is: did it work? Has George taken you back?'

'He hasn't,' said Mummy. 'Just look at her.'

Lorna peeled off her gloves. The absence of her beautiful diamond said all that needed to be said. She felt a deep pang. How she had loved that ring.

'Please tell me you've simply removed it and put it in your bag,' Daddy said, his voice hardening.

'I threw it back at him,' said Lorna.

'You fool!' Daddy exclaimed. 'You should have kept it.'

pleased by the court's lack of interest in the 'secondary matter' – whatever it was.

'In conclusion,' said Mr Justice Hardacre, 'I regard Miss West-Sadler's breach of promise case as flippant, frivolous and profoundly disrespectful to every right-minded and patriotic person who takes the war seriously. Case dismissed.'

Half an hour later the West-Sadlers, together with Mr Wilding and a pair of clerks, were closeted in a small room furnished with no more than a polished table and some chairs. Lorna was cold with shock, right to the very centre of her being. It had never for one moment occurred to her that the case would be thrown out. Mr Wilding hadn't foreseen it either and he was as surprised as anyone. He had told the West-Sadlers that jilted girls always won something, even if it was only a nominal amount. Usually they got a hefty settlement, because only wealthy people could afford to bring a case of this sort and the financial outcome reflected that. But Lorna had been awarded nothing. Worse, the judge had given her a thorough trouncing.

Mummy was in tears and Daddy was furious. His nostrils flared and his face had reddened, both of which were sure signs of anger, but he hadn't become hugely successful in business by letting his feelings run away with him. Lorna saw the moment when he nodded curtly as he set aside his anger for later.

'Right,' he said in a voice of decision. 'Let's get this other business sorted out. At least if I'm dealing with it myself, we can get straight down to brass tacks instead of relying on a judge to pontificate.'

'What is this other business?' Lorna asked, but Daddy and Mr Wilding didn't appear to hear her.

'Perhaps it would be for the best if I were to speak privately to Mr MacPherson,' Mr Wilding suggested.

But Daddy wasn't having that. 'No, thank you. I intend to deal with this issue personally.'

'What issue?' Lorna asked again.

Her father turned to her but immediately turned away again as the door opened. Sir Jolyon Broughton, George and their barrister, Mr MacPherson, walked in. As her gaze clashed with George's, heat swept up Lorna's neck and into her face. Jerking her head away, she found herself instead looking at Sir Jolyon. His lean features and grey-blue eyes made it easy to see what George would look like in the future. Sir Jolyon had never been anything but courteous to Lorna before, but now he flung her a look of scorn that was undoubtedly intended to put her firmly in her place but instead had the effect of stiffening her backbone.

'Perhaps the ladies would prefer to retire,' Mr Wilding suggested.

'If you wish to leave, Mummy, that's up to you,' said Lorna, 'but I won't be banished from the room.'

Her father shrugged his broad shoulders. 'As you wish. Perhaps your presence will remind George of his obligations even though the judge did his best to absolve him of them.'

'You're a poor loser, West-Sadler,' said Sir Jolyon. 'Shall we see to this other matter? It shouldn't take long.'

'What other matter?' Lorna asked loudly, unable to quell the urgency she felt. She had asked several times now and still no one had told her.

Now at last she found out.

'It's the engagement ring,' said Daddy. 'It was given to you and it is yours to keep.'

'That isn't strictly the case,' said Mr MacPherson. 'I understand Miss West-Sadler returned it.'

'She threw it back at me,' George said wryly.

Lorna stared at her father. 'I don't want it back,' she said in a low voice, as if that might prevent the two Broughtons and their legal man from hearing.

'Don't be ridiculous,' Daddy said brusquely. 'You're entitled to it.' He swung round to confront George. 'When you gave my daughter that ring, did you say, "And I'll want it back if I don't go through with the engagement"? Well, did you?'

'Of course not,' said George.

'There you are, then,' said Daddy. 'The ring was Lorna's to keep. She was under no obligation whatsoever to return it – and the fact that she, to quote you, George, threw it back proves that she wasn't thinking clearly.'

'Mr West-Sadler is correct,' said Mr Wilding with a note of cool disdain in his tone that suggested he was not pleased to be involved in this matter.

'Good,' said Daddy. 'That's settled, then.'

'Ah... I think not,' said Mr MacPherson. 'The ring Mr Broughton presented to Miss West-Sadler upon their engagement was in fact a family heirloom. Had Mr Broughton purchased a ring, then you would be correct, Mr West-Sadler, in believing that the ring was your daughter's to keep, but the same rule does not apply when the ring is a family piece.'

Daddy glared not at the Broughtons' barrister but at Mr Wilding. 'Is this true?'

'Indeed it is.'

Daddy snorted. 'Well, it's a ruddy disgrace, that's all I can say.'

'I think that concludes the matter satisfactorily,' said Sir Jolyon.

'I never asked for the ring to be given back,' Lorna said to George, anxious for him to know that, but his only reply was a tight smile.

Her father hadn't finished yet. 'It's highly convenient for the Broughton family, that's all I can say.'

'What d'you mean by that?' demanded Sir Jolyon.

'I mean it's convenient for the gentry to hide behind their family heirlooms when they don't want to pay their debts.'

'Mr West-Sadler, please,' said Mr Wilding.

Mr MacPherson addressed Mr Wilding. 'I suggest you advise your client that he is straying into defamation of character territory.'

'That's enough.' George spoke decisively. 'I will make a payment to Lorna— to Miss West-Sadler to provide recompense for the engagement ring.'

'No!' exclaimed Lorna at the same moment as Daddy asked, 'How much?'

Lorna gazed at her father in disbelief. How could he reduce everything to monetary value like this? And did George really think she wanted compensation? Unable to bear it a moment longer, she rushed from the room, along the corridor and down the stairs. She thought she might have heard George calling her name, but she couldn't be sure and it didn't make any difference anyway. She didn't look back.

CHAPTER SIX

Tuesday was meant to be Mr Overton's last day at the salvage depot, but this had now been changed to Monday. After some discussion Sally and Betty had bought him a smart notebook as a farewell present, and they were surprised and touched by his simple gratitude when they gave it to him on Monday afternoon.

'Good luck in your new position, sir,' Sally said.

'And good luck to you in yours, Mrs Henshaw,' he replied solemnly.

For her part, Sally didn't feel in the slightest bit solemn. Excitement bubbled up inside her every time she thought of her new responsibilities. She had such plans for the depot – *her* depot.

'I bet your Andrew is dead proud of you,' Betty told Sally after Mr Overton had returned to his office to tidy his desk for the final time.

'His mother is too.'

'And your own mum and dad,' Betty added.

Sally hesitated. 'To be honest, my parents are still rather iffy about me working here. They were proud when I worked for the Food Office because it was an office job.'

'But salvage is essential to the war effort!' Betty exclaimed.

'It is,' Sally agreed, 'but it's also manual labour for the most part and that's something they'll never be proud of.'

'They'll feel differently once you start as manager,' said Betty.

Sally smiled, wanting to be positive. 'I hope so.'

'Are you still going to spend tomorrow morning at Mr Atkinson's shop?' Betty asked.

Sally thought for a moment. Mrs Lockwood had arranged this in her usual imperious way and, in spite of Mrs Lockwood's involvement, Sally had been looking forward to it, because she liked Mr Atkinson and she loved anything to do with books. But now she questioned whether she ought to swap places with Betty.

'Actually, maybe you should go instead,' she told her friend. 'I'd rather be here in the depot on my first day as manager. I'll give you the address. Mr Atkinson is expecting you at nine. You can go straight there without coming here first.'

'That means I get a lie-in. What a treat.' Betty smiled and her dimple showed. 'It's a shame, though. Your first morning as manager, and you won't have me here to boss about.'

'Ah, but just you wait until tomorrow afternoon,' Sally teased. 'You'll find out what a slave-driver I can be.'

Tuesday morning brought thick fog. Sally set off early for the depot because it was impossible to walk at her normal brisk pace through the grey blankness that seemed as dense as porridge. She couldn't see more than a couple of feet in front and sounds were muffled too. Even when she knew she must be approaching the depot, she almost walked right past it. She fumbled to let herself in and then felt her way across the yard to wasn't her place to say so, though maybe something showed in her expression.

'The previous bookshop owner had this room as his parlour,' Mr Atkinson explained.

Betty nodded. 'Hence the wallpaper and the mantelpiece.' Also the tulip-shaped shades on the wall-mounted gas-mantels and the fancy plaster ceiling-rose from which hung a central light.

'He was married with a d-daughter,' said Mr Atkinson, 'so they needed the two rooms upstairs as bedrooms. Now there's just me.'

'And your job has sneaked in and tried to take over the parlour,' said Betty. It was easy to imagine Mr Samuel Atkinson taking his work very seriously and then being surprised to find that his shop had grown while his home had shrunk.

There were three doors in the far wall. He opened the middle one, showing a cupboard with coat-pegs and shelves.

'You can put your things in here,' he told her. 'Are you c-cold? You must be after your walk. I'll put the k-kettle on.'

He opened the door on the left and Betty glimpsed a narrow kitchen with an ancient range and a built-in dresser that made it seem even narrower, and a doorway to a scullery with a sink and an old washing-copper at the far end.

Slipping her gloves into her coat pockets, she hung up her coat, draping her scarf over the peg as well. Then she put her hat, gas-mask box and handbag onto a shelf and went to stand in the kitchen doorway. The kettle was on the range and Mr Atkinson had taken the tea-caddy from a cupboard.

'Shall I make the tea?' Betty offered.

'Cer-certainly not. You're a guest.'

'Not exactly,' she said. 'Today I'm one of the workers.'

'Even s-so,' said Mr Atkinson. He stood over the kettle, waiting for it to start singing. 'I'm used to d-doing things for myself. I have a lady who c-comes in and c-cleans for me, but other than that I do everything myself. I'd s-starve if I didn't.'

He glanced at her with a smile and Betty was surprised at how it transformed his serious features. Then she wondered at her own surprise. Everyone looked better when they smiled.

Soon she was sitting at the sturdy table in the parlour-office, drinking tea while Mr Atkinson showed her the work she was here to help with. He drank from a mug and he had given her a cup and saucer with a pattern of harebells round the rims.

'We need to s-sort through all these piles and boxes,' he said, indicating a huge collection of books. 'We have to check that their c-condition is good enough and then put them onto d-different shelves according to where they're going to be sent.'

'How will I know what goes where?' Betty asked.

He picked up some lists from a shelf. 'I've been given some guidance but mostly it's up to us. Put it this way: I d-don't think the troops are looking forward to receiving boxes full of Ursula Bloom and Ethel M D-Dell.'

His voice sounded serious and it took Betty half a moment to spot the twinkle in his hazel eyes. She couldn't help smiling. Mr Atkinson was a likeable fellow, very easy to get along with – easier than she had expected.

'You made the tea,' she said, 'so I'll wash up.'

When she had finished, they got started on the work.

'I've found the best way,' said Mr Atkinson, 'is to sort all the d-donations first so we can s-see what we've got.'

'Sort how?' Betty asked.

'Into general categories. C-classics, romance, d-detective stories, children's books and s-so on. That makes it easier to share them out.'

To Betty's surprise her hands were soon covered in dust that made her skin feel dry.

'I'm s-sorry,' said Mr Atkinson. 'Used books d-don't look dusty but they are. Being packed into boxes d-doesn't help.'

'Good for you,' said Andrew, smiling at her.

Sally smiled back. She drew strength from his loving support.

Mum got to her feet. 'We'll leave you two men to it. I saw Mrs Grant earlier today and I said Sally and me would pop round.'

Sally stood up as well. The two families had been close as could be until Rod Grant had proposed to Sally, who had turned him down because she'd known he wasn't the right man for her. The fact that she had just met Andrew had made things worse because it had looked as if she was throwing Rod over for a new man. There had been a big falling-out over it – mainly people falling out with Sally, including her mum. But then Rod had shown his true colours and everyone had seen for themselves that his good-natured charm masked a vicious temper and a determination to have his own way at all costs. Poor Mrs Grant had been devastated, as had Sally's best friend Deborah, who had previously sided with her brother against Sally, but they couldn't deny the evidence of their own eyes.

Before Sally had turned Rod down, she and Deborah had been best friends all their lives. Now, as the Grant family was living down the shame of what Rod had done, the two girls and their mothers were finding a way back towards friendly ground. To add to the situation, after he had returned to Barrow-in-Furness, where he worked at the shipyard, Rod had thrown himself into a whirlwind romance and had got married in double-quick time.

The Grants' house was only up the road. As Mum knocked, Sally couldn't help remembering all the times she had burst into this house like another daughter. Would she ever do that again? Presumably not. Even if the old friendship was restored in all its warmth, it wasn't as if she lived just a few doors down any longer.

The door opened and Mrs Grant let them in with words of

welcome. She showed them into her parlour, where Deborah was sitting by the fire. She had the same heart-shaped face as her mother but, while Mrs Grant's eyes were light brown, Deborah's were bright blue, the same as Rod's.

The four of them chatted in a general sort of way that felt comfortable enough but lacked the old intimacy.

'Would you like a cigarette?' Mrs Grant held out her packet of Woodbines.

'That's kind, but we'll smoke our own,' said Mum, taking out her packet of Craven A.

Sally couldn't resist the opportunity. 'I hope you don't mind me saying, but, rather than take the packet from the tobacconist, you could empty it when you buy it and leave the box in the shop for salvage.'

'Sally!' Mum exclaimed. 'That's not polite, telling your elders what to do.'

'I'm not,' Sally replied. 'It's just that we all have to do what we can these days. It's called being salvage-minded.'

'You and your salvage,' Mum grumbled. 'Anyway, who wants a heap of loose cigarettes rattling around in their handbag?'

'Betty has made herself a little drawstring muslin bag that she keeps her cigarettes in,' said Sally.

'That's a good idea,' said Deborah. 'I might try that. Have you seen the new fashion pictures in the magazines?'

'Don't you go trying to get Sally on your side,' Mrs Grant cut in quickly. 'I'm not going to agree and that's that.'

'Agree with what?' asked Mum.

Mrs Grant pursed her lips. 'Skirt lengths have crept up a little higher. They might end up above the knee at this rate.'

'No,' said Mum at once. 'That would never happen. It wouldn't be respectable.'

'It's because of having to reduce the quantity of fabric the country uses,' said Sally.

There was a pause and then Mum asked bluntly, 'Have you heard from Rod recently?'

For a split second the air was alive with memories, then Mrs Grant took a deep drag on her cigarette and exhaled a stream of smoke. 'He's doing well at work in the shipyard – and he loves married life.'

'It must be strange for you,' said Mum, 'never having met your daughter-in-law. I know how that must feel, what with Sally wanting to marry a virtual stranger.'

'Mum!' Sally exclaimed.

'It's true,' said Mum. 'You'd no sooner met Andrew than you were hearing wedding bells.'

Possibly wanting to spare Sally any discomfort, Mrs Grant said, 'She sounds lovely, does Dulcie. Doesn't she, Deborah? We've had one or two letters from her, so that's nice. But yes, it is odd, not having met her in person.'

Sally wanted to sympathise, but would that be appropriate coming from the girl Mrs Grant had formerly set her heart on having as her daughter-in-law?

Rod had done a lot of damage – but in fairness Sally had to admit she hadn't been blameless. She had carried on letting him think of her as his girlfriend for some time after she'd known she didn't see her future alongside his, but it had been difficult for her to break free when everyone around them had seen them as the perfect couple.

But the main thing was that she and Mum were here in the Grants' house and fences were being mended. That was the thing that mattered. She and Deborah looked at one another and shared a smile and Sally felt a familiar warmth creep into her heart.

CHAPTER SEVEN

If Lorna had been distraught when George jilted her, she was left utterly beside herself once the so-called gentlemen of the press got their teeth into the story. Mr Justice Hardacre's damning words were reported far and wide and Lorna was ready to die of embarrassment.

Society Girl Puts Cash Before Patriotism

Jilted Rich Girl Shamed By Judge

Judge Lambasts Gold-Digger Fiancée

Columns were devoted to the case, every line loaded with judgement and, in the lower-class newspapers, outright glee at the public and entirely deserved downfall of the snooty Miss West-Sadler. No one had a good word for her. Every word was damaging and there was special nastiness in referring to her as a gold-digger, as if she had set out with the deliberate intention of grabbing herself an important husband. Lorna didn't know whether to dig her nails into her palms in fury or wrap her arms round herself in protection against the humiliation.

Daddy was all but foaming at the mouth, though not over the way Lorna was being presented to the world. No, he was incensed because Mr Justice Hardacre had ordered him to pay George's legal costs.

'It's a bally outrage,' he roared. 'This has made a monkey out of me.'

'What about *me*?' Lorna demanded. 'I'm the one whose name has been splashed all over the newspapers. My reputation is in tatters.'

'You'll have to go home,' Daddy decreed in a voice that said he wouldn't listen to any arguments. 'There's no point in you looking for another husband until this furore dies down. If it ever does,' he added drily.

Lorna was stunned. He made it sound as if she had no genuine feelings for George, and that wasn't the case. What a vile mess this was. Lorna longed to be fussed over and reassured, but there was none of that from her father. Not from Mummy either. She was too busy weeping and wailing as if she was in competition with Lorna as to which of them was the most badly affected.

'How will we ever hold our heads up after this?' she asked, adding, 'We had such hopes when we brought you to London, Lorna,' as if responsibility for the whole debacle could be laid at her daughter's feet.

Frustration consumed Lorna. 'Stop making it sound like my fault.'

'You didn't try hard enough,' Mummy complained.

'That's enough!' Daddy said sharply before a full-scale row could erupt. 'You two are going home to Lancaster. I have some business to finish and then I'll follow.'

The packing was accomplished in record time. The beautiful daytime and evening attire that Lorna had worn with such pleasure vanished into trunks. Open hatboxes sat in a line, awaiting the dainty pillbox with the spotted veil, the brimless fur, the felt trimmed with the pleated bow and the other felt with the upswept brim, all of them hats Lorna had purchased when she was all set to be the future Lady Broughton.

From future baronet's Lady to disgraced ex-fiancée: that was how the world saw her. How was she ever going to recover from the appalling humiliation? Yet at the same time it was easier to think of the disgrace than it was to face the thought of her lost love. Lorna stared down at her empty hands. For a moment she couldn't breathe. George had meant the world to her. Now that they were undeniably separated forever, she realised that she had believed all along that somehow they would get back together. She had to let go of that thought now and face up to life on her own.

If Lorna had hoped that word of her spectacular downfall somehow wouldn't have reached her native Lancaster, she was sorely disappointed. The only good thing was that the London press didn't pursue her, but it was difficult to be grateful when she could see the gleam in the eyes of everyone she knew in her home town.

Some people whom she had known all her life discreetly withdrew when they saw her coming. She hated them for it, but told herself it didn't matter because she still had friends who were standing by her. But she quickly realised that the friends who swarmed around her for the first day or two didn't so much wish to offer moral support as dig for all the gory details. She ended up hating them even more.

When Daddy arrived from London, all Lorna wanted to know was whether the scandal was dying down, but he was full of how America was going to donate some destroyers to the

Royal Navy – elderly destroyers, admittedly, but functional nonetheless.

'Each one is going to be named after a town or city,' he said, 'and one of them is going to be HMS *Lancaster*. It'll take thousands to get her re-equipped. I'll make a hefty donation and join the fundraising committee.'

Lorna couldn't believe her ears. Had he forgotten what she was going through?

Daddy looked squarely at Mummy. 'I'll expect you to stand beside me at all the events, and you can pin a smile on your face too. I've had enough of you looking like a wet weekend.'

Mummy seemed to come back to life. 'Yes, we must do our best for the war effort. When others look at us, we want them to see two proud Lancastrians doing their utmost for their city and their country.'

It was as much as Lorna could do not to drum her heels on the floor. Did they intend to sweep her problems under the carpet? Where was their sympathy? Their understanding?

'I've got something for you, Lorna,' said Daddy. 'It was delivered to our hotel in London.' He held out an envelope.

'You've opened it,' Lorna said indignantly.

'Of course I have. That's George's handwriting, isn't it?'

'You shouldn't open other people's letters,' said Lorna.

'You're not "other people". You're my daughter, and that letter is from the man who jilted you – the man who owes a hefty sum of money as recompense for that dratted engagement ring. I thought he would have made out the cheque to me personally, which is why I opened the envelope, but he's put your name on it.'

'I don't know how many times I have to say it.' Lorna made an effort to conceal her frustration. 'I don't want the money.'

'That's good, because you're my daughter, which means you don't need it,' Daddy replied. 'You can bank the money and make out a cheque to me.'

'But Daddy—' Lorna started to say.

'I'm the one who stumped up for you to be flaunted all over London and, in the absence of an advantageous marriage, I'm entitled to get some money back.'

Lorna pressed her hands into the folds of her skirt, squeezing her fingers into fists. 'It's not as though you need the money, Daddy. As it happens, I've already decided what I'd like to do with it.'

'Now see here, young lady—' Daddy began.

'I want to donate it to the Red Cross. After all,' Lorna added swiftly, 'you're going to make a generous donation to make HMS *Lancaster* battle-ready. Mine will be a second West-Sadler donation to the war effort.'

Daddy looked all set to huff and puff, but Lorna knew he couldn't argue. In fact, he became thoughtful.

'Perhaps we could let the newspapers know what you've done,' he mused.

'No!' The word exploded from Lorna's lips. 'This isn't a stunt to make people think well of me. It's a private thing. I never wanted the money, but since George has sent it this is a good way to use it.'

'Well, maybe,' Daddy grudgingly conceded.

Lorna thought it best to remove herself from the firing line for a spell. Daddy wouldn't take kindly to being bested by his own daughter. She would nip out for a walk while he calmed down.

She left the room and went into the wood-panelled hall, where she dragged on a wool overcoat, fastening the tie-belt unnecessarily tight, and put on her brimless fur hat, then stalked out of the house. She had no destination in mind. She just felt the need to be outside in the fresh air. She glanced into the park, where trenches had been dug to provide protection in the event of an air raid. There hadn't been any raids over Lancaster yet, but the Town Hall and the hotels had set up shel-

'You don't mind, do you?' Sally had asked Betty.

'Don't be daft. Of course I don't. Just make sure you have a good time.'

It was true: Betty didn't mind. In fact, she definitely didn't mind, because she hadn't forgotten the handsome stranger from last Saturday. He'd come back during the week when she wasn't here. She'd kicked herself for that when she had arrived back from the bookshop and found out she'd missed him. Would he – might he drop in again today? It was no use telling herself that of course he wouldn't. No use asking why would he? She just... hoped, that's all. No harm in that.

It was the beginning of November now. Crystals of frost covered the depot yard and Betty's breath fogged in the chilly air as she emptied the daily salvage sacks and began sorting the contents. There were quite a few newspapers and it was impossible not to glance at the front pages – and more than glance.

Society Girl Puts Cash Before Patriotism

Mrs Beaumont, the munitions girls and Betty had all devoured this story at home. Mrs Beaumont had read it out while the girls had breakfast together, constantly chiming in with their thoughts and opinions, none of which was favourable towards the society girl, a Miss West-Sadler.

'The judge was right,' Stella had declared. 'I'd like to see Miss West-Whatsit try her hand in the munitions, working long shifts round the clock and always in danger of being blown to kingdom come if some idiot doesn't follow the safety rules.'

'I bet she's never done a day's work in her life,' Mary had added.

Now Betty opened the newspaper from earlier in the week so she could lap up the tale all over again. There was a photograph of Miss West-Sadler but it was grainy and showed her sideways on, not full face, a hand held out in front of her in an effort to shield herself. She was described in the article as 'a society beauty' and Betty narrowed her eyes, trying to get a clearer look.

In any case, no matter how lovely she might be, it hadn't prevented the judge from giving her a good trouncing – and quite right too.

She put down the paper when a young mother came into the yard, holding hands with twin boys aged about four. The large collar and wide lapels on the young woman's worn coat showed it to be not just pre-war but pre-twins, but the little boys were beautifully turned out in matching coats of navy blue with Peter Pan collars, narrow belts and flap-pockets. Each little fellow wore a cap and knee-length grey socks, though one child's socks were in wrinkles around his ankles. In his free hand, each boy clutched a wodge of string.

After saying a cheerful 'Good morning' to the family, Betty said in exaggerated admiration, 'Goodness me, just look at these two handsome young men. Have you come from the Lord Mayor's office to inspect the depot?'

One lad gazed at her in wonder, while the other turned and buried his face in his mummy's coat, shifting his head slightly so as to sneak a look at Betty, who smiled at the mother.

'Those are very smart coats your boys are in – and you managed to find two of them.'

The young woman laughed, her blue eyes twinkling. 'I'll take that as a compliment. I made them myself, actually. You'll never guess what from.'

Betty settled in for a good natter. 'Tell me.'

'An old blanket I dyed navy blue.'

'Really? What a good idea.'

'I thought so. Every mother wants her children to look smart.'

Betty smiled at the children. 'Haven't you got a clever

over her ration book, together with the jar of Marmite, tub of Ovaltine and carton of Weetabix that Mummy's housekeeper had sent as a contribution to the store cupboard.

Lorna didn't meet her host and hostess until later. Mr Lockwood was a dinky little man who lost his reading-glasses twice in the course of the evening. Mislaying them was evidently a regular occurrence. He was mild-mannered with a warm chuckle and he referred to his wife as the memsahib, as if she was something rather splendid.

'Splendid' seemed a good word for Mrs Lockwood. She had an upright, buxom figure and shrewd grey eyes beneath a broad forehead. Her plummy voice was low-pitched for a woman but there was nothing soft about it. She could probably boom from one side of the parade ground to the other without taking an extra breath.

'Which type of voluntary war work did you do before you came here?' Mrs Lockwood enquired. 'First aid? Fire-watching?'

'Well, none, actually,' Lorna admitted, feeling as if she had come bottom in an important exam.

'None?' Mrs Lockwood seemed to rear up in surprise. 'You'll jolly well do something if you're going to live under my roof.'

'I'm happy to—' Lorna began.

'I'm a member of the WVS and I suggest you join as well. That would be most satisfactory.'

Before she knew what was what, Lorna had agreed to ask her father to send a postal order to cover the cost of her WVS uniform. Mrs Lockwood evidently wasn't the sort of person one said no to.

Once that was settled, Mrs Lockwood gave Lorna what amounted to a short lecture on salvage, concluding with, 'I'll be pleased to have you at my salvage depot.'

Feeling she ought to say something, Lorna asked, 'Am I taking over from someone who has left?'

'Not precisely. Someone has indeed left, but that was the person who ran the depot for me on a day-to-day basis, you might say. One of the existing staff was then given that post and you, my dear Miss Sadler—'

'—will be starting at the bottom,' said Lorna.

'Now then,' Mrs Lockwood said bracingly. 'It's all for the good of the war effort. The most important thing for you to remember is that you should come to me with any questions or concerns. The girl who might seem to be in charge is very inexperienced and I have to watch over her carefully. I take great pride in my salvage depot and expect my staff to do the same.'

'Yes, Mrs Lockwood.'

'Your normal starting time will be eight o'clock but tomorrow you may go in later and I will accompany you. Beforehand I'll take you around the neighbourhood so you can get your bearings.'

'Thank you,' said Lorna.

'It's important that you settle in,' replied her landlady.

Lorna hadn't exactly warmed to Mrs Lockwood, but it was impossible not to admire her. She had thrown herself into war work a whole year before war was declared, when the WVS was busy all over the country assisting local corporations in matters of preparing civil defence and planning ways to reduce suffering in the event of the expected attacks from the air. It was easy to imagine Mrs Lockwood being highly effective not just on a committee but also in the execution of all practical duties. The salvage depot was lucky to have such an efficient and reliable person in charge.

Oh, but how was Lorna going to bear it?

· · ·

The following morning, Mrs Lockwood, looking smart in her green WVS uniform, showed Lorna around Chorlton-cum-Hardy, pointing out the swimming baths and the public library, the post office, the cinemas and the dance-hall.

After that it was time to go to the salvage depot. They walked in through large gates that stood wide open. Although Lorna had braced herself, what she beheld was worse than she was prepared for. Why couldn't Daddy have found her a cosy little desk job? Instead she had to face – this! A yard with crates and sacks and piles of salvage. Paper overflowed from one sack, bits and pieces of rubber from another, while metal and aluminium objects poked out of a row of wooden crates.

Up ahead was a shabby-looking building that filled the width of the yard. The door opened and a girl emerged – dressed in dungarees. Dungarees! And one of those frightful turban-things covered her hair except for a few curls of golden-blond fringe.

'Good morning, Miss Hughes,' Mrs Lockwood boomed. 'This is Miss Sadler. She is starting work here today. Miss Sadler, this is Miss Hughes. She will ensure you are correctly attired.'

Lorna opened her mouth to object and then chose not to. She had opted for the knitted cotton top and plain skirt she had previously worn on a day out on a narrowboat, but the simple, practical outfit now seemed like the last word in elegance and beauty. Even so – dungarees!

'I didn't know we had someone new starting today,' said Miss Hughes. To go with the golden hair, she had blue eyes and a rather lovely peachy complexion.

'Where is Mrs Henshaw?' Mrs Lockwood asked, looking around.

'She's not here,' said Miss Hughes. 'She's out collecting bones.'

'Bones?' Lorna exclaimed, unable to prevent herself from picturing skeletons.

'You know – chicken bones and rabbit bones from cooking,' said Miss Hughes. 'Housewives used to put them in boxes next to the pig-bins in their streets. You can imagine how the local dogs loved that, so Sally – Mrs Henshaw – had the idea of fastening the boxes to lamp-posts instead.'

Good grief, what sort of job was this? A sound behind Lorna made her turn round, to see a girl walking into the yard cheerfully pushing a trolley – the sort that station porters used when they were helping you with your luggage. On this girl's trolley was a stack of small boxes. Like Miss Hughes, she wore dungarees, but instead of a turban she had a headscarf over her dark-blond hair that tied underneath it at the back. She was slender with a heart-shaped face and she looked as if she'd been laughing – until she saw Mrs Lockwood.

The pretty face took on a sort of tightness. 'Good morning, Mrs Lockwood. What brings you here today?'

'Good morning, Mrs Henshaw. I believe you'll find that I do not require a particular reason to necessitate my presence.'

At that moment several dogs of various types came trotting into the yard, making a collective beeline for the trolley of boxes.

The new arrival – Mrs Henshaw – laughed, her expression relaxing again. 'Honestly, collecting the bone-boxes is like being the Pied Piper. Shoo!' She clapped her hands at the dogs. 'Off you go. I'd better get these bones indoors before they get pounced on.'

She pushed her trolley across the yard while Miss Hughes shooed the dogs out.

Mrs Lockwood turned to Lorna. 'I apologise for Mrs Henshaw's lack of good manners, but I'm sure you'll have the opportunity to meet her in due course. Now then, Miss Hughes, if you have finished messing about with those animals, perhaps you will kindly show Miss Sadler where she can get changed. I'll see you at home this evening, Miss Sadler.'

Miss Hughes took Lorna upstairs into a cramped room, where she opened a cupboard containing a stack of dungarees.

'They're all men's so they need altering. Mind you, you're quite tall, so if we can dig out a shorter pair they might not need taking up.'

Lorna had no intention of finding anything to admire about the salvage depot or its staff, but she couldn't help noticing that Miss Hughes's dungarees fitted in such a way as to show off her curvy figure. There was no chance of that with herself. Dungarees would simply make her look even more straight-up-and-down.

'What did Mrs Lockwood mean about seeing you at home?' Miss Hughes asked.

'I'm billeted with her,' Lorna answered.

Miss Hughes's blue eyes widened. 'Crikey.'

Lorna shrugged. 'There are worse things in life than being billeted on the boss.'

'Mrs Lockwood isn't the boss,' said Miss Hughes. 'Sally is – Mrs Henshaw.'

'The girl with the dogs?' Lorna asked, not troubling to hide her disbelief.

'They weren't her dogs. She just sort of attracted them along the way.'

'While she was emptying the bone-boxes,' said Lorna. Honestly, who did Miss Hughes think she was trying to kid?

'Exactly,' said Miss Hughes. 'Mrs Henshaw is the depot manager.'

That settled it. A manager who wore dungarees and collected bones? What a load of old twaddle. Miss Hughes was evidently having a joke. Well, Lorna wasn't going to fall for it. Nobody who had observed both Mrs Lockwood and Mrs

Henshaw would possibly be in any doubt whatsoever as to who was in charge of the salvage depot.

Her first couple of days at the salvage depot did nothing to change Lorna's mind. She felt scornful of Mrs Henshaw. Fancy the person who was in charge, even if only on a day-to-day basis, choosing to wear dungarees like one of the workers. It was bizarre. Of course, she needed to wear dungarees because she mucked in with the work – which was another reason why it was so hard to believe she had any real standing in the depot. Didn't she realise the importance of setting herself apart from Miss Hughes and Lorna? That mattered if one wanted to be respected.

'You have to show people you're above them if you want them to look up to you,' Daddy had impressed upon her more than once.

Even if Mrs Henshaw was too ignorant to conduct herself in such a way, Lorna wasn't. She intended that her new colleagues should realise from the start that, even though she was obliged to be here, she was way above this kind of work. Essential to the war effort it might be, but it was best suited to the working classes, who were used to such things and who would plod away at it unquestioningly.

It honestly astonished Lorna that the other two girls should seem so cheerful about the work. Although they welcomed her to start with, their attitude soon hardened once she made her own feelings clear.

Being sent somewhere to hide away and be protected from those vultures who had written about her in the newspapers was a jolly good idea – but why on earth had Daddy dumped her in this godforsaken job, where she was expected to work *with her hands*, for pity's sake! She might not have minded a desk job so long as they didn't expect her to learn to use one of those wretched typewriter-contraptions. Lorna had more respect for her nails.

Here she was now, Lorna Marguerite West-Sadler, pretending to be plain Lorna Sadler, having to sort through sacks of mixed salvage – *unwashed* mixed salvage.

On her first day Miss Hughes had laughed at her, though not unkindly. 'Your face! There's no need to look so disgusted.'

But Lorna had felt disgusted and, when she didn't trouble to hide it, Miss Hughes's blue eyes had darkened and she'd hauled another half a dozen sacks across the yard and dumped them at Lorna's feet.

'This should keep you busy,' she had declared. 'Try not to look so miserable. When I was little, my mum would say, "If the wind changes, Betty, you'll be stuck like that forever," if I pulled faces.'

Honestly! How rude. Lorna added it to the list of complaints in her head, which she intended to put on paper in a letter home. Surely Daddy wouldn't be so hard-hearted as to leave her here for the duration? And even if he was, Mummy would be horrified and would talk him round. Lorna was counting on it.

When she ate her evening meal of Lancashire hotpot followed by bread pudding with the Lockwoods, Mr Lockwood asked her how she was getting on in her new post. Not wanting to say the wrong thing, Lorna replied with a few safe remarks about the type of tasks she had undertaken so far.

'And what about the other girls?' asked Mr Lockwood. 'Congenial company, are they?'

'We're still getting used to one another.'

'That sounds like a very diplomatic answer,' Mrs Lockwood observed with a quick glance. 'Should I read something into it?'

Lorna smiled and said nothing.

'You can speak freely here, you know,' said Mrs Lockwood. 'I have ultimate responsibility for the salvage depot and it would be of benefit to me to know what goes on. For example, Mrs Henshaw. She hasn't had day-to-day responsibility for very long. How do you think she's coping?'

'It's too early for me to say.'

'Fair enough. Just remember that there's no harm in making observations to me. If anything, you'd be assisting in making the depot run all the more smoothly. You can see the importance of that – can't you?'

CHAPTER TEN

It was obvious that Betty wasn't impressed with Miss Sadler, but Sally wanted to give the new girl a chance. That was what a good boss would do. Clearly Miss Sadler wasn't used to the sort of tasks that working with salvage called for – well, neither had Sally and Betty been when they first started, either, but they had got used to everything. Miss Sadler was finding things harder than they had and she deserved a chance to settle in and find her feet.

Wanting to show her that there was more to salvage work than sorting it out and gathering like things together for collection, Sally took Miss Sadler to Mr Atkinson's bookshop to see how donated books were being sent to the men overseas and to bomb-wrecked public libraries.

Sally was pleased when Miss Sadler showed an interest.

'There's a full set of Anthony Trollope's Barsetshire novels here,' she observed, running her finger along the spines of the books on a shelf. 'Will you send them all to the same place, Mr Atkinson, or will they be split up?'

'I like the thought of readers having access to all of them,' he replied, 'but they c-can also be enjoyed individually. S-spreading them around c-could introduce more people to Trollope. There's no right w-way or wrong way. Wh-what would you do?'

Sally smiled to herself as he and Miss Sadler discussed the matter.

At the end of the visit, Mr Atkinson asked Sally if she could arrange for him to have some assistance again.

'Of course,' Sally said. 'Would another morning's help be sufficient?'

'I've had another c-consignment of d-donations that needs sorting out,' said Mr Atkinson. 'It looks like it's going to be a never-ending job and of c-course I also have to run my shop. Any assistance you c-can provide w-would be gratefully accepted.'

'Have you a telephone in the shop?' Sally asked. 'Write down your number and I'll ring you.'

'I'd be glad to help here,' Miss Sadler said at once.

That felt to Sally like something of a breakthrough. Was Miss Sadler starting to accept her new role? But when they returned to the depot and Sally asked her to hose down some old tyres that were encrusted with mud and heaven alone knew what else, the old Miss Sadler was very much in evidence.

'But that's a filthy job,' she protested, her lips curling in disgust.

'The sooner you get started,' Betty said, 'the sooner it'll be over and done with.'

Miss Sadler rolled her eyes but she did as she was told.

Sally huffed a sigh. She'd been looking forward to having someone new and had liked the thought of being involved in the interviewing process, but instead Miss Lorna Sadler had been foisted on the depot, which had been a bit of a slap in the face for Sally. Not only that, but Miss Sadler lived with Mrs Lockwood. Did that mean they were hand in glove? It was an uncomfortable thought.

'How is the new girl getting on?' Mrs Henshaw asked that evening as she, Sally and Andrew were finishing up the baked jam sponge she had made for their pudding.

Sally's spirits dipped. She hadn't said anything so far at home about Miss Sadler because – well, because she felt as if she'd failed in some way. Then she looked at her husband and his mother. They were both proud of her and interested in what she did. She ought to have confided in them at once.

'I'm not keen on her, to be honest,' Sally admitted. 'I'm all in favour of giving her a chance but she doesn't help herself. She's snooty and she turns up her nose at everything.'

'Oh dear,' Mrs Henshaw murmured.

'She lives with Mrs Lockwood,' Sally added. 'That says it all, really.'

'I can imagine,' said Mrs Henshaw. She knew Mrs Lockwood from the WVS.

'I've tried telling her I'm the manager,' said Sally, 'but I'm sure she sees me as uppity.'

'That must be what Mrs Lockwood has told her,' said Andrew.

'I wish that woman would leave the depot alone,' said Sally.

Andrew took her hand. 'Unfortunately, that won't happen. If anything, this situation plays into her hands.'

Sally smiled ruefully. 'Is that intended to make me feel better?'

'Sorry,' said Andrew, 'but we have to be realistic if we're going to work out what to do.'

That 'we' was all it took to make Sally feel reassured. She caught her mother-in-law's nod of satisfaction too.

Mrs Henshaw stood up. 'I'll clear away while you two talk this over.' Carrying the stacked dishes, she turned in the doorway to say, 'I believe in you, Sally. You'll sort this out.'

Andrew closed the door behind his mother and returned to the table.

'Your mum is so kind,' said Sally, 'but it's difficult to see what I can do.'

'Is this Miss Sadler rude?' Andrew asked. 'Uncooperative?'

'No. She just thinks she's better than we are.'

'She's not even been there a week yet,' Andrew pointed out.

'Do you think I'm not giving her enough of a chance?' Sally asked. 'But if I let her get away with it at the start, it's going to be harder to squash her next week or the week after.'

'That's true. You've got to assert yourself over her. It won't be easy, especially if she goes running home to Mrs Lockwood every evening. I hate to say it, Sally, but this is as much about Mrs Lockwood as it is about Miss Sadler.'

Sally drew in a breath, then deliberately didn't sigh it out. 'I never imagined when I was offered the position of depot manager that my first test would involve a fellow worker's personality. I feel under pressure to handle the matter effectively.'

'I can understand that.' Andrew smiled warmly, his brown eyes full of love. 'Let's talk it through and see what we can come up with.'

The next morning Sally put on her Sunday best, together with her hip-length swing-jacket with its stand-up collar and cuffed sleeves. She could have worn her plain jacket, but Miss Sadler's natural grace combined with the tailored elegance of her clothes made Sally want to show that she too could look fashionable. She slipped her feet into her brown suede shoes with almond-shaped toes and spent some time fussing with her fair hair. She wanted to look immaculate.

She set off early, wanting to be sure of arriving at the depot before Miss Sadler, who, whatever her faults, was prompt. Sally had to go to Star House first.

Mrs Beaumont let her in and she joined Betty in the dining room, where she was having porridge and toast.

Betty was surprised to see her. 'Is everything all right?'

'It's nothing to worry about,' Sally assured her. 'I just came to ask you to go straight to Mr Atkinson's bookshop without coming to the depot first. You can stay there all day.'

'All day?'

'I gather there's plenty to do,' said Sally.

'I didn't know it had been arranged.'

'It hasn't.' Sally smiled. 'Not yet. I'll telephone the shop shortly before nine and tell Mr Atkinson to expect you.'

Leaving Star House, Sally went on her way.

Taking care not to get yesterday's ashes on her hands or her clothes, she got a small fire going in the office to take the chill off the air. After a moment's thought she took the visitor's chair from in front of her desk and positioned it against the wall. She kept her ears open and, the moment she heard Miss Sadler arrive, she stepped out of the office.

'Good morning, Miss Sadler.' She kept her tone brisk and impersonal. 'I'd like to see you in my office at nine o'clock. Please be prompt.'

Sally kept herself busy until a quiet tap on the door heralded Miss Sadler's arrival. She was dressed in her dungarees, with her dark, glossy hair tied back and covered with a scarf. It would take a lot more than being summoned to the office to shake her confidence, but her green eyes held a certain curiosity.

When Miss Sadler placed herself in front of the desk, Sally indicated the chair standing against the wall.

'Would you mind? Thank you.'

Miss Sadler took the chair and put it in position.

'Do sit down,' Sally invited as if Miss Sadler had been waiting for permission. 'Tell me how you think you're getting on here at the depot.'

Miss Sadler looked at her. 'Honestly?'

'Honestly,' said Sally.

'It's not the work I'd have chosen. I'd be much better suited to something in an office.'

'Really?' Sally asked, encouraging her to continue.

'With my education and background, I mean,' said Miss Sadler.

'Ah yes,' said Sally. 'Your education and background. I must admit you seem pretty upper-crust to me.'

Miss Sadler nodded and raised an eyebrow. Sally hadn't known that raising an eyebrow could make someone look satisfied and pleased with themselves, but evidently it could.

'I suppose it must be obvious,' Miss Sadler murmured.

Sally took a breath before she aimed for the jugular. 'It's a shame your breeding is so lacking in patriotism.'

That shook Miss Sadler out of her complacency. 'What?'

'Do you have any idea of the importance of what we do here?' asked Sally. 'It might seem like gathering old junk to you, but a single soap powder box can be made into four aero-engine caskets. One magazine can be turned into the interior components of two mines. And something as small as a single envelope can be made into a cartridge wad. Those are just three examples. There are many more. I'm very disappointed with your attitude, Miss Sadler. Starting now, I expect you to pull your socks up. One of our jobs here is to open the depot on Saturdays and we take turns to do that, but how am I to trust you to do it? If you aren't up to it, I need to know.'

Indignation flared in Miss Sadler's green eyes. 'Of course I'm up to it.'

Sally remained cool and calm. 'Are you? You haven't displayed the right attitude so far. Pride, patriotism and backbone: that's what I need from you. You're not much use here otherwise, Miss Sadler. That's all. You may return to your duties now.'

She made a show of glancing down at the list of salvage collection dates in front of her on the desk. There was a fraught pause, then Miss Sadler stood up. Sally looked up, not reacting to the angry flush of the other girl's cheeks.

'Oh, and would you mind putting your chair back against the wall before you go? Thank you.'

What a difference. The first time Betty had walked to the bookshop, the air had been thick with fog. This time she walked there beneath skies of pale blue. Milky sunshine fell through gaps in wispy layers of cloud. It was lovely not to smell cordite on the breeze. The air raids this week had been short and had concentrated on other areas. There was something rather horrid and unsettling about being glad not to have been targeted when you knew that your own lucky escape meant possible death for other people.

Betty arrived just as Mr Atkinson was raising the blind on the shop door. She smiled through the pane of glass straight at him, clearly taking him by surprise. He opened the door.

'Weren't you expecting me?' Betty asked. 'Mrs Henshaw said she would telephone you.'

He stood aside to let her in. 'That s-solves that mystery. I have elderly neighbours over the road. I help them out by d-doing their shopping for them. I fetched their groceries f-first thing and heard the telephone as I c-came back to the shop, but whoever it w-was gave up just before I got there.'

In the back room Betty went to the cupboard, giving herself a little reminder about using the middle door. About to take off her coat, she turned to Mr Atkinson.

'It is all right for me to be here today, isn't it?' she asked.

'Of c-course. There's always plenty to d-do. Let me help you.'

Moving behind her, he helped her off with her coat, then

gave it to her to hang up. He had such nice manners. Mum had always set a lot of store by good manners. When Betty had put her things away, she found Mr Atkinson making tea. The pretty cup and saucer he had given her last time were on top of the cupboard next to the teapot.

He insisted that Betty must sit at the table to drink her tea, but he moved around, carrying his mug and pointing out various piles of books.

'I've s-sorted out what's going w-where. Today's job is to box up the books and write the address-labels.'

'I like the idea of all these books going off to new homes,' Betty commented.

'I think of it as s-sending them off to do w-war work: entertaining the troops, giving them a means of escaping for a f-few hours; helping the librarians whose customers are anxious for reading matter. Do you like reading, Miss Hughes?'

'I like the film magazines,' said Betty.

'Films are an important part of c-culture. People need stories. W-whether they get them through reading or through watching them unfold on the s-silver screen, it comes down to the same thing: stories are good f-for the soul.'

Betty smiled. He had a real way with words. 'I'll remember that when I'm at the flicks this evening.'

The bell over the shop door jingled, calling Mr Atkinson to serve a customer. Betty could hear the low hum of their voices as she got on with packing the boxes. Mr Atkinson had written all the labels in capitals and Betty pasted them on.

She held up the bottle of glue when Mr Atkinson returned to the back room. 'You're lucky to have this. There's hardly any to be found in the shops these days.'

'I d-didn't get it in a shop,' he told her. 'I w-was provided with it specifically for this purpose and given strict instructions not to use it f-for anything else.'

It took most of the morning to finish preparing the boxes.

Betty did the lion's share because Mr Atkinson had a run of customers. He seemed to know them all and Betty enjoyed the background hum of conversation, pleased to hear that Mr Atkinson's stammer didn't make him clam up.

'You're popular today,' she said when he returned to the back room. 'I'm glad to know folk are still buying books.'

'The quality of new books is going to s-suffer, I'm afraid,' Mr Atkinson replied. 'They'll be printed on the thinnest paper possible, but the main thing is that there will s-still be new books.'

'Do you think the demand will keep up in wartime?' Betty asked.

'Of c-course it will,' Mr Atkinson answered with a smile. 'I told you: people need stories.'

Betty looked at the stacks of labelled boxes. 'All done.'

'Thank you. You've been more than k-kind.'

When Mr Atkinson opened the cupboard and retrieved her coat, Betty looked at him in surprise.

'I'm meant to be here all day. Sorry. I should have said. But if there's nothing else for me to do…'

'There's plenty to d-do – if you don't mind. There are more donations to be s-sorted.'

'Fine. I can do that.'

Mr Atkinson looked uncomfortable. 'It's nearly one o'c-clock. I need to shut the shop for d-dinner.'

'My landlady gave me a sandwich and a jam tart to bring with me.'

'I have to go to an ARP meeting,' said Mr Atkinson. 'I apologise f-for leaving you on your own, but I d-didn't realise…'

'It can't be helped,' Betty said cheerfully. 'Honestly, it doesn't matter.'

In his absence she flicked through a few books as she ate her meat-paste sandwich. Mr Atkinson returned shortly before two, again full of how sorry he was for having been obliged to leave her.

Betty cut off his apologies by asking, 'You're an ARP warden, then?'

He nodded. Not meeting her eyes, he added, 'If you're w-wondering, I c-couldn't join up because I failed the medical.'

'I wouldn't have dreamed of asking,' said Betty.

'I understand that, but I w-wanted you to know.'

'Mrs Henshaw's father is in the ARP. My dad's a police sergeant.'

They spent the afternoon working side by side, with Mr Atkinson occasionally vanishing into the shop to serve a customer.

Betty kept an eye on the clock.

'I'm not being rude,' she assured Mr Atkinson. 'I'm looking forward to going to the pictures after this. The girls I live with are coming here to collect me. I hope that's all right.' She laughed. 'It'd better be, because it's all arranged.'

'You mentioned a landlady before. These girls must be her other billetees.'

'That's right,' said Betty.

'So you d-don't live at home.'

'I'm from Salford,' Betty told him, 'but my work is here. I hated having to leave my dad but I'm happy here now.'

'And your mother?' Mr Atkinson asked gently.

'We lost her a while back. Nothing to do with the war,' Betty added quickly. 'She was wonderful, my mum. I miss her every day. My dad remarried, so I know he's being looked after.'

'Have you any brothers and s-sisters?'

'I would have loved a sister, but I'm an only child,' said Betty. 'What about you?'

'My brother is in the army and my s-sister is a nurse with the Queen Alexandra's.'

Mr Atkinson was quiet for a moment. Aware of being found

unfit for military service? Betty wanted to reassure him that being an ARP warden was a form of service too, but instinct made her hold her tongue. Her saying something would only make his position more obvious.

Presently he said, 'D-do you, um...? What I mean is, I like going to the pictures...' Again his voice trailed off. 'You – w-well, you deserve a nice boyfriend to take c-care of you—'

'You don't always get what you deserve, though, do you?' said Betty. 'If we did, my mum would still be here, enjoying a long and healthy life.'

'Of c-course. I can tell how much you miss her. It's there in your eyes. She must have been a s-special person.'

Betty brushed away a tear. 'She was.' She pulled herself together. 'Sorry. I interrupted you. What were you saying?'

'I was w-wondering if—'

The shop door opened, setting the brass bell jingly merrily.

'Hello! Anyone home?' called Stella's familiar voice.

'Anyone who specially wants to see Errol Flynn romancing Olivia de Havilland?' Lottie added, chuckling.

Five minutes later Betty was on her way. Saying goodbye to Mr Atkinson had all happened in a rush. She'd wanted to tidy up the table and the shelves but he had insisted on doing it himself. What a kind man he was. It had touched her deeply that he'd been understanding about her lasting grief for Mum. What a good friend he must be. She'd like him to be her friend too. In fact – yes, from now on she would think of him as Samuel. She couldn't call him that out loud because it would be forward and inappropriate, but she would think of him by his first name.

Her friend Samuel.

Betty and her chums sat together in the cinema's smoky atmosphere watching the Pathé Newsreel. In Greece the Italians continued to advance and they had bombed Salonika from the air; and in America President Roosevelt had won another term in office – which must surely be good news for Britain. It didn't actually say that on the news but Betty felt certain that everyone in the auditorium, not to mention cinema audiences up and down the country watching the newsreel that evening, was thinking it.

After that they watched the supporting film, and then the lights went up for the interval before the main film was shown. Uniformed usherettes appeared at the front of each aisle, with trays secured in front by straps that went round the backs of their necks. The cinema-goers left their seats to queue up for cigarettes, boiled sweets and ice-cream.

Betty was closest to the aisle, so she collected money from the others and joined the queue.

'Evening, Miss Hughes,' said a voice behind her – a voice that sent delight sky-rocketing through her.

She took a breath to compose herself before she turned round. 'Oh – it's you.' She was so busy feigning surprise that she didn't realise until too late that her pretend nonchalance might have the undesirable effect of putting him off.

But apparently not.

'You know what they say. The proverbial bad penny.'

There was a trace of cockiness in his smile. She ought not to like that but she did.

'I didn't mean to sound offhand,' said Betty.

'Us bad pennies are immune to that.' He gave her a wink that made her pulse race. 'Are you looking forward to seeing Errol Flynn? I bet you're in love with him. All the girls are.'

They chatted about films. As they drew closer to the front of the queue, they agreed that wartime ice-cream wasn't a patch on the creaminess of the real thing.

Then it was Betty's turn and she paid for the four little tubs, giving the handsome young man behind her a shy smile as she passed him. Instead of returning straight to her seat, she hung back a little, standing aside to let others go first. If she sat down, she might not see where her handsome bad penny was sitting. Not that there was any point in knowing, but she wanted to know all the same. She was being daft, but so what?

Then she saw him heading towards the rear of the auditorium. He entered a row of seats and did a sideways walk as others half-stood to let him get past. He sat down – and handed a tub of ice-cream to a pretty girl in the next seat.

Betty felt it like a thump in the stomach. Of course he had a girl, a lovely fellow like that. It was her own fault for being stupid.

But it still hurt.

CHAPTER ELEVEN

Betty wanted to be angry with the handsome fellow with the Clark Gable moustache after seeing him at the flicks. How dare he make himself so charming to her at the salvage depot when he was already spoken for? He had even turned on the charm in the ice-cream queue, possibly with his girlfriend looking on. Poor girl!

But, no matter how much Betty wanted to be vexed and resentful, what she really felt was a deep disappointment. He was so handsome and confident and she couldn't resist those blue eyes beneath the dark sweep of his eyebrows. Ever since the first time she'd seen him, she had wanted to get to know him. She had wanted him to want to get to know her.

She went to the salvage depot, feeling that the last thing she needed today was another dose of haughtiness from Miss Snooty Nose Sadler, but Miss Sadler's attitude had improved. It wasn't perfect but it was better. She now seemed resigned to the work rather than stuck up about it.

That afternoon Sally gave Miss Sadler permission to finish early so she could sign up with a doctor's surgery. After she had gone, Betty couldn't resist mentioning her observation to Sally.

'She was less awful today.'

'I'm pleased to hear it,' Sally replied with a smile.

'Would this have anything to do with you getting rid of me yesterday?' Betty asked.

Sally looked innocent. 'It might have.'

'I don't know how you did it,' said Betty, 'but I'm glad you did. I'm not fishing for information,' she added quickly.

'It wouldn't be appropriate for me to say anything,' Sally answered. 'Sorry if that sounds stuffy.'

'Not at all,' said Betty. 'You're just doing the right thing.'

Just before they started to close up for the day, Mr Atkinson – no, Samuel – walked into the yard. The girls greeted him with smiles and he politely raised his hat.

Addressing Sally, he said, 'I c-came to thank you for sparing Miss Hughes all d-day yesterday. She was of great assistance to me.'

'I was glad to help,' said Betty.

From inside the building came the sound of the telephone bell. Sally excused herself and hurried to answer it.

'D-did you enjoy the f-film yesterday?' Samuel asked.

'Yes, thanks. It was *The Adventures of Robin Hood*. I saw it when it first came out and wanted to see it again.'

'I asked because... w-well, as I said yesterday, I like going to the pictures and I w-wondered if... That is, I hope I'm not s-speaking out of turn, but I wondered if you have a boyfriend who takes you.'

'Huh!' The sound burst out of Betty before she could stop it. 'Since you ask, there's a chap I like – or rather, I used to like him but last night I saw him with another girl.'

'Oh. Right. I'm s-sorry to hear it. I c-can see it's upset you.'

'Why did you ask?'

'It d-doesn't matter. I can s-see this isn't the right moment.'

'The right moment for what?' Betty asked.

Sally reappeared just then.

'I'd better go,' said Samuel. 'I'm sure you ladies need to c-close the depot.'

When he had gone, Betty and Sally closed the big gates, each of them pushing one, and shot the bolts. The gates would remain locked until the fire-watchers came on duty at ten o'clock.

The girls changed back into their own clothes, wrapping up warmly against the chilly evening. Using their torches, they crossed the yard to the door in the fence. Sally went through first. She gave an exclamation, then turned to Betty with a smile. Was it Samuel again? Had he decided to say whatever it was after all? But somehow Sally's warm, humorous smile didn't suggest it was him.

'Someone to see you,' she said.

Intrigued, Betty stepped through the door – and there he was, the handsome man, the bad penny, with his gorgeous blue eyes and his Clark Gable moustache... and the girlfriend. Betty pressed her lips together. When Sally had locked the gate behind them, Betty tucked her hand firmly into the crook of her friend's arm.

'Please,' said the chap. 'I'd like to talk to you.'

Betty made a show of speaking to Sally. 'I have nothing to say to him.'

'I don't know what I've done to upset you, Miss Hughes,' said the man.

Sally gently unhooked Betty's arm. 'Perhaps you ought to hear him out.'

As Sally walked away and was lost in the pitch-darkness of the blackout, even the faint beam of her tissue-dimmed torch fading to nothing, Betty glared at the young man, hating that he knew her name when she still didn't know his. But what did it matter? It didn't. Him and his dratted girlfriend.

'Go on, then,' Betty challenged. 'Say whatever it is you've come to say.'

'I was going to ask if you'd come to the flicks with me.'

'What, you, me and your girlfriend, you mean?' Betty tossed her head so sharply, she nearly dislodged her film-star hat. 'Don't bother denying it. I saw you together last night.'

He nodded slowly. 'I was worried you might have.'

'Does she know you go around asking other girls out?'

He held up his hands in surrender. 'Look, you're right. I did have a girlfriend, but I don't any more. The thing is – well, she's a lovely girl and all that, but after I met you...' He shrugged and pressed his lips together into a crinkly line that was both rueful and appealing. 'I know you're not the sort to go out with a fellow who's spoken for. I could tell the first time I met you that you're the decent type. If you say you don't want to see me ever again, I swear I won't trouble you, but I want you to know that I don't go out with the girl you saw any longer. Even if you never want to see me again, I've broken it off with her for good because I know now that she's not the right girl for me. I want you to understand that I wouldn't normally approach a girl in this way. I'm far too shy normally, believe it or not. But there's something about you, something special, and I'm hoping you'll give me another chance.'

It was another busy night for the WVS. Lorna spent the first part of her shift at the site of a severe incident on the far side of Chorlton Park, where, beneath skies filled with the clamour of aircraft engines, anti-aircraft fire and the crashes and thunderclaps of explosions, a pair of semi-detached houses had collapsed into a mound of rubble.

'Just dropped like stones, they did,' a shocked woman told Lorna. 'A second or two – that was all it took. There was no time for any of them to get out.'

The families were now trapped in their respective cellars.

Please let them still be alive. Lorna wrapped a blanket round the woman's shoulders.

'Here. You need to keep warm,' she told her. 'Come and have a cup of tea.'

She drew the woman towards the mobile canteen, where tea and sandwiches were on offer. Lorna had in recent nights done her share of dispensing these not just to the newly homeless and the rescued but also to exhausted but still determined rescuers.

An ARP warden approached Lorna. 'Digging through the ruins of the two houses is going to take several hours. I suggest you take these folk over to the rest centre. There's no point in them stopping here.'

Lorna nodded. The public shelter at the end of the road hadn't taken a direct hit, but the explosion that had done for the two semis had compromised its structural integrity, rendering it unusable until it had been checked by a civil engineer.

Taking care where she put her feet as she crossed the brick-strewn road, Lorna gathered together the people from the public shelter.

'Come with me. I'll take you to the rest centre.'

'We want to stop here and wait for news,' said a man who was gaunt with shock. 'They're our neighbours in those cellars.'

'There's nothing you can do,' Lorna said firmly. 'If you want to do something, then help me with these other people.'

After a moment he nodded and soon Lorna was leading the group to MacFadyen's – or, to give it its full name, MacFadyen's Memorial Congregational Church, which was the local WVS's headquarters and also the rest centre, where people were brought when they had lost their homes. Not everyone who came here was homeless. Sometimes people swarmed in because the ARP had turfed them out of the Anderson shelters in their back gardens, thanks to an unexploded bomb in the vicinity.

COURAGE FOR THE HOME FRONT GIRLS   113

Lorna shepherded her group across the large, lofty hall and settled them, then went to fetch a tray of tea. That was probably all these folk needed. Once she had supplied the hot drinks, Lorna set about helping those whose dirt- and dust-encrusted forms showed that they had been bombed out. For now they needed to get warmed up and be provided with soap and water. Later, fresh clothes and footwear would be provided and the WVS women would help them to fill in the forms associated with having lost everything they possessed.

Lorna boggled at the efficiency of it all. What she felt ran deeper than admiration. She loved being a part of this. It had given her purpose at a time when her life had been in ruins. She might have been pushed into joining the WVS by the formidable Mrs Lockwood, but now she was more glad of it than she could express. The work done by these stalwart women was essential and Lorna took a growing pride in being a part of it. She also liked the thought that her mother too was involved with the WVS.

Lorna's WVS duties engaged her in a way that her job at the salvage depot couldn't hope to. She had discovered something new inside herself. All her life, she had been the obedient daughter; then she'd been the adoring fiancée. But now she was somebody in her own right, and she could feel a new confidence growing inside her.

It gave her the ability to step back from the feud between Mrs Lockwood and Sally Henshaw. Mrs Lockwood was always on at her to spill the beans about what Mrs Henshaw was up to, and it was true that Lorna required no convincing that Mrs Lockwood needed someone better than Mrs Henshaw to see to the depot for her on a daily basis, but she was careful not to get involved. To criticise Sally Henshaw to Mrs Lockwood, and then work alongside Mrs Henshaw as if she'd never uttered a word, would have been both petty and complicated – and Lorna had had far more than her share of complications in recent weeks.

It wasn't just the depot feud she wanted to distance herself from. She had to put George behind her as well and try to shut down her feelings for him. He was part of her past and she needed to move on.

His name was Eddie Markham and he didn't have a girlfriend. No, wait – yes, he did – her! Betty was jubilant. She could almost feel her face shining with happiness. How soon could she start calling him her boyfriend? You probably had to go out together a few times before you could do that, as if you were trying one another out, so to speak.

Not that she and Eddie needed to do any trying out. Of that Betty was perfectly sure. She was special. He had said so. He had parted company with his previous girl specifically so as to go out with Betty with no complications. It showed what a gentleman he was.

He took her to the pictures on Saturday and they sat in the middle of the auditorium. He didn't try to persuade her to go to the back row, where everyone knew the canoodling took place. Mind you, the thought of canoodling with Eddie made Betty feel all fluttery and breathless.

Eddie had insisted that they see *Wuthering Heights* with Merle Oberon and Laurence Olivier, which was doing the rounds again.

'Are you sure?' Betty asked. 'Wouldn't you rather see *The Hound of the Baskervilles*? I know that's on. I've never seen *Wuthering Heights* and I'd love to, but I'm not sure it's going to have the same appeal for a man.'

'Can't you see I'm trying to impress you?' Eddie asked.

He said it in a jokey way but at the same time there was something in his voice that suggested he really meant it and

Betty felt a little surge of delight. She had wanted a boyfriend for ages and now it was even better than she'd imagined.

That was on the Saturday evening. On Sunday afternoon he took her to a tea-dance where, before the music started, they had fruit scones and Betty was mother with the teapot. She admired the china, which was decorated with a pattern of violets round the rim. The tables, set with crisp linen, were positioned around the dance-floor.

'I thought you'd like it here,' Eddie said. 'You have to bring a pretty girl to a pretty place, don't you?'

Ought she to feel embarrassed? She wasn't. She was thrilled. Eddie was such a gentleman. He was obviously trying to please her, to impress her. It was very flattering.

It was lovely as well to be asked questions about herself. He said he wanted to know all about her.

'What job did you do before you worked at the salvage depot?' he asked.

'I worked in a grocer's shop from when I left school. It wasn't anything special, just a corner shop.'

'Don't call it "just" a corner shop. They're the lifeblood of any local area. Did you enjoy it?'

Betty nodded. 'I did. The Tuckers were good to me.'

'I can imagine you being good at shop work,' said Eddie. 'You've got a lovely smile. A friendly manner is what you need when you work in a corner shop.'

Betty raised her teacup to her lips to hide her blush.

'And then you packed it in to do war work,' Eddie said admiringly.

Should she tell him? Shouldn't she? She couldn't bear him to think ill of her, yet she also wanted to speak the truth. You couldn't keep secrets from your boyfriend.

The man who was running the event, a dapper old boy who was very light on his feet, called for silence and announced that, in the few minutes left before the dancing started, raffle tickets would be for sale.

'All proceeds to the Red Cross,' he finished encouragingly.

Eddie immediately got up and went to the table where the tickets were being sold. He came back with a handful and presented them to Betty.

'For me?' she asked in surprise. 'You shouldn't.'

'Of course I should,' he replied. 'Nothing is too much for my best girl.'

Emotion welled up inside Betty. 'You're spoiling me.'

'It's only some raffle tickets.'

'It's more than that. It's this whole afternoon – the tea and scones, the dance. It's a lovely occasion and it's so kind of you to get tickets for it, and then to support the raffle as well.'

'It's in a good cause.' Eddie seemed determined to brush aside her appreciation – which made her all the more appreciative.

'The thing is,' Betty confided, leaning closer and dropping her voice, 'I don't have much money left over for treats at the moment. I – I owe my dad quite a bit of money. You see, the reason I had to leave the grocer's was because...' She drew in a breath. 'I was sacked.'

'You never pinched the stock, did you?'

'No!' she exclaimed, astonished that anyone could imagine such a thing of her. 'Nothing like that. It was the stupidest thing. Have you heard of the tests that people from the Food Office do? They go into a shop and try to get the shopkeeper to break the rationing rules and then they take him to court. That was what happened to me. I sold some butter to someone who wasn't registered with Tucker's, only it was really someone from the Food Office – and poor Mr Tucker ended up in front of the magistrate.'

Eddie blew out a low whistle. 'Crikey. What happened?'

'He was fined and so was I. It was horrible. He had to write a cheque there and then to cover both fines or I don't know what would have happened to me. He'd already kept back my wages to cover any fine, but of course that wasn't anything like enough. So then my dad had to pay back Mr Tucker – and now I'm saving up a little bit every week so I can pay back Dad.'

'Is it a lot?' Eddie asked.

Betty nodded, but she was too embarrassed to admit how much. Honesty had its limits.

'That's why I'm enjoying this afternoon so much,' she said. 'It's nice to be spoiled.'

'And there was me thinking you were here for my good looks,' Eddie teased.

Betty was flustered but in a pleasant way. She knew he was joking. 'I'm not here just to have money spent on me. I like your company. You know that.'

Eddie nodded. He sighed deeply, which made him sound satisfied with life. 'It's good to hear you say it, Betty. To have a pretty girl – and not just any pretty girl but this particular pretty girl – telling me she likes my company, that's made my day, that has. It's made my year.'

Betty was thrilled. Would it be right for her to call him her boyfriend now he'd said that? The question sent a thrill of delight skittering through her.

She wasn't alone in being happy. Mrs Beaumont was thrilled to see her happy and the munitions girls wanted all the gossip.

Sally was pleased for her too.

'What's he like?' she asked as the two of them fiddled with long pieces of string, untying all the knots.

It wasn't so easy for them to chat these days. They used to talk all the time before Miss Snooty Boots had turned up, but her presence had largely put the mockers on that. She was inside the building at present, sorting rags into different types of fabric.

Betty let loose a happy sigh. Eddie was her new favourite subject. She could talk about him until the cows came home.

'You've seen what a looker he is,' she said to Sally. 'And he has beautiful manners. He makes me feel special.'

'I'm so glad for you,' said Sally. 'What does he do? Why hasn't he been called up?'

'Flat feet.' Betty giggled. 'Not that you'd ever know. He's a wonderful dancer.' She hesitated, wondering whether to say it. Yes, she would. 'The first time he took me in ballroom hold, my skin tingled all over.'

'It sounds as if you're smitten,' Sally said, her hazel eyes shining as she smiled.

Betty's heart gave a thud. Was this the moment when her friend warned her to be careful? Betty desperately didn't want Sally to pour cold water on her happiness.

But Sally said, 'It reminds me of Andrew and me. I was officially Rod's girlfriend when we met but I knew Andrew was the right man.'

'That's exactly what happened to Eddie,' Betty exclaimed. 'He already had a girlfriend but then he met me when he came in here needing directions.'

'And later he came back to see you again but he found me instead, looking like Mrs Mop,' Sally added.

'When he turned up here after work and I didn't want to speak to him, it was because I'd seen him at the pictures the night before with this girl, but he'd come to tell me he'd finished things with her.'

Sally nodded. 'He was in a difficult situation. I knew I couldn't possibly get involved with Andrew until I'd told Rod the truth. In fact, I told Andrew I couldn't ever see him again.'

'You never!' breathed Betty.

'I did. It all seemed so complicated, but I would never have two-timed Rod.'

'And Eddie didn't two-time me,' said Betty. 'He waited until he'd said goodbye to the other girl before he asked me out.'

'Andrew makes me feel complete,' Sally said softly. 'I've never been happier in my life. That's what it's like when you meet the right person. You just *know*.'

Sally was in the yard with Betty and Miss Sadler, the three of them sorting through that morning's sacks of mixed salvage, when three headscarfed women, who were probably in their thirties, turned up at the depot pushing a handcart loaded with books.

'That's a lot of books,' Betty said by way of greeting.

'It's a lot of pushing,' said one of the women. Her nose and chin looked sharp but her eyes were kind. 'We had to borrow the window-cleaner's cart to get 'em here.'

'We wanted to bring them all in one go and get it over with,' said another, whose tightly curled fringe bubbled out from the front of her headscarf.

'Are you sure you want to part with them all?' Sally asked.

'Yes,' said the third. The others had rosy cheeks from the exercise, but her face was pale and she had shadows under her eyes. 'They belonged to Grandad – the children's grandad, that is – and he's no longer with us so we're doing a big sort-out.'

'I'm sorry that you've lost him,' Sally said politely.

'We're the daughters-in-law,' said the one with the bubbly fringe, 'and our husbands have left it to us to get the house emptied.'

'The old man loved books and collected them all his life,' said the pale-faced woman. 'Each of the grandchildren has taken a couple to remember him by, but as a family we want the rest of them to go towards the war effort.'

When the books had all been carried indoors and the sisters-in-law had departed, Sally took a quick look through the various titles. A number of the books dated back to the previous century, though that in itself didn't necessarily make them valuable. She went to the office and put through a telephone call to Mr Atkinson's bookshop. Absurd as it sounded, it gave her real pleasure to do so. Much of her work involved the same old tasks as always, but making this call meant she was the depot manager.

She explained to Mr Atkinson about the sizeable donation and asked him to come along to pick out anything rare or costly that he could sell for the proceeds to be donated to the war effort.

'You might also want some of the books for the troops or for public libraries,' she added. 'I could stay late one evening if you want to come after shutting the shop.'

'There's no need for that,' said Mr Atkinson, 'but thank you f-for offering. I'll c-come when I shut for d-dinner. Would today suit you?'

Sally rearranged her own dinner-break to fit in and was ready when Mr Atkinson arrived. She liked him. He was always polite and agreeable. His gangly appearance made him seem as if he might be clumsy, but he never was. He took off his overcoat and took a moment to wipe the lenses of his spectacles on a clean handkerchief before he started sorting through the books.

'Shall I leave you to it?' Sally asked. 'Put any that you want over here. Would you like a cup of tea?'

'Thank you. Most kind.' He looked around at the heaps of books. 'I might not have time to go through them all now. I might have to c-come back.'

'There are rather a lot of them,' said Sally.

She went off to make the tea. Returning a few minutes later, she crept into the room, not wanting to disturb him.

He glanced round. 'Thank you.'

'I'll leave you to it.'

'Before you go,' he said and stopped.

'Yes?' Sally asked.

'I w-wonder if I might ask you s-something.'

'Of course,' said Sally.

'It's a d-delicate matter and I don't w-want to speak out of turn.'

Good heavens, whatever could it be? 'I can't imagine you saying anything you shouldn't,' Sally assured him.

'It's... w-well, it's Miss Hughes.'

'What about her?' Had Betty made a terrible blunder at the bookshop last time she was there?

'I know you're her f-friend.' Mr Atkinson's narrow face was flushed and he wasn't quite facing Sally, but the way he had planted his feet firmly showed his determination to say his piece. 'I w-wonder if you think I might have any ch-chance with her. She mentioned being interested in a man but he already had a girlfriend, so I w-wonder—'

Sally jumped in. 'Eddie stopped seeing the other girl. Betty – Miss Hughes—'

It was Mr Atkinson's turn to jump in. 'I see. Thank you. I'm s-sorry for—'

'No harm done,' Sally said. 'I won't say a word to Miss Hughes, I promise. This is just between us.'

He nodded and bent so far over the books that he looked as if he was trying to climb inside them. Sally hurried from the room, her heart beating fast. Well! That was the last thing she'd expected. Poor Mr Atkinson.

At home, when they were having a cup of tea in the parlour after their evening meal, Sally was delighted to report the improvement in Miss Sadler's attitude. 'It's clear she's still not pleased to be lumbered with working at the depot, but she has stopped showing such obvious distaste.'

'You handled the situation very well,' Andrew praised her.

'I'm proud of you. It was a good idea to appeal to her patriotism instead of hauling her over the coals.'

'It seems to have worked,' Sally agreed. 'It's not her fault she was brought up to think so well of herself.'

'But this is wartime and everyone has to do their bit, regardless of any other considerations,' said Mrs Henshaw. 'We'll all end up rubbing shoulders with people we'd never have met before the war. We're all the same now and the sooner your Miss Sadler learns that the better.'

Sally got up from her seat and bent over her mother-in-law to give her a hug. 'Let's hope she does. If not, I'll bring her here and you can give her a good talking-to.'

'Hey, what about me?' asked Andrew. 'If there are hugs going on, don't leave me out.'

He stood up as well, and leaned down to put one arm round his mother while drawing Sally closer with the other. Sally snuggled up. Her own parents weren't huggers and she had been brought up to keep her hands to herself. Meeting Andrew hadn't just had a powerful effect on her heart. It had seemed to affect her arms too, making them want to hold the people she loved.

With one last squeeze, the family broke apart.

'Thank you both for taking such an interest,' Sally said, resuming her seat.

'Of course we're interested,' said Mrs Henshaw. 'I'm glad the matter with the posh girl is sorted out.'

Sally didn't say so but there was something else that needed to be sorted out: Mrs Lockwood's attitude towards the depot. Sally felt sure that one reason why Miss Sadler had been a bit of a so-and-so to start with was because she was Mrs Lockwood's loyal follower. Since Sally had taken over the depot, Mrs Lockwood had visited more often, and seemed set upon undermining Sally's authority at every opportunity.

Recently she had swanned in, exuding efficiency and

supremacy, to demand the latest figures of salvage quantities. The salvage was measured by weight on a large set of scales rather like the 'I Speak Your Weight' machine on a seaside pier.

Sally had been reluctant to share the information with Mrs Lockwood, but she was the official Salvage Officer with the WVS so she had no option. Mrs Lockwood copied the figures and went on her way, leaving Sally shaking her head in relief to see the back of her.

But the following day, Sally had found out from one of the delivery drivers that she, as manager, ought to have sent in the figures to the Town Hall. Something inside her had slumped. This made her look inefficient, but Mr Overton hadn't exactly trained her up for this post and she was learning as she went along.

And then Mrs Lockwood had returned to the depot and announced that she had personally delivered the statistics.

Sally gasped in outrage and started to object.

'Don't be ridiculous,' Mrs Lockwood boomed. 'The Town Hall required the information and I provided it. What's wrong with that? You should be grateful.'

Grateful? Sally had been furious. Humiliated too, not least because she saw the cool scorn in Miss Sadler's green eyes.

'I've got to do something about this,' Sally confided to Betty when the two of them were sitting together on folding chairs on the depot roof, nursing hot drinks as they faced a long, bone-chilling night on fire-watching duty.

'But what?' Betty asked. 'The woman is a human steamroller.'

'I've been thinking,' said Sally. 'Mrs Lockwood is well known in the local community.'

'Mrs Beaumont says she was a do-gooder before the war.'

'I need to get myself known. Specifically, I need to make sure people associate me with the depot.'

'You want to give talks, you mean?' Betty asked. 'Like the one we arranged for Mr Overton to do.'

'Exactly,' said Sally. 'It would be good for the depot as well, because the more people know about salvage the better for the war effort. I need to give talks, especially in schools. Children are getting involved in salvage collection and I think it's something to be encouraged. I can help organise competitions between schools for who can collect the most waste paper or the most milk-bottle tops. I could get the Scouts and the Guides involved as well.'

'That's a good idea,' Betty said admiringly.

'You don't think it looks like I'm blowing my own trumpet?' Sally asked. 'Just to get one over on Mrs Lockwood?'

'Crikey, no,' Betty said at once. 'This is your way of taking your work seriously and doing the best you can for the depot.'

Reassured, Sally started to put her plan into action, her determination only increased by the news of the terrible destruction that had been visited upon poor Coventry by the Luftwaffe. Coming just days after the sorrow of Remembrance Sunday and the anniversary of Armistice Day, the devastation of Coventry was even more of a blow.

Sally spent Friday getting in touch with local schools and putting dates in the diary to visit them. She also made a list of knitting circles, soup kitchens, first-aiders and any other groups she could think of. She would start getting in touch with them next week.

It was her turn to work on Saturday. She went over the road to introduce herself formally at the police station and then showed two police officers, Constable Arnold and Constable Collins, around the depot. They promised to spread the word while they were out on the beat. She had also been invited to meet Sergeant Robbins in the police station that afternoon. She went to the police station at three o'clock.

Sergeant Robbins was middle-aged, a tall man with an

upright posture that suggested he kept his shoulders pushed back at all times so as to look as smart as possible in his uniform. Sally sat in his small office and answered questions about her background. She told him about her work in the Food Office and explained that marriage had brought her to Chorlton and the salvage depot.

Sergeant Robbins chuckled. 'Life takes some funny turns. What about your colleagues?'

Sally didn't know how Miss Sadler had got assigned to the depot. It embarrassed her not to know, so she concentrated on Betty. Somehow or other she ended up telling Sergeant Robbins the story of Betty and the butter she shouldn't have sold when she worked in the grocer's.

The sergeant's face clouded. 'Miss Hughes broke the rules, you mean?'

Sally immediately wished she could take everything back. 'Well, yes, but—'

'Did the matter go to court? What was the outcome?'

'The grocer was fined and so was Miss Hughes.'

'So she landed her own boss in the soup as well, did she?' Sergeant Robbins shook his head. 'Poor fellow. No one deserves an employee like that.'

Sally sprang to her friend's defence. 'I assure you that Miss Hughes is a law-abiding citizen.'

'Oh aye?' The sergeant's eyebrows climbed up his forehead.

'She made a mistake, that's all, and she's learned her lesson.'

'I hope so, for your sake, you being her new boss.'

Sally tried again to smooth things over. 'Some shopkeepers are obviously on the fiddle and they need to be stopped, but then you get someone who falls for the sob story.'

'And Miss Hughes was one of those?' Sergeant Robbins asked in a voice that said he had no intention of being swayed.

'Yes, she was,' Sally insisted. 'I know because...' She lifted her chin. 'I was the person who tested her.'

Sergeant Robbins laughed, though not in a way that suggested amusement. 'And now you're working together?'

'Yes, we are, and we've become true friends, so I know what I'm talking about when I say she's a good person.'

'A good person who broke the rules.'

'A good person who trusted a stranger.'

'Easily led, is what you're saying,' Sergeant Robbins remarked. 'I suggest you bear that in mind, Mrs Henshaw, you being in charge of the depot.'

Sally was deeply disappointed. This was far from the impression she'd come here to project. Sergeant Robbins moved the conversation along and she told him about the planned school visits and the inter-school competitions she intended to set up.

'The kids will enjoy that,' said the sergeant. 'It'll make a change from hunting for shrapnel.'

Afterwards Sally trailed home, feeling guilty for having discussed Betty's past so freely. She wished she could say that Sergeant Robbins had winkled the information out of her, but she knew he hadn't. It was her own fault for letting her tongue run away with her.

CHAPTER TWELVE

What with war work and overtime, plus the voluntary civil defence work that kept people out all night and the air raids that kept them up when they spent the night at home, everyone was tired – everyone except Betty. She was too excited and happy. Her cheekbones seemed to be permanently lifted from smiling so much – and all because she had a handsome, attentive boyfriend. This was what she had dreamed of for such a long time.

Eddie Markham was perfect and she didn't know what she had done to deserve him. When she was in his company, she had to force herself to drag her gaze away from him. She loved those teasing blue eyes surrounded by lashes as dark as his hair. There was something else about him too, something that was both attractive and intriguing. Anxious to let him know how much she thought of him, Betty tried to put it into words.

'You have such an air of confidence,' she told him and then cringed inwardly in case it was a daft thing to say.

But Eddie preened. 'That's because I know how to take care of myself.' He snatched a kiss. 'I know how to take care of my girl an' all,' he added, his lips close to her cheek, his words sending her all tingly.

Eddie's confidence wasn't just in his personality. It was a physical thing too. It was there in the lift of his chin and the set of his shoulders, even in the way he walked. A delicious shiver tumbled through Betty. It wasn't just his handsome face she adored. That physical confidence made her daydream about him dragging her into his arms and wrenching kisses from her.

'You look pleased,' Eddie said, his arm firmly round her waist as they stood in the queue for the cinema.

Prior to this, Betty had always thought that girls who allowed such familiarity in public looked flighty, but now she felt proud and wanted all the world to see she was Eddie's girl. She looked up at him, breathing in the scent of his tobacco. He held his Woodbine between two fingers of his free hand and angled his head upwards each time he exhaled, blowing the smoke over her head.

'I am pleased,' she told him. 'This coming weekend would have been my Saturday for working, but I helped Sally by doing her Saturday when she had a family birthday, so she's paying me back this week. I've got the day off.'

Her heart pitter-pattered in anticipation. Would he suggest spending the day together?

But Eddie looked at her tenderly, saying, 'I've got something on. I wish I'd known before so I could have taken you out for the day.'

'That would have been lovely.' Betty lowered her face for a moment before looking up brightly. It was silly to be disappointed. 'I think I'll go home for the day.'

'Tell you what,' said Eddie. 'If you're free on Monday evening, you can tell me all about it. Where is home?'

'Salford,' said Betty.

'You're a bit of a distance away from your ever-loving

family, then,' said Eddie. 'Does that mean you've got nobody close by to keep an eye on you?'

Betty dared to say, 'Only you,' and her reward was a tightening of the arm at her waist.

'Good girl,' Eddie whispered huskily.

At Dad's house on Saturday, Betty chose her moment carefully. Although she had felt like bursting through the front door and proclaiming the wonderful news that she had a boyfriend, she had held her tongue until she and Grace had cleared away after the meal and the three of them were sitting in the parlour, having a cuppa and a smoke. Betty would really have preferred to tell Dad on his own, but she knew better than to exclude Grace.

She looked affectionately at Dad, loving the sight of his beloved, habitually serious expression. After Mum died, anguish had left his face pinched and there had been a dullness in his eyes. Give Grace her due, she had restored steadiness and companionship to Dad's life.

'I've got something to tell you,' Betty announced.

'You haven't lost your job, have you?' Grace said at once.

'Of course not,' Betty answered indignantly.

'Well, you can't blame me for asking,' said Grace. 'We already know you're not good enough to be promoted.'

'Let her speak,' said Dad, but, instead of sounding as if he was leaping to Betty's defence, it seemed more like the patient sort of voice he would use as a copper dealing with a minor altercation between neighbours who ought to know better.

Betty took a moment to compose herself. She wanted this to be perfect. Unable to suppress a smile, she said, 'I've got a boyfriend.'

Grace's light-brown eyes widened. Her mouth widened too. 'Oh, *Betty!*' she cried in delight.

Dad laughed, a surprised sound. 'That was unexpected.'

Grace took over. She left her armchair and sat beside Betty on the sofa, taking her hand. She had never done that before.

'Haven't I always said what a lovely girl our Betty is and what a wonderful wife and mother she'll make one day? Haven't I always said that, Trevor?' She stroked Betty's hand. 'Oh, Betty, this is the best news. I'm so pleased. We want to hear all about him – don't we, Trevor?'

Here was Grace calling her 'our Betty', but Betty's surprise was swept away by pleasure. It was a long time since she had been the centre of attention in a good way under this roof.

'What's his name?' Grace asked.

'And what does he do?' asked Dad. 'Is he a soldier on leave? It's a difficult business being involved with a soldier, Betty. I'm only thinking of your happiness.'

'His name's Eddie and he's got flat feet,' said Betty. 'You'll like him, I promise.'

'Is he handsome?' Grace asked in a cosy way, as if Dad wasn't there and they were having a girly chat.

'Very.' Betty didn't dare say more for fear of sounding like a schoolgirl with a crush. 'I met him when he came into the depot asking for directions.'

'How romantic,' breathed Grace.

'I'd like to meet him,' said Dad. 'I don't care for the thought of you going out with a chap I don't know.'

'Oh, Trevor,' said Grace, 'Betty's a good girl and very sensible.'

'I never said she wasn't. I still won't feel right about this until we've met him.'

'You'd better invite him round, then, Betty,' said Grace.

'I'd love to,' said Betty. 'I want you to meet one another. You'll like him, Dad. You'll see.'

Compared to Grace's warm approval, Dad's reserve felt odd, but it was only to be expected that he would feel protective. Betty had never been in favour with Grace before. Of course, Grace was hearing wedding bells and telling herself that Betty really and truly would be gone for good. Betty was sure of that, but Grace's favour tasted sweet all the same.

Betty spent Monday afternoon in the bookshop. More donations had arrived and needed to be sorted. Betty was happy to get on with it on her own while Samuel was busy in the shop. She felt she knew what she was doing and she liked the thought of Samuel trusting her.

As she worked, she thought back to her Saturday visit to Dad and Grace and a smile curved her lips.

'You look happy.'

Glancing round at Samuel, Betty laughed at herself. 'I am,' she said simply.

'Good,' he replied. 'It's nice to s-see.'

What a kind man he was. 'I saw my dad on Saturday – and my stepmother, of course.'

Betty felt a bit guilty for adding Grace as the usual afterthought. After the way Grace had embraced Betty's new status as a girl with a boyfriend, she deserved more of an acknowledgement than that, even if her real motive had been to get Betty married off and out of her old home once and for all.

'I hope you f-found them w-well,' Samuel said politely.

'Yes, thank you. They're both fine.' She couldn't keep it to herself a moment longer. 'I had good news for them. I told them about Eddie – my boyfriend,' she added, feeling a self-conscious glow in her cheeks. How wonderful to be able to say 'my boyfriend'.

There was a pause before Samuel spoke, but that was probably because he was starting on a 'w' sound. 'W-well, I'm sure that made them happy.'

'It did, especially my stepmother. She was thrilled for me.'

'And your f-father?'

'Oh, him an' all, but you know what dads are like with their daughters. He wants to meet Eddie.'

'And make s-sure he's good enough f-for you,' Samuel finished.

Betty laughed. 'Like I said: dads and daughters.'

Aware of having stopped working, she rose to her feet and started putting the various piles of books onto different shelves.

'S-so you'll s-soon be taking Eddie to meet them.'

'Definitely,' Betty confirmed. 'I can't wait – and neither can Dad and Grace.'

'And Eddie,' said Samuel.

'Oh aye. He can't wait either.' She bit her lip, trying to remember if Eddie had actually said so. It didn't matter if he hadn't. She knew how keen he was on her.

She finished shelving the books and turned round. She had an odd feeling, as if there was a silence behind her – which there was because Samuel hadn't answered – but it felt like more than that, more than a simple gap in the conversation.

Samuel smiled at her. His hazel eyes appeared warm and tender, which must have been something to do with being behind the lenses of his glasses, a kind of optical illusion. 'W-what can I s-say except to give you my best w-wishes? It gladdens me to s-see you happy.'

'Thank you.' Satisfaction spread throughout her body. 'I've never been as happy as this before.'

That evening Betty couldn't wait to see Eddie. She put on her tweed skirt and the cherry-red jumper knitted by Mum. Would the colour make Eddie think it made her hair look more golden, like Mum used to say? Grace had given her a half-full jar of Snowfire Cream.

'Take it. I've got another. I bought them when war was declared.'

Betty had been delighted. She looked in the mirror now, thinking of the 'divinely smooth and fair' complexion promised in the advertisements in *Woman's Illustrated*. She smiled on purpose to make her dimple appear. Sally had told her about Eddie referring to her as Miss Dimple. Betty had never cared for her dimple before but now she loved it.

She went downstairs to wait for him in the sitting room. Mrs Beaumont was knitting. The munitions girls were all upstairs getting ready to go out dancing. When the doorbell rang, Betty switched off the hall light before opening the door a crack.

'Come in and say hello,' she said.

'Not this time. I can't wait to have my girl in my arms.'

Betty slid through the gap and found herself in Eddie's embrace.

As they walked, he asked her about her visit to Salford. Betty gave a few details, then issued the invitation.

'Dad and Grace would love to meet you.'

'Grace? Is she your sister?'

'My stepmother. My mum died a while back.'

'I'm sorry to hear that. A girl needs her mum.'

Betty's heart expanded as she absorbed his words of understanding.

'What's your stepmother like?'

Crikey. She couldn't bear to deceive Eddie but she couldn't speak the truth. She settled for, 'She used to be a neighbour so it isn't like having a stranger in the house. Anyroad, Dad wants to meet you. Grace an' all, of course.'

'Sorry. I was forgetting you'd just issued an invitation. It took me aback to hear you'd lost your mum. All I could think of was your distress.'

How lucky she was. 'Will you come?'

'Well...' Eddie stopped and turned to look at her, holding

both her hands. 'It's a big step for a bloke to meet a girl's parents. Having to go all the way over to Salford makes it even more of an occasion. It's not like if Star House was your home and I could pop in and shake your dad's hand.'

Betty broke their eye contact so he wouldn't see her disappointment. 'Oh, I see.' But she didn't, not really. Had she been too keen? Had she made a fool of herself?

Eddie lifted her chin, keeping his knuckles underneath it. 'I'm not trying to dodge out of it, honest I'm not. But I need us to be a couple for a while, so I can show your dad how serious I am. I need him to believe in me. I can't expect him to think well of me until I've been taking you out for some time. I have – I have to prove myself.'

He stopped to kiss her. Often his kisses were demanding, but this one was tender. It lasted a long time and left Betty wanting to swoon.

Eddie started to speak, stopped, then started again. 'It scares me how much I care for you.'

A small gasp emerged from Betty's throat. This was the kind of thing that happened in the romances she loved to read – and now it was happening to her.

CHAPTER THIRTEEN

It was past the middle of November now. The days were getting ever shorter, the blackout longer. The trees were increasingly bare and the sight of ruined houses and heaps of rubble made the grey days feel dismal and dreary, but the rich, gleaming red of japonica berries and holly berries added a welcome touch of brightness to relieve the gloom.

When Sally and Andrew visited Sally's parents on Sunday, Dad was busy digging his vegetable patch. He removed his pipe from his lips to kiss Sally, and put it back in again to shake hands with Andrew.

'What are you doing?' Sally asked.

'Getting on with the digging.'

Sally smiled. 'I can see that. I was hoping for more detail.'

Andrew and Dad shared a glance.

It was Andrew who replied. 'Getting on with the digging is a time-honoured tradition that doesn't require any further explanation.'

'It's all to do with keeping the ground in fine fettle,' said Dad. 'You go along in and say hello to Mum. I'll be in shortly.'

Mum had got the parlour nice and warm. Sally hoped she

hadn't been overgenerous with the coal, leaving her and Dad with not enough, but she didn't comment.

When Dad came in, the four of them sat and chatted. As always, the first topic was the war. They hadn't seen one another since before the Coventry blitz, so that was top of the list. As an ARP warden, Dad had reliable information about what Coventry had suffered.

'Over five hundred tons of high explosives,' he said sombrely. 'And somewhere between seven and eight hundred incendiaries.'

Sally shivered. 'No wonder there's this new word – "coven-trated" – to mean something has been smashed to smithereens.'

'It doesn't bear thinking about,' said Mum. 'It makes the attacks on Wythenshawe and Stretford earlier this week seem small.'

'They won't have seemed small to the people involved,' said Andrew.

'Betty and I were on fire-watching duty that night,' said Sally, 'and we saw all the fires.'

'At least nobody died in Wythenshawe,' said Dad, his silence about Stretford telling its own story.

Mum put down her empty cup and squashed the tip of her Craven A into the ashtray.

'Have you finished your tea, Sally? Let's go up the road and see the Grants.'

Sally was glad of the suggestion. She had intended to pop in and see Deborah and was wearing the short necklace of blue beads that her friend had given her last Christmas.

Putting on their coats and hats, she and Mum linked arms as they walked along. Mrs Grant and Deborah were both at home. Deborah was wearing a sunshine-yellow jumper that Sally recognised. It made her glossy dark-brown hair look even closer than usual to being black.

'I remember your nan knitting that for you,' said Sally.

'She always did like bright colours,' said Mum, unintentionally reminding them that she and Deborah's nan had been more or less the same age and had in fact been at school at the same time.

'That's the necklace I got you, isn't it?' Deborah looked pleased and Sally was glad she'd worn it.

'Yes. It's so pretty.'

'Blue is your colour,' said Mum.

'I'll put the kettle on,' said Mrs Grant.

'Not for us,' said Mum. 'We've only just had some.'

Sally asked after Dulcie because she wanted to show she was comfortable doing so. It still felt odd to think of Rod being married to someone else. Not that she begrudged him his whirlwind romance – far from it – but she had her own opinion of Rod Grant and she sincerely hoped that Dulcie was happy.

'She's fine,' said Mrs Grant. 'We've had another letter from her.'

'That's nice,' said Mum. 'You're getting to know one another.'

Mrs Grant sighed and there was a glint of resignation in her brown eyes. 'Go on. Say it if you want to. The whole neighbourhood is thinking it, so you might as well come right out with it.'

'Mum doesn't mean to stir anything up,' Sally said.

'Of course I don't,' said Mum. 'I hope you know me better than that, Edith Grant. I feel for you, I really do. I know what it was like for me when Sally took up with a chap from Chorlton, so I know a bit of what you're going through.'

'Mum!' Sally exclaimed.

'It's true,' said Mum. 'You might as well have taken up with the man in the moon. That's one thing about this war. In normal times, girls get together with local men, boys they went to school with or that live round the corner, and everyone already knows one another. The families already know one another. That's how it's meant to be. It's to do with being part of a community.'

Deborah chimed in, a note of determination in her voice. 'We'll feel better after Rod has brought Dulcie here for a visit, won't we, Mum?'

'Is that on the cards?' Sally asked. She couldn't help feeling curious about the unknown Dulcie.

'Not yet,' said Mrs Grant.

'What job does she do?' Sally asked.

'She's a clerk at the shipyard,' said Deborah. 'That's how they met.'

Sally nodded. Rod was a caulker, making ships watertight. Before the war he had worked on the docks at the Manchester Ship Canal, but once the war started he was ordered to report to the shipyards in Barrow-in-Furness to work on actual ship-building rather than the repairs he had done in Manchester. All the neighbours hereabouts had regarded him as a hero when he was sent away at short notice to support the war effort.

'Dulcie must be every bit as keen to meet Rod's family as you are to meet her,' said Mum.

'I've been sending her a bit of advice about Rod,' said Mrs Grant. 'His likes and dislikes, things like that. After all, they haven't known one another very long.'

'I'm sure she appreciates it,' said Mum.

Deborah rolled her bright-blue eyes expressively at Sally. Sally wondered what it must be like for Dulcie to receive 'advice' from her unknown mother-in-law. She thanked heaven all over again that her own mother-in-law was so downright likeable.

'I've chosen them a nice Christmas card,' said Mrs Grant. 'Well, in so far as it's possible to get good cards this year. The quality has gone right down. I know, I know.' She held up her hand to stop the obvious responses. 'There's a war on and there are more important things than cards.'

'I think it's still important to send them,' said Mum. 'At a time like this, we want to show our family and friends we're thinking of them.'

'And it doesn't take a high-quality card for the sentiment to be appreciated,' said Deborah.

'Cards can be put to good use afterwards,' Sally added. 'I don't know exactly what a Christmas card is worth in terms of salvage, but it takes twelve letters to make one box for rifle cartridges, so it must be about the same for thin wartime cards.'

Shortly after that Sally and Mum went home.

'I hope you enjoyed your little visit up the road,' said Dad.

Sally gave a sigh of pleasure. 'We did.'

Mum looked at her. 'But did you have to bring up' – and Sally expected her to say *Dulcie* but instead she ended the question with, 'salvage?'

'Salvage?' Sally repeated in surprise. Then she laughed. 'Why shouldn't I? I only said that paper is used to make boxes for rifle cartridges.'

'There's no need to shout about your job from the rooftops,' said Mum. 'That's all I'm saying.'

'Being the manager of the salvage depot is something to be proud of,' Andrew said loyally.

Sally knew there would be no reasoning with her mother. She turned to Dad, asking him with her eyes for his support.

'I'm glad you're happy in your work, Sally,' he said, 'but it honestly surprises me that you find it satisfying. It's *salvage*.'

'It matters,' said Sally.

'It's essential,' Andrew added.

'That goes without saying,' said Dad, 'but let's face it: it's something for children to do. That's why Sally has got these competitions going between the schools. Don't get me wrong: I'm all in favour of children getting involved in the war effort. But it's children's work, Sally – and you're better than that.'

. . .

Despite her parents' words, Sally had been delighted to be asked to give a talk at the church hall on the subject of salvage. There was a good turnout and all the seats were occupied. Sally felt nervous but pleased too.

'If you give your talk first,' said Mr Avery, an ARP man who had organised the evening, 'we'll then open the floor for questions and comments. These things always go better when people feel involved.'

Mr Avery started by giving the audience instructions about what to do in the event of an air raid, raising a few chuckles when he added, 'But Jerry hasn't got a ticket so let's hope he stays away.' Then he introduced Sally.

She was standing to one side, her heart beating faster than normal. Led by Mr Avery, the audience gave a smattering of applause to welcome her and she stepped forward. She had her notes in her hand, but she had practised so many times that she knew everything more or less by heart, which meant she could look out at her listeners. Strictly speaking she didn't look straight at them, but directed her gaze just above their heads so they felt they were being looked at.

She started off by listing some random items that could be given a new wartime purpose.

'Lace curtains become sandfly netting. If any of you are golfers, golf balls can contribute towards the making of gasmasks. The rags you donate might be made into maps for bomber crews and tank crews. Old mattresses can become life jackets. After the "Saucepans for Spitfires" campaign, we all think of our saucepans being made into planes, but they are used for other things too, such as helmets.' Sensing that everyone was listening attentively, Sally decided to go for a laugh. She hadn't been sure whether she would use this piece of information, but it seemed safe to. 'And guess what goes towards making parachutes and chinstraps.' She paused for half a moment before announcing, 'Corsets!' for which she was rewarded with a ripple of laughter.

Heartened, she started to enjoy herself. She had learned a lot about salvage since she'd started working at the depot, and here was the chance to spread some of that knowledge; but she was careful not to go on for too long. When she finished, she glanced across at Mr Avery, who stood up and led some polite applause.

'Thank you very much, Mrs Henshaw. I'm sure we all found that most informative. Now we move on to the part of the evening when the audience can pose questions and raise any matters they wish.'

Sally nodded encouragingly at the rows of faces. 'It's important to look for new ways to boost the war effort by thinking more widely about what can be salvaged.'

A man immediately leapt to his feet. 'I'm glad you said that. I want to discuss this idea of removing railings and melting them down.'

This was something that was currently being widely talked about, so Sally had come prepared with a few facts and figures – but she could barely get a word in. There were so many opinions. Questions, too, though most of them didn't get answered or discussed, because things got pretty heated and Mr Avery did more gasping like a fish out of water than keeping control in the church hall.

'I heard someone on the wireless saying that the railings from our front gardens or from around our local parks can go off to join the fight against Hitler. As if railings are soldiers!'

'What if our parks get flooded with undesirable people? That's what I want to know.'

'What d'you mean by "undesirables"?' challenged a woman with perfectly painted lips.

'I just mean people will feel free to roam, that's all. We have boundaries for a reason.'

'Never mind the parks. What about my garden? I don't want dogs and cats wandering in willy-nilly. You know what dogs are like for digging.'

'What about railings round churchyards? It wouldn't be respectful to remove them.'

'I understand your concern about this,' Sally put in, 'but I think that they wouldn't be exempt.'

'What about inside the cemetery?' demanded a man with a square face and a large nose. 'What happens when a private tomb has its own railings? Would they have to come down?'

'What if I give up the railings outside my house but my next-door neighbour doesn't want to give up his?'

'He should be forced to by law.'

'Are you saying there should be a law making everybody give up their railings?'

Again Sally managed to put in, 'I believe there will be certain grounds for exception, such as historic or safety,' though she wasn't sure how many people actually heard her.

'There's a good reason for everyone to have to give up their railings,' called out someone else. 'It will make everyone's houses look the same. You can't have a street with half the railings gone and the other half still in place. That would look shabby.'

'And you think that having chicken-wire instead of railings isn't going to look shabby?'

'What about good old-fashioned neighbourliness?' asked a woman. 'In our road, we hang our carpets and rugs over our railings when they need a beating and we have a good natter at the same time.'

'I'm more concerned about the damage,' said a man with a fleshy face and red-veined cheeks. 'Most houses that have railings have a low curtain-wall of brick with railings set into the top. Take away the railings and that's going to make the bricks come loose.'

The arguments about the removal of railings took up the remainder of the time. Sally was rather taken aback. Disappointed, too, after the way her talk had been received. All the same, she made a funny story out of it when she got home.

'Did all those people sit politely through my talk just so they could have their say about railings afterwards?' she asked humorously.

She was reluctant to make light of it at the depot the next day, though. Betty would have loved the anecdote but Sally felt iffy about sharing it with Miss Sadler. She hated the idea of suggesting that there was any difference of opinion regarding salvage in front of the depot's new recruit. Was that daft of her? Miss Sadler was undoubtedly working harder now, but the occasional soft sigh or cool glance still made it clear she considered herself born to better things.

So Sally opted to keep mum about the railings controversy. She would tell Betty at the end of the day when they walked together along Beech Road, heading for their respective homes.

In any case, as the three girls sorted rags, string and twine in one of the depot's rooms, Betty couldn't stop talking about how keen her dad was to meet Eddie and how Eddie was anxious to prove himself first by being a fixture in her life for longer.

'It must be serious if you want to introduce him to your family,' Miss Sadler observed.

Sally looked at her in surprise. She didn't normally join in with personal conversations. Then she felt a stab of guilt. Maybe she and Betty didn't encourage her to – but then, why would they?

But Betty seemed too bubbly to notice. She laughed and blushed, her creamy cheeks staining a pretty pink. Sally's heart melted. She loved seeing her friend like this. She dearly wanted Betty to enjoy the same sort of loving relationship she herself had with Andrew – stable and strong but also exciting and passionate. If Andrew and Eddie liked one another, then the two couples could go out together.

Looking self-conscious, though by no means in an uncomfortable way, Betty answered Miss Sadler's question. 'Yes, it's serious, but it's all happened very quickly and Eddie wants my dad to see how serious he is by the two of us going out together for some time. I agree with him. I want Dad to feel confident about us an' all.'

'Of course you do,' said Sally.

She hoped with all her heart that Betty wouldn't have to face anything like the kind of objections and offishness that she'd endured at home after meeting Andrew.

The door was flung open and Mrs Lockwood filled the doorway.

'So this is where you are, Mrs Henshaw. I should have known you'd be hiding yourself away somewhere.'

Sally gasped; but, if there was one thing she had learned about dealing with Mrs Lockwood, it was the importance of fighting back right away. It was either that or be trampled. She was also desperate to conceal the humiliation she felt at being spoken to in such a way in front of the other two.

'I'm not hiding, Mrs Lockwood, and I'm surprised you would think so. If you need to speak to me, let's go to my office. There's no fire yet but I'm sure your indignation will keep you warm.'

So saying, she put down the bundle of string she was unravelling and glared at her visitor. Would she refuse to budge from the doorway? With a toss of her head, Mrs Lockwood turned and marched off as if the office was hers and she was entitled to lead the way. Short of thrusting her way past, there was nothing Sally could do.

Mrs Lockwood opened the office door and didn't stop walking until she stood behind the desk – as if it was *her* desk.

The effrontery astounded Sally, but Mrs Lockwood gave her no time to react.

'I've been hearing about you, Mrs Henshaw, about your comings and goings.'

'I don't know what you mean,' said Sally.

'Don't you indeed? Putting yourself about as a public speaker: that's what I mean. Swanning around, talking to various groups, visiting schools. It won't do. Do you hear me?'

Aiming for a tone of quiet dignity, Sally replied, 'I'm informing people about the importance of salvage, what uses are made of it, and why everyone should be involved.'

'Goodness me, what would the war effort do without you?' Mrs Lockwood's light, mocking voice, at odds with her customary forceful manner, was surprisingly hurtful. 'Do you imagine people haven't seen the posters or read the government leaflets? Do you imagine the population of Chorlton to be illiterate, Mrs Henshaw?'

'Of course not,' Sally snapped, dignity forgotten, 'but the more information people have the better.'

'If it were necessary to go around giving talks on salvage, I would have done it myself,' Mrs Lockwood announced. 'I don't expect you to do it.'

'As the manager of this depot—'

'As the so-called manager,' retorted Mrs Lockwood, 'your duty is the day-to-day running, nothing more, and certainly not gallivanting around the neighbourhood like a music hall act. You're getting above yourself, Mrs Henshaw, and I shan't stand for it.'

Sally and Andrew were both due to go out on duty that night. Mrs Henshaw was also going to be out all night, working for the WVS.

Mrs Henshaw went upstairs to get changed and came back down wearing her smart green uniform. She always got changed before Sally and Andrew. Nothing was ever said but Sally sensed it was so she and Andrew could have a bit of privacy upstairs. It was embarrassing to think of Andrew's mother apparently imagining them indulging in a spot of hanky-panky before putting on lots of layers ready to go on duty in the freezing cold.

As soon as the bedroom door closed behind them, Andrew wrapped Sally in his arms and kissed her thoroughly. She surfaced feeling breathless. But it wasn't just the physical intimacy of their relationship that mattered to her. She also treasured their conversations. She wanted every kind of closeness with her husband. She wanted them to share everything. If they were to cherish and support one another to the fullest extent, honest communication was essential.

'Tell me about your day,' she whispered, taking Andrew's hand and drawing him to the bed to sit side by side. Instead Andrew lay back propped against the pillows and patted the space beside him, inviting her to lie snuggled up to him, her head against his chest.

'That's better,' he said before relating a few incidents from his day at school. 'Then I did some minor repairs in a couple of houses that had got a bit shaken in the raids. I really did do repairs,' he added with a touch of humour. Often he had to tell others, including his mother, that this was what he'd done when really he'd been engaged in his other, secret work. 'What about your day?' he asked.

Sally explained about Betty being excited at having gone home to Salford with news of having a boyfriend.

'She's a sweet girl,' said Andrew. 'She deserves to be happy.'

'She certainly thinks she's found happiness with Eddie,' said Sally. 'From what she says, he sounds just as keen.'

Andrew kissed the top of her head. 'Does it remind you of anyone?'

'I can't think what you mean,' she teased, turning her face up to receive his kiss. When she snuggled down again, she told him about Mrs Lockwood.

Andrew was indignant on her behalf, just as she'd known he would be. Lying in his arms washed away the anger and hurt from earlier on.

'You know what's at the bottom of this, don't you?' he asked. 'It means you're doing well at the depot.'

'Do you think so?'

'Definitely. You're making your mark. Mrs Lockwood is kicking herself for not having done all the things you're now busy doing.'

'Thank you,' Sally said. 'Your support means everything to me.'

'My support comes at a price.'

Sally paid him with a kiss. While their faces were still close together, she whispered, 'Don't ever forget that I want to support you too.'

'I know.'

'I think every single day about your secret work. I know what a strain it can be for you. I don't want to push you into talking but I want you to know that I'm always here to listen if you need me. You're so brave to do what you do.'

'Making coffins doesn't take courage.'

'Yes, it does,' Sally insisted. 'It takes huge courage to have to face thoughts of the war dead every day and to know that you're preparing for the imminent deaths of people who are currently leading ordinary lives.'

'In so far as any of us can lead a normal life in wartime,' said Andrew.

'You know what I mean.'

'Yes, I do,' he said. 'I love you, Sally Henshaw. Marrying you was the best thing I ever did.'

'I love you too,' Sally whispered.

CHAPTER FOURTEEN

'Well, you needn't think I'm doing *that!*' Lorna exclaimed. The words had burst out before she had time to consider them, but she couldn't regret what she'd said. She didn't care if she sounded unpatriotic. She was not, absolutely categorically not, going to haul disgusting old tyres out of a filthy pond.

Mrs Henshaw gave her a look. Was she about to lay down the law? Let her try. Lorna managed not to roll her eyes. Honestly, did Mrs Henshaw not understand how inappropriate it was that a person from her walk of life should be in a position of authority over a girl of Lorna West-Sadler's standing? In her head Lorna seemed to hear Daddy saying, 'Good grief!' in his most exasperated voice.

Lorna pulled her shoulders back as she returned Mrs Henshaw's level gaze. She had learned not to argue about the jobs she was given, but she intended to fight to the death over this one. Dragging tyres from a pond? Never!

Before either of them could speak, Miss Hughes said brightly, 'I'm happy to give it a go.'

'I'm not,' said Lorna.

'You better jolly well had be,' Miss Hughes retorted, fire

appearing in her usually soft blue eyes. 'If you don't pull your weight, I'll push you in.'

'There won't be any need for that,' Mrs Henshaw declared. She grinned – yes, positively grinned, much to Lorna's surprise. To Miss Hughes she said, 'You and I will do it. D'you remember what a lark it was when we went round delivering the pig-bins. It'll be like that.'

'Oh, that was great fun,' said Miss Hughes, the fire in her eyes giving way to a lively sparkle.

And that was that. The two of them got ready and set off, giggling like schoolgirls, leaving Lorna to hold the fort. She watched them walk through the gates. She meant to turn away, but instead something drew her forwards to stand in the gateway and watch them walk along Beech Road, pushing the sack-trolley.

Fancy getting excited about dragging a pond. Lorna expected to feel scornful. She expected her lips to twist into a sneer.

Instead what she felt was – envy.

Envy? No. Impossible. But there was no other explanation for the quick heartbeat and the tugging sensation deep inside.

She envied them their camaraderie, the personal trust and friendship that spilled over into the way they worked together. She might work alongside them but she was emotionally separate from them – which was absolutely right and proper, of course. She was from the top drawer and they were from the bottom drawer. She was only here because of the appalling way the newspapers had treated her.

But, goodness, she was lonely. She yearned for friendship, for the warm companionship she saw between the other girls. She longed for what they shared.

Urged by her parents, before now she had dedicated her adult life to seeking a suitable husband.

But what she most wanted now was a friend, a true friend.

. . .

Mrs Henshaw and Miss Hughes returned with a couple of tatty tyres balanced precariously on the sack-trolley. One tyre fell off but, instead of clicking their tongues in vexation, both girls laughed and helped one another lift it back on. Their eyes were bright, their cheeks flushed from their outing in the chilly air.

'This will boost our rubber weights next time you send in the figures,' said Miss Hughes, laughing.

Lorna observed the two of them with a sort of consternation. How could they find pleasure in pulling old tyres from a pond? That wasn't fun. Fun meant the finest silk, a breath of French perfume, expensive cigarettes and sophisticated conversation. It meant elegance on the dance-floor, demure smiles across candlelit tables, an understanding of all the social nuances. It meant knocking back a plate of sandwiches before going out for the evening so as not to be tempted to display anything more than a wisp of an appetite. Fun was about beauty, money, appearances, the most handsome man, the loveliest girl. Fun was *serious*.

And it most emphatically did not involve ponds and tyres. As for Mrs Henshaw and Miss Hughes – well, honestly, how childish.

Lorna busied herself removing paperclips from waste paper. It was a mind-numbingly boring task but at least it felt vaguely ladylike compared to other jobs. When it was time to stop for their tea break, Lorna felt sure the other two would have preferred to have theirs without her, and frankly she wouldn't have minded this herself, but they were all too polite to go down that particular road.

They had their break in the office, where a small fire burned in the afternoons. The real staffroom was up above the office. Betty had told Lorna about it.

'The fireplace up there was boarded up until recently. Mrs

Henshaw got the fireplace reinstated so we could have the room for our breaks, but we haven't got enough coal to set a fire in there.' She smiled. 'So that will be our summer staffroom.'

Summer! Would Lorna still be here next summer? The thought made her shudder. Surely Daddy would come round long before that and send her somewhere more suited to her station in life. She hadn't heard from him personally, but then she hadn't expected to. The same as when she was at boarding school, she addressed her letters to *Dear Daddy and Mummy* and the replies were always written by her mother and signed, by her, *Love from Daddy and Mummy*.

As Lorna and the others drank their tea there was a noise outside, followed by the main door banging open.

'Knock knock,' called a young woman's voice.

Miss Hughes got up. 'That sounds like Stella.' She looked pleased but mystified too. Opening the door, she called, 'In here.'

A tall girl appeared. From beneath a frankly unflattering woolly hat, glorious red hair spilled over her shoulders.

'Sorry to barge in,' she said. 'I've come to share the good news. We've got a new billet.'

'Congrats,' said Miss Hughes. She looked at Mrs Henshaw. 'I told you the munitions girls wanted to move nearer to Trafford Park, didn't I?'

'Yes,' said Mrs Henshaw. She smiled at the newcomer. 'Good place, is it?'

'I don't think we'll get looked after the way we do at Star House, but it's clean and comfy and there's space for all three of us. We didn't want to be split up.'

'Have Lottie and Mary seen it?' asked Miss Hughes.

'They're at work,' said the redhead, 'so I had to make the decision.'

'Couldn't it have waited?' Lorna asked.

The other three looked at her as if she was mad.

'Don't be daft,' said the redhead. 'It would have been snapped up by someone else. Good places always are.' She looked enquiringly at Miss Hughes, who immediately responded.

'This is Miss Sadler. This is Stella Reeves. We're in the same billet – for now, anyroad.'

Miss Reeves thrust out a hand and shook Lorna's.

'When are you leaving?' asked Mrs Henshaw.

'We have to give a week's notice. We're going to ask Mrs Beaumont if we can have a little farewell party at the weekend. We're all free on Saturday night. How about you? Are you fire-watching?'

'No, we're both off that night,' said Miss Hughes.

'Good-o,' said Miss Reeves. 'You'll both come, won't you?'

'Thanks,' said Mrs Henshaw. 'I'd love to.'

Lorna hid her surprise when Miss Reeves turned to her. 'Would you care to come? I know you've never met us, but you'd be welcome.'

Lorna opened her mouth to decline. As if she wanted to attend a harum-scarum impromptu party with strangers! But then she pictured another evening of listening to the wireless at the Lockwoods' house. A Saturday night too. She had been considering volunteering for an extra WVS shift.

She heard herself say, 'Thanks. It's kind of you to ask.'

Every time Lorna thought of the munitions girls' party in the run-up to it, and as she got ready for it, and even as she rang the doorbell and then slid into the unlit hallway of Star House, she had told herself she was only attending so as to give herself something to do. Lying low in a place where she had no chums was a crushing bore.

It was Miss Hughes who let her in. She shut the front door and swished a curtain across it, then switched on the light.

Lorna saw a long hallway with a dark-green runner. A runner of the same colour went up the stairs. Along the walls, including the staircase wall, were framed photographs of stars of the music hall, all of them signed.

'Give me your things,' said Miss Hughes.

She hung up Lorna's coat and scarf on an already overburdened hat-stand and tossed Lorna's hat onto a shelf before leading the way into the sitting room, where an upright piano stood against one wall and there was a tall cabinet with drawers below and glassed-in shelves above. As well as several girls in their twenties, there was a middle-aged woman with blue eyes, her improbably jet-black hair worn scooped away from her face, with fashionable waves down to her shoulders.

Miss Hughes performed the introductions.

'Evening, love,' said Mrs Beaumont. 'It's nice to meet you.'

Love? Lorna had never in her whole life been called 'love'. She didn't know whether to feel amused or outraged.

'Now then, we're all friends here tonight,' said Mrs Beaumont. 'Everyone here knows Stella, Mary and Lottie, so it's first names all round even if you've never met before. What's your name?'

Lorna blinked. 'Lorna.'

'That's a pretty name,' said Miss Hughes. 'I'm Betty – very ordinary.' She pulled a face but smiled at the same time, and a dimple showed in her cheek. 'And Mrs Henshaw is Sally.'

'I know,' said Lorna. 'I've heard you using one another's names.'

All along she had considered that, even if they were friends outside work, it was inappropriate to use such familiarity in the workplace. But it had also made her feel unwanted, and, even if the salvage depot was the last place on earth she wanted to be, she had hated feeling excluded... even though she had told herself that Mrs Henshaw and Miss Hughes were the last people by whom she wished to be accepted.

Introductions followed. As well as Sally and Betty, there were the three munitions girls who currently lived here – redheaded Stella, whom Lorna had already met; sandy-haired Lottie; and sweet-faced, blue-eyed Mary. Some others from the factory had been invited too, a mixture of girls in their twenties and women a little older.

Lorna had come armed with a bottle of port. Daddy had given her two to wrap carefully inside her jumpers when she was getting ready to come here.

'Alcohol will soon be nigh on impossible to get,' he had told her, 'so one of these is a gift for the people who are taking you into their home and you can give them the other bottle at Christmas.'

Christmas! The thought of still being in exile at Christmas had made Lorna feel as if she'd been punched in the stomach. She had counted on being freed from exile in Manchester long before then. But no, as far as Daddy was concerned, she was doomed to stay away until everyone had forgotten the name of Lorna West-Sadler – and Daddy didn't care how long that was going to take.

Coming here tonight, aware that Sally and Betty wouldn't exactly be thrilled by her presence and worried that they might have gossiped about her to Stella, Mary and Lottie, not to mention Mrs Beaumont, Lorna had elected to bring the second bottle of port with her partly out of politeness and partly, she had to admit, as a kind of passport into her fellow partygoers' favour.

'I'm sorry it isn't champagne,' she said. In her world, the real world where she belonged, parties involved champagne. 'But I gather that's impossible to get since France fell.'

There was a moment of astonished silence as all eyes fixed on her. Had she said the wrong thing? Then there was a gale of laughter.

'I think we can make do with port and lemon if there's no

champers, can't we, girls?' said Mrs Beaumont. 'Fetch the glasses, Betty. There won't be enough to go round, so get the best teacups an' all.'

Which was how Lorna found herself sipping port and lemon out of a teacup – a teacup! Her instinct was to sneer secretly but somehow, surrounded by everybody else's good humour and laughter, she found herself relaxing instead. It must be the port.

Mrs Beaumont had an old-fashioned gramophone with a huge horn on the side, and the background music was soon turned up for a hearty singalong to a mixture of old music hall tunes and modern singers like Gracie Fields and the Andrews Sisters.

Mrs Beaumont put on a new record. 'This is your song, Sally,' she said, laughing.

The sound of Gracie Fields singing 'Sally' filled the room. Lorna, who'd had singing lessons – along with lessons in the piano, drawing and ballroom dancing – was the only one who could effortlessly hit the song's highest notes. At the end the others cheered her, which was oddly exhilarating to a well-bred young lady more accustomed to a polite round of quiet applause at the end of a tasteful performance.

Mrs Beaumont stood up. She blew a final stream of smoke into the air, then removed the spent cigarette from its holder and stubbed it out in the ashtray.

'Time for something to eat,' she announced. 'Mary and Lorna, come and lend a hand.'

The kitchen was tiny compared to Mummy's – or rather, compared to Mummy's cook's kitchen. Mummy never set foot in it. When she and Cook conferred about the menu, Cook came to the morning room and stood in Mummy's presence.

Mrs Beaumont took a fly-net off a bowl. 'There are jars of meat-paste that can be spread on crackers. You can do that for

me, Mary. Lorna, you can stir the soup while it warms through.'
She gave Lorna a wooden spoon.

'What kind is it?' Mary asked.

Lorna heard Mrs Beaumont say, 'Oyster' and was impressed.

'Oyster?' she repeated. 'Delicious.'

'Oyster?' It was Mrs Beaumont's turn to repeat it. Then she laughed. 'Chance would be a fine thing. I said, "mock-oyster". In other words, fish-trimmings, artichokes and herbs.'

Mary gave Lorna a nudge. 'But you're right about it being delicious. Mrs B's cooking always is.'

'Mind what you're doing with that spoon, Lorna,' said Mrs Beaumont. 'You'll slop the soup all over the show if you stir it that fast. Anyone would think you'd never stirred soup before.'

'I haven't,' Lorna admitted.

'Right,' Mrs Beaumont said briskly. 'Give me the spoon and I'll show you. Gently, like this. Now you try. That's better. You have to keep it moving to stop it sticking to the pan. I'll get the dishes.'

These proved to be a mixture of soup-plates and pudding bowls, just as the spoons were a hotchpotch of soup-spoons and dessert-spoons. Lorna hoped she'd get a proper soup-plate and spoon and then wondered why it should matter. The atmosphere was chummy and convivial and the need for extra crockery and cutlery stemmed from having invited plenty of friends. Mummy wouldn't have agreed but Lorna rather thought that this mattered far more than the correct china.

After supper – and Mary had been right: it was indeed delicious – Mrs Beaumont lifted the lid on her upright piano and belted out tunes from the shows followed by a medley of Glenn Miller numbers that had everyone on their feet and pushing the furniture out of the way to make room for dancing.

The evening ended with everyone doing the Charleston for simply ages until they had to beg Mrs Beaumont to stop playing.

Lorna dropped onto the sofa to get her breath back. She was flushed and dishevelled and must look a fright. Mummy would have had kittens.

But Lorna knew something that her mother didn't. Fun wasn't meticulously planned and perfectly executed. Fun was... fun.

On Monday at the depot, Lorna was aware of the other two looking at her through fresh eyes, and she felt a moment's resentment. Why should it come as a surprise to them that there was more to her than her dislike of salvage work? Then she shook off the feeling and admitted to herself that, if they'd had a narrow view of her, they'd had good reason.

Sally – or should it be Mrs Henshaw? Lorna expected to return to their previous formality – spoke before she could.

'Betty and I have been talking. We hope you're happy to continue with first names. It makes the depot a pleasanter place.'

Lorna nodded. 'Suits me,' she said, although she wasn't altogether sure it did. This was a place of work and it was meant to be formal. On the other hand, why not? She remembered how isolated she had felt before. She was hungry for friendship.

'Just one thing,' said Sally. 'Using first names doesn't give you an excuse to slack.'

'When have I ever slacked, apart from at the very beginning?'

'Do the words "tyres" and "pond" mean anything to you?' Betty enquired.

'That was different. That was... *disgusting*.' But she remembered how the other two had returned to the depot in high spirits. 'Anyway, I won't take advantage.' She handed Betty a folded sheet of paper. 'Please would you give this to Mrs Beaumont? It's a thank-you for her hospitality.'

Betty smiled with real warmth, her dimple appearing and remaining on show. 'She'll appreciate that. Thanks.'

Lorna got on with her work, feeling better about life in general than she had felt for some time. She missed George and was bitterly sorry that things had gone so badly wrong for them. She wanted to hate him. He ought never to have paid attention to the gossip about her family. All wealthy parents of girls took their daughters to London in the hope of an advantageous marriage. That was what the Season was for. One only had to read romantic novels to know that. So it was preposterous for the gossips to suggest that George had been hunted down by Lorna's family—

'Lorna.' Sally's voice broke into her thoughts. 'I'm sorry for saying you might think that using first names could help you get away with slacking. It was uncalled for and I apologise.'

'Thank you.' Lorna was surprised, but she appreciated the courtesy and wanted to be civil in return, especially now that the atmosphere between her and the other two was so much better. 'It wasn't uncalled for. I can understand what made you say it.'

Sally smiled, her hazel eyes softening as she gave a nod of acceptance. 'I've had a telephone call from the salvage depot in Urmston. They've been hit by a sickness bug. The manager has found cover for tomorrow and Wednesday but she needs another pair of hands this afternoon. I'd like you to go, please. I'll give you directions.'

A peace-offering for the 'uncalled-for' remark? Or a token of faith in Lorna's improved attitude? Whichever it was, Lorna was pleased. Just a few days ago she had felt lonely. Now maybe she would be able to put that urgent, empty feeling behind her.

Soon after midday Mr Atkinson appeared, his hazel eyes earnest behind the lenses of his glasses.

'Good afternoon, ladies.' He raised his trilby politely. 'I'm s-sorry to turn up unannounced but I've had two more d-deliveries of donated books and I'm in d-danger of vanishing beneath them.' To Sally he said, 'I'm hoping to prevail upon your good nature yet again by asking if I might have some assistance this afternoon.'

'Of course,' said Sally.

Betty smiled broadly.

'Perhaps Miss S-Sadler would like to help,' Mr Atkinson suggested.

'I'd be happy to,' said Lorna, 'but I'm already down to do something else.'

Betty stepped forward. 'I'll do it.' Belatedly, she looked at Sally for permission.

Sally nodded. 'It'll leave me on my own here but we're up to date, so I can manage.'

When Mr Atkinson had gone, Betty said to Lorna, 'I wonder why he asked you. No offence, but I'm his regular helper.'

Lorna shrugged. 'Sally took me to the bookshop when I started here and I expressed an interest. Maybe that's why. You don't mind that he asked me, do you?'

'Mind?' Betty laughed. 'Why on earth would I mind?'

But she did mind. Silly as it sounded, she did mind.

CHAPTER FIFTEEN

'It's good of Mrs Henshaw to let you s-spend the afternoon here at s-such short notice,' said Samuel. 'Well, no notice at all, really. And with it leaving her on her own at the depot too.'

'She's keen for the depot to support the war effort in every way it can,' said Betty.

They were in the shop's back room once again, sorting through stacks of books. Betty had been looking forward to one of their companionable sessions, but Samuel seemed rather quiet. Not that he was ever the life and soul, but she couldn't help thinking that he seemed a little – well – distant. Distant towards her or distant in general? She couldn't tell. Maybe he had a lot on his mind. It must feel as if he was never going to come to the end of these donated books; and, as an ARP warden, he carried a lot of responsibility.

Hoping to draw him out, Betty chatted.

'It's December already. Who'd have thought? It was Stir-Up Sunday yesterday. Does your family do Stir-Up Sunday?'

She smiled at the memory of Mum making the Christmas pudding on the first Sunday of the month and getting Dad and Betty to stir in the ingredients.

'Yes,' said Samuel. 'W-we used to go to my gran's house f-for it when I was a boy.'

'Mrs Beaumont, my landlady, used a new wartime recipe because of all the shortages. Her pudding includes carrot, potato, prunes and stale cake crumbs. My mum used to put in nutmeg, cinnamon, dried fruit and the grated zest of an orange and a lemon. The whole house would smell fruity and spicy.'

'It sounds d-delicious.'

'Oh, it was,' Betty enthused. 'She was a very good cook.'

The shop door opened and Samuel went to serve his customer. They had a long conversation – about books, presumably. There certainly didn't seem to be any distance or reserve on Samuel's part. A couple more people entered the shop and he was busy for some time. But even though he had talked at length with his customers, he retreated into his shell when he returned to the back room.

Betty pressed her lips together. Should she ask? If she didn't, she might afterwards wish that she had.

'Have I done something wrong, Mr Atkinson? Have I upset you?'

For the first time that afternoon he looked straight at her, with a gentle smile. 'Of c-course not. I'm s-sorry if I gave that impression. Why don't you f-finish for today?'

'There's another hour to go,' said Betty.

'W-we've come to the end of the first lot of books, s-so it's a good stopping point. Thank you f-for your help. I appreciate it.'

He was already opening the cupboard door. Betty had no alternative but to fetch her things.

Betty was surprised and confused by the way Samuel had sent her away from the shop. Her only consolation was that he had sounded sincere when he'd said she hadn't done anything wrong. And it was true that it had been a good point to stop, so maybe she was reading too much into it.

Anyroad, she was seeing Eddie this evening, and thoughts of him swept aside everything else. More than anything, she wanted him to meet Dad and Grace. Previously she had always bobbed along through life, taking everything as it came, but now she had a future of her own to look forward to and she couldn't wait.

She didn't want to wish the time away but oh, how she longed for springtime. She wanted Eddie to take her for walks on the meadows. She imagined holding a buttercup under his chin to see if he liked butter and then teasing him about rationing. Mainly, though, she wanted him to see her in light-weight dresses, blouses and skirts instead of wrapped up in her winter woollies. She wanted to be at her prettiest for him. He was so attractive that she was sure he could have any girl he wanted. Every time they were together, she felt thrilled and grateful that he had chosen her.

As they walked to the cinema, her gloved hand held protectively inside the crook of his arm, she told him about spending the afternoon helping Mr Atkinson at his bookshop.

'I'm not sure I like the sound of that,' said Eddie.

'Why not? It's in a good cause.'

'I don't mean that,' said Eddie. 'I mean you going to this bloke's shop. Helping with sorting out a few books, my eye! It seems to me he wants to be alone with you.'

Eddie was jealous! Betty was delighted because it showed how much he cared. But she was also keen to reassure him he had nothing to be scared of.

'It's not like that. It's just that there are a lot of donated books to send out.'

'I'm not happy about this,' said Eddie.

'Honestly, there's nothing to be concerned about. I don't give a fig for him.'

'I should hope not,' said Eddie. 'You're my girl.'

My girl. Eddie's girl. Betty struggled to contain her smiles.

Eddie stopped walking, straightening his arm so that her hand fell away as he turned to face her.

'You know how much you mean to me, don't you, Betty?'

'Yes,' she whispered. Was this the moment when he told her he loved her?

'I've never felt about any girl the way I feel about you. I can't bear the thought of that other bloke wanting to get his hands on you.'

Betty's lips parted in shock. 'He wouldn't. He's a gentleman.'

'I want to be a gentleman an' all, Betty,' Eddie said huskily, 'but it's all I can do to keep my hands off you.'

Betty filled with emotion. Her throat closed over and she couldn't speak.

'If you knew how much I cared... but I can't show you because I respect you too much,' Eddie continued. 'I know you're a decent girl. I know you don't put it about. Sorry. That was a coarse thing to say. You do care about me, don't you, Betty?'

'I love you.' Damn and blast. She hadn't meant to say that but it had slipped out. Everyone knew the man was supposed to say it first. At the same time, she felt elated at having finally expressed what was in her heart.

'My darling,' Eddie murmured.

He bent his head to hers. He didn't touch her with his hands, didn't draw her to him. He just let his mouth play across hers, his lips nudging hers apart, the tip of his tongue darting into her mouth and making the flesh tingle all over her body. He kissed her gently, lingeringly. The kiss deepened and still he didn't hold her. Betty couldn't wait any longer. Her arms snaked round his neck and she clung to him.

At last Eddie's hands moved, but not to her waist or round

her back to draw her to him. Instead he cupped her face, his kisses becoming more intense.

Finally Eddie ended the kiss, his breathing deep, his chest rising and falling. Betty was dazed. Her lips felt swollen.

'My girl,' Eddie whispered.

They went to the pictures. Betty barely paid any attention. Normally there was nothing she enjoyed more than watching a glamorous Hollywood couple falling in love on the silver screen, but tonight her own real-life romance was far more enthralling.

Originally Betty hadn't been due to go out with Eddie on Tuesday evening but, after they'd been to the pictures on Monday, he had made her promise to see him again the next evening. Betty could have wept for joy. Her helping sort through a heap of books with Samuel had certainly had a thoroughly desirable effect on Eddie. She loved the way his jealousy had brought his feelings to the fore.

On Tuesday evening, she dressed with her usual care, eager to see what plans Eddie had for their extra evening together.

Looking uncertain, Eddie said, 'I want to take you somewhere special... only I'm not sure you'll want to come.'

His hesitation was so sweet she could have eaten him for breakfast. The way he always wanted to please her was everything a girl could possibly wish for.

'I'm sure it will be perfect if you've chosen it,' she said trustingly.

'Come on then.' Suddenly Eddie was smiling. He caught her hand and pulled her along. 'We'll catch the bus.'

'Where to?' asked Betty.

'You'll see.'

On the bus Eddie sat close to her. Betty entwined her fingers with his, enjoying the mystery of where they were going. When the clippie came along with her ticket machine at the ready, Eddie asked for two to Fallowfield. Betty smiled to herself. She might now know where they were going, but at the same time she didn't really know, because the local geography of the south of Manchester didn't mean much to her.

When they got off, Eddie took her down a couple of streets. It had a familiar feel to Betty because she came from somewhere like this, with a shop on nearly every corner. She stopped to look at the display in a grocer's window, impressed by the large quantity of jars and cartons, everything from jelly crystals and Mazawattee Tea to Weetabix and porridge oats, from Wright's Coal Tar Soap and Bluebell Metal Polish to Duraglit and Rinso.

When she admired the display, Eddie laughed. 'Don't believe everything you see, Betty. All those cartons and whatnot will be empty. They're just there to tempt you to go inside – where you'll find hardly anything on the shelves.'

They carried on along the road and stopped outside one of the terraced houses. He let go of her hand and stepped away from her. Puzzled, Betty automatically took a step after him.

'No,' he said gently. 'I don't want you to feel you're being pushed into something you're not ready for. This has to be your choice and I won't say a word to stop you if you say no. I'll just take you straight back to Star House.'

'Is this where you live?' Betty asked.

He nodded. 'I'd love to show you my home, but I'd understand if you think it's not appropriate.'

Why on earth would it be inappropriate? Betty couldn't think of anything that would make her happier.

'I'd like to see inside,' she said softly.

Eddie unlocked the door onto the dark hallway but, before Betty could step inside, he scooped her up in his arms.

'Got to carry you over the threshold, haven't I?'

And he walked inside with her in his arms as if she was his bride. It was the most romantic thing that had ever happened.

Even more thrilling, instead of setting her on her feet, he kept holding her as he lowered his mouth to cover hers in a deep kiss that sent her senses reeling.

When he finally put her down, she stumbled. Eddie caught her by her waist and pushed her against the wall to kiss her again. Grabbing hold of her good sense, Betty pushed him away and wriggled free.

'Sorry,' Eddie whispered.

He took her into the parlour and switched on the light. Betty formed a swift impression of a clock on the mantelpiece above a tiled fire-surround, a single armchair and a sofa that didn't match, a worn square of carpet, and tobacco-stained patches on the ceiling above the seats.

Betty frowned and bit the inside of her cheek as a feeling of uncertainty washed through her. 'Where's your mum?' Eddie hadn't brought her to an empty house, had he? Of course not.

'I don't live with my mum,' Eddie told her. 'She died when I was a nipper. I live with my nan.'

'Oh, Eddie, I'm so sorry. I didn't know.'

'I don't talk about it. My nan's out at the WVS tonight – but she knows you're here,' he added. 'She was meant to be here too but she had to stand in for somebody who's poorly.'

'That's a shame,' said Betty. 'I'd love to meet her. When I do,' she couldn't stop herself adding, 'does that mean you'll be ready to meet my father?'

Eddie placed his hands on her shoulders. 'No, love. I told you. I have to prove myself to him by being your chap for a decent amount of time. How else is he to take me seriously? You deserve the very best, Betty Hughes, and I intend to give it to you, just like your dad wants for his little girl.'

Betty felt torn. She wanted Eddie to meet Dad, but, on the other hand, she could see things from Eddie's point of view. She made a show of looking in the mirror, touching her hat as if it needed straightening and patting the hair that lay on her shoulders.

Eddie looked at her through the reflection. 'Do you want to see the rest of the house?'

Betty was more than happy to see where Eddie lived. It would add substance to her daydreams. She thought of Sally living with Andrew's mother and imagined herself living here with Eddie's nan. Behind the parlour was a kitchen with a table and chairs, a fireplace and a couple of doors, one to the scullery and the other presumably to the cellar. Eddie let her glance in but that was all. Well, he was a man, after all. He had no interest in mundane things like kitchens.

Back in the hallway, they stood at the foot of the stairs. Eddie's fingers tangled with hers.

'Do you want to see upstairs? It's all right to say yes, Betty. It's safe and it's proper – because we're engaged.'

Betty's heart all but jumped out of her chest. 'Are we?'

Eddie nodded soberly. 'I can't ask you properly yet. I can't go down on one knee and give you a ring. I need to ask your father's permission first. That's the right thing to do because I respect you and I respect him – but I can't ask you until we've been together for long enough.' He dropped a kiss on her mouth. 'As far as I'm concerned, we're engaged.' Another kiss. 'What d'you think, Betty? Please say yes.' Another kiss. 'Please say yes.'

'Yes,' she breathed.

Eddie groaned and swept her into his arms, crushing her to him as his mouth captured hers once again. When the kiss ended, he laughed.

'We're unofficially engaged. That means you can come upstairs in my house – if you want to. I wouldn't expect you to enter my room. That really wouldn't be respectable. But would you like to see my nan's room – the room where I was born, the bed where I was born?'

'Really?' Betty was enchanted.

'Really,' said Eddie.

'Well – I suppose...'

'Good girl.'

Eddie took her hand and the next thing Betty knew she was on the landing. Eddie switched on the light and opened a door, displaying a room with a double bed with a brass frame and a faded patchwork quilt. A basketwork chair that had seen better days stood in one corner and a china jug stood inside a matching bowl on top of a small cupboard in the opposite corner.

Standing behind Betty, Eddie cupped her shoulders in his hands, pulling her gently so she leaned against him.

'Shall we seal our engagement here, now, in this bed? There's nothing wrong with that, Betty, because we're a proper couple and I can't wait for it to be official. You're so beautiful.' He nibbled her earlobe. 'I can't believe how lucky I am. The most gorgeous girl in the world is my girlfriend and we're unofficially engaged.'

'Eddie...' She wanted to turn to face him but he kept her turned away.

'It's all right, love. I shan't push you into anything. But if we... If you let me... Well, it wouldn't be unofficial any more, would it? I mean, we still wouldn't be able to tell anybody because we'd still have to wait until I can ask your dad, but we'd know. You and me, we'd know. We'd know we'd made it official. It'd be our secret.'

Now he did turn her round to face him, kissing her before she could speak, before she could give voice to her doubts.

Eddie whispered in her ear. 'You can't fall for a baby the first time, Betty. Everyone knows that.'

'Eddie, we shouldn't...'

'I know that, my darling, I really do, but you're so lovely. How am I supposed to wait?' He looked deep into her eyes. 'How are *we* supposed to wait? You want to seal our engagement, don't you? Please tell me you love me as much as I love you.'

Betty pressed her lips together. 'No,' she whispered.

'Yes,' was his answering whisper.

Betty spoke more firmly. 'No.'

'But we're engaged.'

'Even so, it's not right. We shouldn't, not before we're married.'

'You aren't still thinking the old-fashioned way, are you?' Eddie asked, his eyes dark and intense. 'It's wartime, Betty. We have to make the most of every moment.'

'I know there are girls who are going all the way, who would never have dreamed of doing that before the war,' said Betty, 'but – but I'm not one of them.'

Eddie leaned forward and nibbled her ear. 'Are you sure about that?'

'Yes, I'm sure.' She wished she hadn't come upstairs. Had she led him on? She hadn't meant to. 'I'm sorry,' she whispered, her voice cracking.

'Why are you sorry?' he asked softly.

'I don't want to let you down – but I can't do what you want. You know I can't.'

Eddie laughed softly. 'It's all right, Betty.'

She looked up at him. How had she got herself into this pickle? From somewhere came the thought that her friend Samuel would never put a girl in this position.

'But you don't blame me for trying, do you?' Eddie asked.

'What?'

'You're so lovely. How was I supposed to resist? You won't hold it against me that I tried?'

'No, I won't,' said Betty.

Eddie clicked off the landing light and headed downstairs. Betty followed, glad to reach the hallway.

'I think we should leave now,' she said.

'Fair enough.' Eddie caught her hands and looked into her eyes. 'You don't blame me, do you?'

'Of course not,' she replied.

But in her heart she knew it wasn't entirely true and that she was saying it because it was what he wanted to hear. Deep down in the furthest corner of her heart, Betty knew he shouldn't have tried to persuade her.

CHAPTER SIXTEEN

Last weekend Lorna had worked her first Saturday at the depot. Strictly speaking, it ought to have been Betty's day, but she and Sally had previously done a swap and now Sally was paying it back. She had suggested that Lorna do the day with her.

'When I did my first Saturday, and when Betty did hers, we each did them on our own. This would give you the chance to see what Saturdays are like but without being alone.'

'Are Saturdays different?' Lorna had asked, not seeing how they could be.

'The work is the same,' Sally had explained, 'but we can get quite a few people dropping in. They've been at work or at school from Monday to Friday and Saturday is their chance to come here. And of course there are still the daily sacks to see to: the same number of sacks but no one to help you with the sorting.'

Lorna hadn't really wanted to work the extra day with Sally, but the memory of the carpeting she'd received in her first week prompted her to do it. She didn't want to be accused of a lack of patriotism again. She might not enjoy her war work but it was her duty to make the best of it.

At the end of Saturday's work, when they were busy closing up, Lorna had thanked Sally for the experience because she realised that Sally had intended to help her.

'You're welcome,' Sally replied with a smile that brought a glow to her tawny eyes. 'It's Betty next Saturday and you the Saturday after.'

Lorna had no qualms about being on her own at the depot. She wasn't her father's daughter for nothing, even though she wasn't bombastic like he was.

Now it was midweek and the collection vans were due at the depot that afternoon. The girls had to ensure that everything was ready. It was doubly important on a day like today, when persistent drizzle meant nobody wanted to be out in the open more than they had to.

When the collections were going on, it all got a bit confused at one point because two vans arrived at the same time, one of them an hour early, and then two extra vans turned up that they weren't expecting at all, so there was a scramble to get the additional salvage ready for the off. In the middle of it all, Mrs Lockwood appeared and stood, oblivious to the grey mist of drizzle, in the centre of the upheaval, her gaze flashing this way and that, missing nothing.

She addressed one of the collection men. 'You're here for the rubber, aren't you? You'll find it over there – and there's more over in that corner, though why it isn't all in one place I can't imagine.'

Her voice boomed out over the sound of voices and footsteps, squeaky trolley-wheels and a hunk of metal being dragged across the yard. Then all at once four engines started up and the vans set off for their next calls. The depot was suddenly quiet.

Mrs Lockwood turned to Sally. 'I wasn't intending to come here today but it's a jolly good thing I did. You made a proper pig's ear of that, Mrs Henshaw. Perhaps I ought to make a point of being here for every single collection.'

Lorna frowned. Sally had had everything in hand. Lorna had trusted Mrs Lockwood's judgement before this, but was the WVS woman being unfair?

'Good riddance,' Betty murmured as Mrs Lockwood strode from the depot onto Beech Road.

Sally looked annoyed, but was too professional to respond to Betty's comment. All she said was, 'Let's get the yard tidied up.'

Another van turned in through the gates and stopped.

'Not another one,' Betty joked. Then she saw who was sitting beside the driver. 'It's—' She caught herself up before she could use his first name. 'It's Mr Atkinson.'

Samuel opened the door and got out, as did the driver.

'This is my f-friend, Tom W-Watson of Perkins and Watson, the builders.'

Tom Watson was older than Samuel, maybe in his early fifties. Old enough to have fought in the last war, anyroad. His eyes were blue, his expression earnest. As he tipped his cloth cap to the girls, Betty saw his hair was silver.

'What brings you here?' Sally asked pleasantly.

'Among the d-donated books I've received,' said Samuel, 'there are some that aren't in good enough c-condition. They ought to go for s-salvage. I've been saving them up.'

'Let's get them unloaded,' said Sally.

With five pairs of hands, the job was soon done. Then Sally and Mr Watson got chatting about how busy his building firm was, thanks to Herr Hitler. Outside school hours, Sally's Andrew worked for the Corporation, doing minor repairs, so it was natural for Sally to be interested. Betty took the opportunity to have a word with Samuel.

'It's a good thing you didn't arrive fifteen minutes earlier.'

She described how the four vans had all turned up at once, making it sound amusing.

'I c-can imagine Mrs Henshaw thriving in a s-situation like that. She's always struck me as being a good organiser.'

'Yes, she is.'

Betty was pleased to hear her friend being praised, and she wished Mrs Lockwood could have heard it too. She was glad that Samuel recognised Sally's good qualities. It was his honest opinion too. She knew that. He wasn't the sort to say something just for the sake of it. You could trust his word.

That made her remember telling Eddie she didn't blame him for coming on strong with her. She wished he hadn't got fresh with her; but then, she had gone upstairs with him, so maybe the whole episode had been her fault. Had she led him on? Shame burned her cheeks and her breathing hitched. What would Mum have said?

She was seeing Eddie again tonight. That would make three nights in a row. Three! She was thrilled at the thought but at the same time she felt worried and unsettled after what had happened yesterday, more so after being with Samuel. He was always a gentleman and she knew she was right to trust him.

In the event, however, Eddie maintained a respectful distance, ducking his head diffidently.

'I'm sorry about... well, you know what. You're a good girl and I got carried away.' His gaze met hers at last. 'I love you so much that I couldn't help myself. The excitement of getting engaged, of knowing you're going to be my wife, swept me along. I've thought of nowt but you all day.'

'Likewise,' said Betty.

'You've thought about you an' all?' he teased. He lowered his head to murmur throatily in her ear. 'Do you realise what you've done to me, Miss Betty Hughes? You've driven me wild, that's what you've done, driven me wild. It made me forget to behave like a gentleman.'

Eddie enfolded her in his arms and kissed her. As the kiss ended, Eddie rested his face beside hers, his breath warm against her skin.

'You're gorgeous, Betty. I'm the luckiest man in the world. You've taken my mind off my troubles.'

Betty tried to angle her face so she could see his, but he was holding her too close.

'Troubles?' she asked.

'Aye.' With a sigh, he released her. 'Well, not so much my troubles as my mate's. But I'm loyal, see, so his troubles are my troubles. That's the way I see it, even more so now that we're at war.'

'I can understand that,' said Betty. After the way he had tried it on with her, she wanted to be able to feel close to him again. Close – and safe. You couldn't be close to someone if you didn't feel safe with them.

'I knew you would,' said Eddie. 'You've got a big heart. You're always thinking of others. I'm going to be proud to have you on my arm as my wife.'

'What problem has your friend got?' Betty asked. 'If you don't mind saying.'

'I don't mind, not to you. I'd never keep summat from you. It's very simple, actually. His mum got bombed out.'

'I'm sorry to hear that.'

'It's a common problem these days,' said Eddie. 'She was one of the lucky ones. Plenty of folk, as well as losing their home, lose every blessed thing they ever possessed, but she didn't. Quite a bit of her stuff remained intact. She's gone to live with her friend, but what's to become of all her stuff, eh? That's the real problem. Places that hire out storage space are already full to the brim and, to be honest, she's not got the money to pay for storage, anyroad.'

Betty murmured sympathetically.

A bright note entered Eddie's tone. 'I've just had an idea.'

'What?' Betty asked.

'No, I couldn't ask it of you.'

'Ask what of me?'

'Well, since you ask,' said Eddie, 'you've got that socking great depot building, haven't you? And I know it isn't anywhere near full because you told me so that time we took shelter in the cellar. I just wondered if – well, if you'd let me park some stuff in there, just temporary like. You know, to help out my mate's mum.'

'I don't know,' Betty answered uncertainly. 'I'd have to ask.'

'No, don't do that,' Eddie said at once. 'Your friend Sally sounds like a stickler for the rules and you've told me about that other lady who watches over her just waiting for her to make a mistake. I'd understand if you're not keen to help. It's a lot to ask. It's just that my mate's mum is beside herself with worry.'

'I do want to help,' said Betty, 'but I don't want to go behind Sally's back.'

'But you have to. You can't ask her to bend the rules. That wouldn't be fair on her. Just imagine if the old battleaxe found out.'

Betty couldn't help smiling. Mrs Lockwood was a battleaxe all right. She was starting to feel more at ease with the idea. 'It would be temporary?'

'I promise.'

'I suppose we could manage it.'

Eddie pulled her close and kissed her. 'I knew you'd do it. I knew you wouldn't let me down. You're the best girl ever. I'll bring the things round tomorrow evening in between the depot shutting for the day and the fire-watchers arriving. Half-seven? Eight? You can be there then, can't you? And you can sort out a suitable room for me during the day. It has to have a lock.'

Betty was taken aback by how quickly the plan had unfolded. 'I'm not sure about this.'

'And you know why, don't you? It's because you're a decent

person. You don't like breaking the rules or going behind Sally's back. I respect that. Oh, you're going to fetch our children up to have such high standards. I don't deserve you.'

'Yes, you do,' said Betty.

'So you'll do this little favour for me?' Eddie asked. 'To help out a lady who's in a fix.' He kissed her. 'You're a good girl, Betty.'

Lorna was surprised and delighted to receive an invitation from her old friend Melissa to attend her birthday party up in Lancaster. *My last fling before I join the Wrens,* Melissa had scrawled across the bottom. The party was to take place on Saturday but the invitation didn't arrive until Friday. It was waiting for Lorna when she arrived back at the Lockwoods' house after work. It had originally been sent to her parents' house, from where it had been sent on. Lorna frowned at the handwriting that had redirected the envelope to the Lockwoods' address. It wasn't Mummy's or Daddy's. It must be the house-keeper's.

Railway journeys were notoriously long these days, what with passenger trains having to give way to trains full of troops or loaded with munitions to be sent abroad or supplies of food or coal being delivered to the four corners of the kingdom, so Lorna rose early on Saturday morning, creeping about so as not to disturb the Lockwoods. Mind you, the loud snores emanating from their bedroom suggested that one of them was too deeply asleep to notice; and if the other could slumber on in spite of that racket, then Lorna's tippy-toeing about wouldn't make any odds.

She felt a buzz of excitement as she went on her way. She had booked a taxi to take her to Victoria station. On her way there she just had time to send a telegram to Mummy to say she was coming home. There wasn't time to send one to Melissa –

not if she wanted a seat on the train. But Melissa would be, if
not exactly expecting her tonight, then at least very much
hoping she would be able to come.

Even though she caught an early train it was already almost
full, and she was lucky to get a seat. Her heart felt light. She
couldn't wait to go to the party tonight. She might have enjoyed
the munitions girls' leaving bash at Mrs Beaumont's, but really
and truly wasn't that because she'd been starved of her proper
social life? This party tonight was going to be the real thing.

Ah, the real thing. Silk and satin, the best cigarettes,
cultured conversation beneath twinkling chandeliers, a dance-
band. Of course, it was important to support the war effort too
and there would undoubtedly be quizzes and a beat-the-clock
crossword to raise funds for the Red Cross.

Sitting beside the carriage window, Lorna gazed out, but
what she was seeing was her array of evening gowns. She
mentally sorted through them, lingering over each one as she
wondered what to wear. The dusty-pink silk with the sunray-
pleated skirt or the crêpe de Chine with the wide shoulder-
straps and the three-tiered skirt? The ivory taffeta with puff-
sleeves, its floor-length skirt prettily covered by an overskirt of
spotted net, or the turquoise-and-cream satin with the pearl-
edged neckline and the saucy little train at the back? George
had told her that the turquoise made her green eyes look like the
colour of the Mediterranean.

The train pulled into Lancaster station and Lorna alighted,
closing her eyes for a moment as she breathed in the air of
home. Mummy had brought the motor to meet her. Daddy
didn't believe in women driving but, when Mummy had signed
up to join the WVS and they had found out that her husband
possessed a motor, she had been ordered to learn to drive so she
could ferry people with minor injuries to hospital.

As they drove home, Mummy said, 'This is an unexpected
pleasure, darling.'

'Melissa invited me to her birthday party. It's all very last-minute.'

'How did she get in touch with you?' Mummy asked.

'She didn't,' said Lorna. 'The invitation was sent home and was posted on.'

'Not by me – and your father wouldn't have.'

Lorna felt a flash of resentment. Honestly, it was as if her parents were ashamed of her. 'Anyway, I'm here now and that's what matters.'

'I hate to think of you having to live in Manchester, with all the bombings.'

'As you can see, I'm safe and sound,' said Lorna. 'Are you doing much driving for the WVS?'

'The idea was for me to take people to hospital during air raids, but we still haven't had any, thank goodness. I drive for the pie scheme most days. Pies and pasties are baked here in town and delivered to land girls and farm workers to ensure they get good meals. I was glad when you wrote to say you'd joined the WVS.'

Lorna grinned. 'I wasn't given a choice. Mrs Lockwood is a leading light. I think I'd have had to look for a new billet if I'd tried to say no. Recently I've been working with the Central Hospital Supply Service part of the WVS. We cut and label bandages, swabs, gauze and operating gowns. Then there are the pillowcases, bedjackets, nightdresses, instrument bags and covers for hot-water bottles. It's all done on a conveyor-belt basis. Each person does the same thing over and over again and passes on to the next person. We've been given new anaesthetic masks to do that are more economical than the old pattern; and we make and mend blankets.'

'Don't tell me you're actually sewing,' Mummy said, openly amused.

'Measuring and folding.'

'At least working with the WVS is something to be proud

of,' said Mummy. 'Not like that frightful salvage work Daddy found for you. I keep asking him to find you something else, but he simply refuses. He says it's a good hiding place.'

Lorna pressed her lips together. She had considered pleading with Daddy this weekend, but evidently there was no point.

'When you go to Melissa's party tonight,' said Mummy, 'make sure you have your story ready. Don't say anything about Manchester and above all else don't say a word about salvage. Sorting rags and collecting chicken bones – I never heard the like. When I read that letter about you dredging a pond for old tyres, I positively shrieked in horror.'

'I didn't do that,' said Lorna. 'The others did.'

Mummy wasn't listening. 'You must never tell anyone about that. So *infra dig.*'

Lorna firmly set aside all thoughts of salvage work as they arrived home. It was such a pleasure to be back; a relief too as she breathed in the scent of the wood-panelling and feasted her eyes on the gleam of rosewood and brass. When she went upstairs and threw open her wardrobe doors, she felt like climbing inside, opening her arms as wide as she could and hugging all her gorgeous clothes to her. Nostalgia and longing overwhelmed her. She couldn't wait to dress up in her finery.

This was her life as it was meant to be.

CHAPTER SEVENTEEN

On Saturday evening shortly before seven o'clock Betty stood in the hallway, wrapping herself up against the cold. In the front room *Can I Help You?*, which tonight was hosting a discussion about the training and employment of women in munitions factories, was coming to an end on the wireless and would shortly be followed by *In Town Tonight,* which was one of Mrs Beaumont's favourite programmes. The landlady and her friend from up the road were having a cosy evening together, knitting comforts for the troops. As she slipped out of the house, Betty told herself that she too was providing comfort, though of a different sort. She was giving some unfortunate bombed-out folk peace of mind by giving Eddie access to one of the rooms in the depot.

To her astonishment, he had turned up on Thursday evening in a van. A van! She hadn't really thought about it but she had sort of imagined him bringing a couple of boxes and maybe a sack of linen. An amount he could carry in his arms, anyroad.

Instead of letting him sneak in through the door in the fence as she had intended, she'd had to open the gates so he could drive the van inside the yard. She couldn't get the gates closed behind him fast enough.

'Don't look so scared,' he had said to her. 'You're doing my mate's mum a big favour.'

Betty had pulled herself together. 'I just didn't expect there to be so much stuff that you'd have to use a van.'

'That's why I need a good amount of storage space,' Eddie explained.

'Is the van yours?' Betty asked.

He hesitated. 'I nearly said yes because I want nothing more than to impress you, but it's more important to tell the truth, so no, it isn't.'

'I'm impressed that you know how to drive,' said Betty.

'I've borrowed the van from the mate whose mum we're helping, as a matter of fact.'

So saying, Eddie opened the back of the vehicle. His friend's mum had some nice things. Some of the boxes were closed but others had no lids, and Betty noticed a silver teapot and milk jug that looked old, some pretty ornaments and a black marble clock. Catching her looking, Eddie opened a polished wooden box containing a full set of bone-handled cutlery for her to admire.

'She was lucky that so many of her belongings were saved,' said Betty.

'They'll be safe here in the depot,' said Eddie.

'How long for?' Betty had asked him. She hated to ask but she needed to know.

'Just until she can find herself a new place.'

Betty suppressed a flutter of panic. 'That could take ages, with all the bombings and the damage. Folk who move in with family or friends on a temporary basis don't get priority because they've already got a roof over their heads.'

Eddie frowned. 'You don't sound all that keen to help.'

'Oh, I am,' Betty had been quick to assure him. 'It's a bit of a worry, that's all.'

'What is?'

'Taking advantage of the depot.'

Eddie had immediately taken her into his arms. 'My darling Betty,' he whispered. 'This is exactly why I respect you so much – because you're a decent person who follows the rules. That means that when you bend the rules, you do it because you're following your heart.' He kissed her. 'If asking you to provide a room in the depot is too much, don't give it another thought. I don't want you to be unhappy. Just say the word and I'll take everything away again and you can forget you ever saw it.'

'There's no need for that,' Betty had said at once. 'I never meant you to do that. In fact, the room I've chosen has plenty of space for more than you've got in the van, if you need it.'

Which was how Betty now came to be on her way to the depot on a bitterly cold Saturday evening. When the words about the room's space had slipped from her lips on Thursday, she'd wanted to show Eddie she truly wanted to help, but even so she hadn't really thought he would take her up on the offer of filling up the space. But he had told her about other people he knew who were desperate to find safe storage for the precious belongings.

'It's a kind of war work,' he had told her. 'We all have to help one another when we can.'

This time Betty had the gates standing open ready so he could drive straight into the yard. When Eddie jumped out of the vehicle, so did another man. They swung the gates shut and shot the bolts home.

'Who's that?' Betty snatched Eddie's arm. She kept her voice quiet but she felt alarmed.

'This is my mate Leon,' Eddie said nonchalantly.

'What's he doing here?'

'What d'you think?' Eddie replied. 'Lending a hand. It was

his mum you helped by letting me use that room. Leon! Come and meet my girl, Miss Betty Hughes. You owe her a big thank-you. Betty, this is Leon Hargreaves. We were at school together.'

Leon was muscular and thickset, with the kind of figure that would turn to flab one day if he didn't watch out.

He touched the brim of his cloth cap. 'How do. Eddie's told me what a cracker you are. Thanks for helping my mum,' he added with a grin.

Betty smiled politely, willing to like Leon for Eddie's sake, though she wished Eddie hadn't brought him here this evening. It made Eddie's use of the room feel worse somehow.

Eddie opened the back of the van and Betty stared at the quantity of goods. She dragged him to one side.

'What's the matter?' he asked.

'Everything. You bringing your friend here – and then a whole vanload of goodness only knows what.'

'You said it was all right,' Eddie pointed out.

'I know I did, but it doesn't feel all right this time.' Betty struggled to explain herself. 'When it was just Leon's mum, it felt fine. But all this... It feels more serious. It feels like taking a liberty with the depot.'

Eddie gave her a lopsided grin that raised one side of his Clark Gable moustache. 'Don't go getting cold feet on me now, Betty love. I'm relying on you. Leon's mum is relying on you. All these folk,' and he waved an arm to indicate the van's contents, 'are relying on you. It's a fine thing you're doing.'

Betty steadied herself. Eddie was right. She had agreed to this and heaps of people needed her help. She mustn't lose her nerve. She nodded. She wanted Eddie to kiss her and make her feel better, but not with Leon watching.

They all mucked in and emptied the van. Many of the boxes had lids but in those that didn't Betty spied leather goods, a writing case, a dram flask, some pictures, various items of stoneware, a pair of decanters, and some clocks.

'There's a whole box of candlesticks,' she remarked, her gaze roving over a variety made from brass and cut-glass.

'They belong to someone's old auntie,' said Eddie. 'She collects them.'

'How many people are you helping?' Betty asked.

'How many are *we* helping?' he corrected her. 'What makes you ask?'

'Well... all these mantelpiece clocks. Six of them.'

'Then we must be helping six families, mustn't we?' said Eddie.

Betty nodded. That must be why she could see three coal-scuttles and four toast-racks. She was glad to help but a bit scared too. All these people were counting on her to keep the secret from Sally.

Betty locked up the building and Leon drove the van out of the yard, leaving her and Eddie to shut and bolt the gates. Betty covered her mouth with one hand as relief coursed through her, but she quickly dropped it before Eddie could see. She went to open the door in the fence but Eddie reached over her shoulder and held it shut.

'You haven't let me thank you yet.'

Turning her to him, he kissed her, and any reservations Betty still had melted away.

Lorna had had a simply wonderful time trying on dress after dress. She never used to do this. She usually knew exactly what she wanted to wear and on it went. This evening, though, she had behaved like a little girl with a dressing-up box.

At last she had chosen the dusty-pink dress with the sunray-pleated skirt. Its soft hue made her hair seem even darker. She scooped it away from her face and held it back with enamelled combs. She arranged a plump roll of hair at shoulder-length, setting it with sugar-water, and she teamed the dress with an ivory silk shawl with a hem of long tassels, then chose silver evening shoes and a matching bag.

She imagined driving herself to the party. Not that she knew what to do behind the wheel, but now that Mummy was driving, Daddy couldn't object if she wanted to learn too. It would be a modern and sophisticated thing to be able to do after the war.

She travelled by taxi to Melissa's parents' house. Before the war there would have been coloured lanterns to guide guests up the curving driveway. Now drivers only had their dimmed and restricted headlamps.

When Lorna tapped briskly using the lion's-head door-knocker, the door opened a fraction and she slid inside into the vestibule, which had all its glass panes blacked out. She entered the hall, her spirits rising as she heard the sounds of music and voices. A burst of masculine laughter suggested that Melissa had managed to nab some army officers for the evening.

The person who had let her in was Melissa's schoolboy brother, Terence. Lorna caught a whiff of tobacco about him. She glanced sharply at him but he merely shrugged and took her coat, dumping it on a carved wooden bench. Behind him, one of the double doors to the drawing room opened and Melissa appeared. She was all smiles – and then she saw who had arrived.

'Lorna!' she exclaimed. She quickly pulled the door shut behind her and scooted across the hall. 'What a surprise.'

Lorna laughed. 'Didn't you think I'd be able to come? Of course I came. I only received the invitation last night, but here I am.' She extended her arms out to the sides, showing herself off like a prize.

Melissa grasped her hand and pulled her into the library. The room had no fire, no guests, no music. What was going on?

'Why have you come?' Melissa asked.

'You invited me,' said Lorna, puzzled.

'Yes – for old times' sake.'

'Friends from the cradle, and all that.' Lorna kept her voice light and bright, but she was struggling to understand.

'I sent you the invitation late so that, even if it was posted on, it would be too late for you to accept.'

Lorna went cold. 'You mean you don't want me here?'

'No, I don't mean that,' said Melissa. 'Of course I want you here. It's just that... well, that business of the breach of promise caused an awful scandal. Listen. You're lovely and I adore you, but I'd rather not be seen with you just now. You do understand, don't you?'

Lorna stared at her old friend. Could she still count Melissa as her friend? She felt wretched. Her eyes filled but she blinked away the tears, determined not to let them fall.

Melissa shuffled her feet. 'I know this is hard on you, Lorna, and I never meant to hurt you. I truly meant it as a kindness when I sent the invitation.'

'The invitation I wasn't meant to accept,' said Lorna.

'Well – yes.' Melissa had the grace to look ashamed. 'I did it because I wanted you to know I was thinking of you. I wanted to give you a little boost. I never for one moment imagined you'd come racing here at the last moment.'

Lorna drew back her shoulders and planted a smile on her face. She desperately wanted to appear dignified. 'I'll slip away quietly. I'm sure you understand.'

'Terence will telephone for a taxi,' Melissa offered.

'That's all right.' All Lorna wanted was to escape. 'There's a telephone box near the end of the drive.'

'I'm truly sorry about this,' said Melissa.

Lorna didn't trust herself to say anything more. She simply nodded, then went to open the door. Thank goodness Terence hadn't spirited her coat away. She picked it up and put it on. Oh, how she wanted to hug it tightly around her body, but she was too proud.

The drawing room door burst open and several couples quickstepped through it. Lorna froze. Instinct urged her to dive back into the library, but it was too late. She had been seen. The couples stopped dancing.

It took every bit of willpower Lorna possessed to hold herself upright. 'Good evening. I hope you're all enjoying yourselves. I just dropped in because I haven't seen Melissa in simply ages. Now I'm on my way... somewhere else.'

Everyone else still had their eyes fixed on her and Lorna couldn't understand why. They should say, 'Good evening.' They should say, 'Lovely to see you,' and 'What a shame you can't stay.' Politeness dictated it. Weren't good manners supposed to be the bedrock of high society?

And then – and then – she battled with a sensation of light-headedness as the couple closest to the vestibule turned to face her and the man was George. The old spark flew between them but, at the same time, the atmosphere in the hall underwent a subtle transformation. The people who moments ago had been shocked at the sight of her now regarded her with open curiosity, their glances flicking between her and George.

'There'll be fireworks in a minute,' someone whispered.

Lorna wanted to say, 'No, there won't.' She wanted to say, 'I'm not the person the press portrayed me as being.'

Instead, hideously self-conscious but with her head held high, she walked across the hall to the door to the vestibule.

George left his partner and it seemed he might be about to stop her.

Lorna paused but only for long enough to say in a quiet voice for him alone, 'I always loved you, George, but I have to leave now.'

With her dignity intact but her heart in shreds, she hurried from the party.

CHAPTER EIGHTEEN

Mrs Henshaw normally made a point of undertaking her WVS duties at times that ensured she could be at home in good time to cook the family's evening meal, but today she was helping to look after a lady who was convalescing at home after leaving hospital and so she was due to be out all day Sunday. Andrew was going to be out as well on an all-day training exercise, so in the afternoon Sally went over to Withington to see Mum and Dad, leaving their house in plenty of time to get home before Andrew.

Even though it was a shame about the lady who'd had to have her appendix out, Sally was thrilled at the prospect of arriving home to cook a meal for her husband and sit down with him at the table, just the two of them, as if the house was theirs alone. She prepared a winter vegetable bake, cooking and frying various vegetables and loading the bottom of the pie dish before making a sauce of flour, milk and leek-water, together with cheese and seasoning, to pour over the top.

She knelt down on the hearthrug to lay the parlour fire to take the chill off the air before Andrew got home. She wanted the house to feel cosy as he walked through the front door. Sally loved her mother-in-law dearly but the chance to play at being a couple in their own home was nothing short of wonderful. She laughed at herself. Some young couples might seize the opportunity to dash straight upstairs to bed, and here she was dying to put a plate of food in front of her husband.

Hearing the key in the door, she hurried into the hallway to greet Andrew. As he enfolded her in his arms, Sally breathed in the scent of fresh air that clung to his clothes and his skin.

'Take off your jacket and come and sit down,' she said. 'We've got a while before we eat.'

Andrew chucked his cap onto the shelf above the coat hooks, asking, 'How was your visit?' at the same moment as Sally asked, 'How was your training?' They looked at one another and laughed.

'You first,' said Andrew, leading the way into the parlour, where they sat together on the sofa. He leaned back, hooking an arm round Sally's shoulders and drawing her back to lean on him. 'How are your mum and dad?'

'They're fine, thanks,' she told him. 'They send their best. Dad said to tell you he hopes today went well.'

'That's good of him.'

'He likes having a son-in-law.' Then Sally corrected herself. 'He likes having *you* as his son-in-law.'

Andrew chuckled. 'That's because I lend a hand with the vegetable patch. Seriously, maybe he and I should get an allotment together next spring.'

Sally was delighted. 'He'd love that.'

'Don't say anything to him yet,' Andrew cautioned. 'I need to work out how much time I'd be able to give it every week.'

'I won't breathe a word,' Sally promised. 'I'm glad you and Dad get along. Me and your mum hit it off the very first time we met and it grieved me that my parents didn't exactly welcome you with open arms.'

'That's way in the past,' said Andrew. 'They've accepted me

now and that's what matters.' He sniffed. 'Something else that matters now is feeding your husband. I warn you that if we don't get to the table pretty sharpish, my tummy is going to start rumbling in a distinctly unromantic way.'

Laughing, Sally got to her feet. The savoury aroma of the winter vegetable bake was filling the downstairs. Going to the kitchen, she put on the oven-gloves to take it out.

The meal was a success.

'It's like when we were together in the Worker Bee before we got married,' said Sally.

Andrew laughed. 'When we were young and fancy-free, you mean. Look at us now, an old married couple.'

Sally cleared away while Andrew smoked a Capstan and perused the newspaper. She was just about to boil the kettle for tea when the siren started up. Her heart sank. Her perfect evening!

But there was no time to dwell on that. She and Andrew hurried round the house doing what was necessary before they went out to the Anderson shelter in the small back garden. The pitch-dark evening vibrated under the sound of waves of enemy aircraft and the searchlights split the black skies apart, homing in on individual planes for the ack-ack guns to target.

Sally and Andrew played cards for a while, but Andrew's heart obviously wasn't really in it.

'I'm sorry,' he said. 'I'm finding it hard to concentrate. I keep wondering what's going on out there.'

'Are you worried about your mum?' Sally asked.

'I'm wondering what arrangements have been made for the convalescing lady and whether she's out of bed. In hospitals, if patients are bed-bound and can't get down to the cellars, they have to take what shelter they can underneath the beds. If this lady can't get to the shelter, Mum won't leave her.'

The raid, which had commenced around seven o'clock, dragged on for an hour and a half before Andrew stood up.

'We're both on duty tonight. There's no point in waiting. We have to go now.'

'We're needed even more on a night like this,' agreed Sally.

They dashed inside and upstairs to get changed into their warm togs. Sally tried not to flinch each time a bomb came crashing to earth. It was easier to gauge how far away the explosions were now that they were in the house. When you were in the Andy, all explosions sounded as if they were happening close by.

They shared a meaningful kiss and then left the house, heading in different directions to do their duty. As Sally ran down Beech Road, she had to dance to one side so as not to bowl Betty over as she emerged from Wilton Road. Together, they hurried to the depot, unlocked the door in the fence and dragged the big gates open before running upstairs to the attic to climb the ladder to the skylight that gave them access to the roof.

As she emerged, Sally immediately lifted her binoculars to her eyes, her heart beating hard as she turned around on the spot, watching the masses of lights falling in long lines that meant string upon string of high incendiaries had been released. Beside her, Betty did the same. Together, they noted where fires had sprung up. As always, Sally gazed in the direction of Withington as she sent up a prayer for her parents and all her old neighbours, especially the Grants.

After a few minutes of surveying the distance and getting a feel for the extent of the raid, they settled down to watching the nearby area. They were responsible for the safety of the depot, its yard and a stretch of Beech Road. Every building of significant size or purpose and every road in the country had its own team of fire-watchers, who took turns to be on duty every single night.

'Look!' Betty exclaimed. 'Down there.'

Incendiaries had landed further along Beech Road, beyond their own patch.

'I'll go and help,' said Sally. 'You stay here. I'll be as quick as I can.'

She hurried down the ladder, not caring that the rungs jolted beneath her feet, and raced down the stairs. Grabbing two buckets of sand, she hastened as best she could under their weight along the road. People were darting about, yelling to each other as they dealt with the deadly weapons. Dumping one bucket on the pavement, Sally approached an incendiary quickly but not too quickly – safety was paramount – and upended her sand on top of it, then stepped away briskly. She picked up the full bucket and emptied its load on another incendiary, then ran back to the depot, buckets clanking, for more sand.

When all the incendiaries had been dealt with, Sally ran back to the depot, breathless but invigorated, and resumed her position on the roof.

'Any more fires?' she asked.

'No. Not yet, anyroad.'

'Let's hope it stays that way.'

As the raid continued, flames lit up other districts, but the immediate vicinity remained safe. Sally thought of Andrew and what he might be facing as part of a rescue squad. *Please let him come home safe and sound.*

In the early hours Chorlton came under attack. The two girls watched and listened in horror as the bombings drew closer. Beech Road and its surroundings weren't hit but over there, towards the Mersey – and over that way, in the direction of the swimming baths – and the other way, towards Southern Cemetery, there were explosions and the whole earth shook. A further explosion and a flash of flames straight upwards towards the sky declared that a gas mains had been hit.

'Please don't let them hit the water mains,' breathed Sally. 'We need all the water we can get to put the fires out.'

At last, at long last, Jerry had dropped his entire load and the German planes disappeared, leaving fire, smoke, craters and rubble to be faced. The all-clear sounded and Sally lowered her binoculars, her shoulders feeling taut and numb at the same time.

'Thank goodness that's over,' said Betty. 'What's the time?'

Sally shot back her cuff. 'Coming up to half-four. Do you want to put the kettle on or do you want to stay on watch?'

Soon they were supping tea.

'I thought tea was meant to revive you,' Betty remarked, 'but I can feel waves of tiredness washing over me.'

'It's been a long night,' said Sally. 'All that concentrating.'

'And the fear,' Betty added. 'I've got my Eddie to worry about now, not just Dad and Grace.'

'I'm glad you met Eddie,' Sally said with an affectionate smile for her friend. 'It's good to see you happy.'

'Do I look happy?'

'You glow,' Sally told her.

Betty laughed, but she was obviously pleased. 'Not right now, though. I'm too tired to glow.'

'Save your glowing for Eddie,' said Sally, and Betty clearly loved hearing that too.

At six o'clock it was time to go home. They made their way down through the building. They locked up, closed and bolted the gates and left via the door in the fence, locking that too – though it wouldn't be long before everything had to be unlocked and opened up again.

Sally walked home, hoping Andrew wasn't still in the middle of a rescue. She hated having to set off for work without having seen him. And what of Mrs Henshaw? Had she ended up staying with the patient all night?

Smells of soot, rubble and cordite accompanied Sally on

her way home. As she turned the final corner, the aromas intensified and her skin prickled all over. Their road had been hit. On this side, several yards of paving stones had been tossed up into the air and had landed any old how, forcing Sally to wrench her gaze away from what she wanted, needed, to look at – the houses – and watch where she put her feet as she negotiated her way past. It wasn't just the paving stones. There were individual bricks and bricks in clumps, roof-tiles, glass, lumps of plaster, even a front door. The air was heavy with a mixture of smells, the sharp and the musty. Sally's eyes stung and something unpleasant caught in the back of her throat.

Getting beyond the worst of the rubble that was strewn all over the place, she lifted her face and looked along the road, her heart bumping at the sight of a pair of semis without a top half. The roofs were gone as well as both sets of upstairs. Yet there wasn't a mark on the lower parts of the houses. Even the windows were intact. Oh, the poor Lundys and the Graftons. What a dreadful thing to happen to their homes. Please let them have had time to evacuate and get to their shelters. The thought of them being caught in their beds—

Sally wrenched her gaze away, her attention suddenly caught by another house on the opposite side of the street. You sometimes saw photographs of this in the newspapers – where the whole of the front of a house had been stripped away, leaving its innards on show, letting you see things you should never see, like the bedroom wallpaper.

A family round the corner from Mum and Dad's house in Withington had been well known locally for having the poshest home in the neighbourhood, all chintz upholstery and fringed pelmets, with Wedgwood on display in a glass-fronted cabinet, and a leather-bound set of the complete works of Shakespeare complete with gold lettering on the spines. Then the front wall of their house had been blown to smithereens and, lo and behold, their upstairs had shown a very different state of affairs, with barely a stick of furniture to be seen.

Why was she thinking about that now? Sally knew the answer to that. It was because, although her eyes could see whose house had lost its front, her brain was doing its best not to believe it.

Mrs Henshaw kept saying, 'Oh my goodness, oh my goodness,' over and over in a soft voice. It was the first time Sally had ever seen her mother-in-law look vulnerable. She had been widowed young and had brought up Andrew on a woman's wage, no easy task. Sally remembered meeting her for the first time and how severe her face had looked, showing competence and reliability in every line. Then she had smiled and kindness and generosity had filled her blue eyes as she welcomed Sally into her home. Sally had felt liked, and above all accepted – which was more than her own parents had made Andrew feel.

Now Mrs Henshaw appeared dazed and incredulous. Sally hugged her. She was shocked too. Her home had gone – her first married home. But however hard this was for her, it must be a hundred, a thousand times worse for her mother-in-law, who had moved into that house as a bride and ended up working long hours in order to keep it after her husband died. She had worked until Andrew had been earning enough to support the house and had insisted it was his turn to look after her.

'You come on in with me, Mrs Henshaw.' Mrs O'Grady from next door but one took Mrs Henshaw's arm. 'A nice cup of tea will set you up. There'll be plenty to do later on. You an' all, love,' she added, looking at Sally.

'Thank you but no. I'll stay here.' Though what that might achieve, Sally couldn't have said. She gave her mother-in-law a little push. 'You go.'

'You'll let me know the minute Andrew comes back?'

'Yes, of course.'

Mrs Henshaw cast one last anguished look at the ruins of her home and allowed herself to be led away.

Sally couldn't take her eyes off the house. The awful thing was that she had got used to the idea of this happening to other people. Her throat tightened with guilt. It was one of those things that you never truly understood until it happened to you.

An ARP warden approached her. He was an elderly man, his face streaked with grime beneath his tin helmet. Sally thought of Dad. Had he been on duty last night? Did he look this way right now, weary but determined?

'You can't go in there yet,' he told her. 'You know that, don't you? The building has to be checked to see if it's safe.'

'What about our things?' Sally asked. 'What's left of them, anyway.'

'You just stay put for now,' said the warden.

Sally felt vaguely ashamed for asking about their belongings. As if possessions mattered compared to people.

Where was Andrew? She desperately wanted him to return so she could seek refuge in his arms. At the same time she didn't want him to come. All the while that he wasn't here, he didn't know and was spared this appalling shock.

Something made Sally glance round, and here came Mrs Henshaw, pale and drawn but grim. The cup of tea had worked its magic, together with her mother-in-law's stout spirit.

'I know what we need to do,' she said. 'Goodness knows, I've helped enough homeless people at the WVS rest centre. Don't worry about a thing, Sally. You go to work as normal and I'll sort us out with everything: clothes, toiletries, somewhere to stay.'

'Are you sure?' Sally asked, concerned.

'Of course I'm sure. It's no good giving in. That's what Hitler wants us to do. I've had my weepy moment and I'll be all right from now on.'

Andrew must have been involved in a rescue, because he didn't appear before Sally had to go to work. As she walked down Beech Road with the smells of smoke and rubble in her nostrils, the sweet scent of the privet surrounding the rec sprang at her, bringing tears to her eyes. How bizarre to feel cheered by a privet hedge, of all things.

'Sally!'

Betty was coming along Wilton Road from Star House. She had changed out of her fire-watching clobber. Sally glanced down at the slacks, two jumpers and an old jacket of Andrew's, together with the tin hat dangling from her fingers, that made up her own fire-watching gear.

Betty put on a spurt. 'Sally! You haven't got changed. What's happened?' She gasped. 'Don't say...'

Sally nodded. It ought to be easy to nod. It was such a simple thing to do, but somehow it required a great effort. 'The house is gone – well, the front of it. We'll never live there again. We aren't allowed inside yet to look for our things. It's got to be checked.'

'Oh, Sally, I'm so sorry.' Betty took her arm. 'Come with me. Mrs Beaumont will look after you.'

'I've got to open the depot.'

'Lorna can do it,' said Betty. Taking a firm hold of Sally's arm, she led her to Star House. Opening the door, she called out, 'Mrs Beaumont! Sally's been bombed out. Can she have some tea?'

Mrs Beaumont appeared. Over her skirt and blouse she wore a wraparound pinny patterned with an array of flowers in vivid colours – roses, peonies and daisies against a background of green foliage. The pinny together with her bottle-black hair made her appear exotic.

'Bombed out?' she said. 'Come in, my lovely. Let's have a cuppa and see what's what. Take her into the dining room, Betty.'

Soon the three of them were sitting around the table, drinking tea and smoking. Sally inhaled deeply on her cigarette. She normally smoked for pleasure but she could understand now why folk said it was good for their nerves. She closed her eyes as she exhaled smoke.

'Can you bear to talk about it?' Mrs Beaumont asked sympathetically.

Sally gave herself a moment. She didn't intend to make a fuss. 'You know when you see houses with the front blown off and everything on show? That's what's happened to ours.'

'I'm sorry to hear it,' said Mrs Beaumont. 'What about your furniture and so on?'

'We're not allowed in yet. I don't know how much we'll be able to retrieve when we do get in.'

Mrs Beaumont raised her long cigarette-holder to her lips and inhaled, then removed it to breathe out. 'Have you got anywhere to go?'

'My mother-in-law works at the WVS rest centre, so she knows the system.'

Mrs Beaumont took a sip of tea, her little finger cocked. 'I've got space here now that the munitions girls have moved on.'

Betty caught her breath. 'Oh, Mrs Beaumont, do you mean it?'

'I'm not in the habit of saying things I don't mean,' said Mrs Beaumont. 'Stella had Vesta Tilley, which is a double, so Sally and her husband can have that, and that leaves a choice of Florrie Forde or Vesta Victoria, which are both singles, for Mrs Henshaw. Don't look so startled, Sally. You're not hearing things. All my rooms are named after the great stars of the music hall.'

It was a good thing Sally was sitting down, because she felt wobbly with relief. 'That's so kind of you.'

'It is and it isn't,' said Mrs Beaumont. 'It's a way for me to choose who I have here instead of having people foisted on me by the billeting officer.'

'Like I was, you mean,' said Betty, but her eyes twinkled and her dimple appeared.

'The offer's there, Sally,' said Mrs Beaumont. 'Think it over and let me know.'

CHAPTER NINETEEN

Lorna was surprised to be the first to arrive at the depot. Even though she was always punctual, it had never happened before. When there was no sign of the others by the time she had got changed, she pressed her lips together, but her annoyance immediately vanished as concern took its place.

When Sally and Betty walked in through the open gates, Lorna found herself hurrying towards them – only to stop dead when she realised that, although Betty was dressed normally, Sally looked distinctly workmanlike.

'What's happened?' Lorna asked.

'Sally's been bombed out,' said Betty.

'*No*,' Lorna breathed. 'Was anyone hurt?'

Sally shut her eyes for a moment. When she opened them, they were glistening. 'We were all out last night, but thanks for asking. Honestly – thank you.'

Lorna might have spent the past few weeks firmly believing that salvage work was beneath her – and she still believed it, even though she was now on a friendlier footing with Sally and Betty and was starting to have second thoughts about Mrs Lockwood – but, if there was one thing she had learned during her time both here and working for the WVS, it was the importance of putting the kettle on.

'Come in and sit down,' she said. 'You look shattered and I don't just mean physically. You're the first person of my acquaintance this has happened to. I'll make the tea.'

'I'm already awash with tea from Mrs Beaumont,' said Sally.

'Just half a cup, then,' said Lorna. 'It's good for shock. While I'm doing that, you two go in the office and Betty can get the fire going, then she can stay in there for a while with you, Sally, and you can talk things through.'

'I'm not an invalid,' Sally protested.

'Maybe not,' said Lorna, 'but a spot of looking after wouldn't go amiss. Don't worry about the daily sacks or getting the collections ready. I'll see to all that.' She made shooing motions with her hands. 'Chop-chop. In you go.'

She made tea for the others, then returned to the yard to sort through the latest sacks, which was one of her least favourite jobs. Mind you, every job felt like her least favourite when she contemplated tackling it.

Presently Betty appeared, now dressed in her dungarees and with her beautiful golden hair covered by a headscarf.

'How is she?' Lorna asked.

'Pretty stunned but determined to carry on.'

'Good for her,' said Lorna. 'It's what everyone has to do in her position.' She tried to picture it happening to herself.

'She's getting changed,' said Betty.

That prompted Lorna to ask, 'Were her clothes lost in the bombing?'

'She doesn't know yet,' Betty answered. 'They won't be allowed back in the house for a while – or maybe not at all. But her mother-in-law works for the WVS, so she knows the drill.'

'That'll make things more straightforward,' Lorna observed. 'Sorry,' she added. 'That sounded as if I was dismissing it and I'm not.'

Soon Sally appeared and threw herself into her work. To take her mind off her troubles? Or working harder to defeat Jerry?

When their tea break came round, the three of them sat in the office, which had warmed up nicely.

'Let's talk about something different,' Sally requested.

'Fair enough,' said Betty. She turned to Lorna. 'Did you do anything special at the weekend?'

Lorna was all set to lie through her teeth, but somehow Sally having lost her home called forth the truth.

'I went up to Lancaster to attend a friend's party.'

'Tell us all about it,' said Sally. 'I'd like to hear something nice.'

'Well, you won't hear anything nice from me, I'm afraid,' Lorna replied bluntly. 'It was dire. It turned out that my friend didn't want me there at all.'

Betty frowned. 'Then why did she invite you?'

'Politeness? Kindness? I've no idea,' Lorna said breezily. 'She sent the invitation at the last possible moment, never imagining I'd be able to go. She claimed she'd done it out of the goodness of her heart to cheer me up, and she was right: it did give me a boost. But when she uttered the immortal words, "I'd rather not be seen with you just now," the boost faded away toot sweet.'

'How horrid,' said Sally. 'What did she mean?'

Lorna looked at the other two. They were both puzzled, but not in a nosy sort of way. There was concern in Sally's fawny-hazel eyes and Betty's blue ones. Everything that had happened to Lorna in recent weeks ever since George had broken off their engagement welled up inside her and pain expanded inside her throat, making it impossible to speak. Then she went very still, realising that the moment had come to shed some of her burden.

'Did you read in the papers about the breach of promise case brought by a Miss Lorna West-Sadler?'

'Yes,' said Betty, followed a moment later by, 'Oh. But you're...'

'My father made me ditch half of my surname when he sent me here to hide from the publicity.'

'You're Miss West-Sadler,' breathed Sally.

'Didn't the judge say...?' Betty's voice trailed off.

'The judge said all kinds of things,' Lorna answered crisply, 'none of them flattering. I'd rather not be reminded of them, if it's all the same to you.' The old hurt washed through her. 'But for the record, I didn't personally bring the breach of promise case. That was my father.'

'Lumme,' said Betty. 'I don't know what to say. Fancy you being her.'

'Please don't tell anyone,' said Lorna.

'We won't,' Sally assured her. 'Does Mrs Lockwood know?'

'Lord, no, and that's the way I'd like it to stay.'

'Fair enough,' said Betty. 'You can count on us.'

'So that's why my friend didn't really want me at her party,' said Lorna. 'That's why she sent such a last-minute invitation.'

'You poor love,' said Sally. 'It must have been dreadfully upsetting.'

Lorna closed her eyes for a moment. Sally didn't know the half of it. The scene with Melissa had been bad enough, but seeing George afterwards had ripped Lorna's heart in half.

'You went all that way thinking you were going to have a lovely time,' said Betty, 'only to find your friend didn't want you.'

The backs of Lorna's eyes burned and she had to blink away tears. 'I didn't think you'd react this way. I thought you might say I deserved it, but here you are being kind and understanding. Sally's just gone through a traumatic event but you're both making time for me.'

'Of course we are,' said Betty. 'Why wouldn't we?'

'I've lost my home,' said Sally, 'which is grim, to say the

least, but it's only bricks and mortar. What happened to you, Lorna, went right to the core of your feelings. So yes, Betty and I do want to be kind. We want to support you. That's what friends do for one another.'

Mrs Henshaw came to see Sally at the depot that afternoon to give her an update. She had arranged with someone from the WVS in Withington for a WVS lady to call on Sally's parents to reassure them that the Henshaws were safe and well.

'Thank you for that,' Sally said warmly.

'Right now our house is being cleared of whatever contents survived and any furniture will go into storage.' Mrs Henshaw looked stricken for a moment. 'All said and done, what really matters are the things of sentimental value, the photographs, the cigarette-box Andrew's father made, things like that, but even those don't matter compared to the three of us being safe.'

'Have you seen Andrew?' Sally asked.

'Yes. He's been given the afternoon off school to help with emptying the house.'

'Is he all right?' Sally thought of him going through the ruins of the house he had lived in all his life and her heart ached.

'He's shocked but, as he said, he's seen it often enough through being part of a rescue team. Don't fret about him. He'll manage.'

'We all will,' said Sally, 'as long as we're together.'

'That's another thing,' said Mrs Henshaw. 'We shan't be together. It's often hard to billet a married couple together, but the WVS have found a place that can take in a couple, though unfortunately there isn't room for me to come too. You and Andrew will be moving over to Wythenshawe.'

'What about you?' Sally hated the thought of their little family being split apart.

'Not to worry. I can move in with my sister.'

Sally pictured Andrew's Auntie Vera, short, easy-going, her old-fashioned boned corsets giving away their presence by creaking occasionally. She could imagine Auntie Vee providing a warm welcome, but she had good news for her mother-in-law.

'We can stay together. Mrs Beaumont, Betty's landlady, has offered to take us all in at Star House. She's got space because her other lodgers have left. It's much better for Andrew and me than being billeted on strangers, and of course you must come too.'

Mrs Henshaw let out a huge breath. 'What a relief. I never imagined us being able to stay together.'

'Star House is in Wilton Road opposite the rec,' Sally told her. 'Pop round there now and introduce yourself. I'm sure you'll like Mrs Beaumont.'

Mrs Henshaw looked as if a great weight had been lifted from her and Sally smiled as she saw her on her way. Relief and gratitude bubbled up inside her, feelings that surged to the fore again later when Andrew appeared at the depot.

Sally was upstairs when he arrived and she saw him from a window. Uttering a cry, she raced downstairs and into the yard, throwing herself into the arms that he flung wide to pull her to him. Within the comfort of his embrace, it was impossible not to shed some tears as the shock and distress of losing their home rose inside her.

Andrew murmured soothingly in her ear. 'It's all right. We're safe. That's what matters.'

Sally nodded, her forehead moving against his chest. She tipped back her head to look up at him through a mist of tears. 'I know. We can manage without the house but we can't manage without one another – and your mum,' she added. 'She's safe too.'

'I saw her on my way here. She says we're all moving into Star House.'

'Isn't it wonderful? We can all stay together – and we'll be with Betty. It's because the munitions girls moved out.'

'Lucky for us they did,' said Andrew.

'How strange to be talking about luck when we've just lost our house,' said Sally.

'Everyone who is still alive is lucky,' said Andrew.

That reminded Sally. 'Do you know if the Graftons and the Lundys are safe? I saw what happened to their houses.'

'They're fine,' Andrew assured her. 'Well, they're shocked and upset, of course, but aside from that they're fine.'

'Like us,' said Sally. 'Shocked and upset but still here and still together. That's really all that counts. Are you going to Star House now?'

'No,' Andrew replied in a firm voice. 'I'll come back here to the depot at closing time. We'll fetch Mum and then the three of us can go to Star House together. That's the right way to do it when you move into your new home.'

Early that evening the Henshaws headed for Star House, bringing their surviving clothes and a distressingly small number of other bits and pieces, plus some essentials – combs, toothbrushes, shaving tackle – provided by the WVS. After the warmth and optimism Andrew had made her feel earlier, Sally fought against a slump in her spirits.

'Are you all right?' Andrew asked quietly as he shifted the cardboard boxes in his arms so he could open the garden gate.

Sally pinned a smile on her face. 'I think it's starting to sink in that our home is gone.'

'Chin up,' he whispered.

She nodded, determined not to let everyone down. 'I'm fine,' she whispered back.

Up the path they went. The front door opened before they got there. The blackout meant that no light spilled out in welcome, but Mrs Beaumont appeared in the dark doorway with Betty behind her.

'Come in, all of you,' their new landlady called with a smile in her voice. 'Let's get this door shut and then we can put the light on. Put your boxes and bags down here for now and hang up your coats on the stand. Then come into the sitting room. We've got a nice fire going. Betty, be a love and pop the kettle on.'

'Welcome to your new home,' Betty said with a grin before disappearing towards the kitchen.

In a matter of moments the Henshaws were in the sitting room, where the promised fire burned brightly.

'Make yourselves comfortable,' said Mrs Beaumont, 'and when we've had a cup of tea, I'll show you up to your rooms. The beds have been aired and I've put lavender sachets in the hanging-cupboards and the drawers. If you don't care for laven-der, I've got some rose-petal ones as well.'

'Thank you,' said Mrs Henshaw, with a tremor in her voice at the kindness. 'This is so good of you.'

'Not at all,' Mrs Beaumont answered firmly. 'This is your home now for as long as you need it and I'm sure we'll all get along famously.'

Betty pushed the door open with her hip and Andrew stood up to hold it open for her as she came in with the tray.

'Tea up,' she sang out, her blue eyes twinkling.

'You'll have to give me your family's ration books, Mrs Henshaw,' Mrs Beaumont said as she poured tea for everyone.

'I've told my butcher and grocer that in future we'll come under Star House,' Mrs Henshaw replied. 'I've had to apply for new ration books. It serves me right for keeping the old ones in the drawer. That old sideboard got a good shaking when the house was hit. I didn't go inside afterwards but I could see it from the pavement. The cupboard doors were hanging off and the drawers were open. I suppose our ration books got picked up in the blast. They must be halfway to Timbuktu by this time.'

'I know that the reason for you being here at Star House is perfectly awful,' said Betty. 'Losing your home is a horrid thing to happen – but, since it has happened, I'm very glad you're here.'

'It's nice of you to say so,' Mrs Henshaw told her with a smile.

'It's been quiet here since the munitions girls left,' said Mrs Beaumont, 'so it'll be good to have a full house again – well, almost. There will still be one empty bedroom. In my days as a theatrical landlady, it was always a source of great pride to me to keep a full house. I wonder who that is,' she added as the doorbell rang.

'I'll go,' said Betty, standing up.

When she returned, she had Mr Atkinson with her. He smiled shyly at the assembled household. Betty introduced him to Mrs Beaumont.

'I know who you are,' she told him. 'I've been in your shop, but we've never been formally introduced. Do you know the Henshaws?'

'I know Mrs Henshaw,' he replied, looking at Sally.

'This is my husband,' said Sally, and Andrew stood up to shake hands. 'And this is his mother.'

'Good evening, Mrs Henshaw.' Mr Atkinson shook her hand. 'I was s-sorry to hear about your house.'

'How do you know about that?' Sally asked.

'Air raid w-wardens hear most things,' he answered. 'That's wh-what has brought me here.' Uncertainty flickered in his hazel eyes. 'I hope this isn't inappropriate but I have brought something for your f-family.'

'How kind,' said Sally, 'and how unexpected.'

Mr Atkinson produced a book. 'It's about the music halls. I

know it's not the s-sort of practical gift you need when you've been bombed out, but it c-comes with my best wishes.'

'And it'll mean you always remember the time you lived in Star House,' Betty exclaimed.

'That w-was what I thought,' said Mr Atkinson.

'I'm sure it won't take a book to help us do that,' said Mrs Henshaw, 'but it's very good of you, Mr Atkinson.'

'Yes, it is,' Andrew concurred. 'A kind thought. Just what we needed today.'

'Thank you,' Sally added. 'We'll keep it always. It'll remind us of you, as well as Star House.'

'Would you care for a cup of tea, Mr Atkinson?' Mrs Beaumont offered. 'I'm sure I can squeeze another out of the pot.'

'No, thank you,' he answered. 'I must be getting along.'

After he had departed, the others finished their tea, then Mrs Beaumont led the way upstairs to show them to their rooms. Mrs Henshaw was given a single room and there was a double for Sally and Andrew. On the top floor, it was above Betty's room, which meant that in daylight they would have a view over the old recreation ground, which was now mainly given over to allotments. As well as the large bed with its pale-blue candlewick bedspread, there was a chest of drawers and a matching wardrobe with a long mirror inset in one of the doors. In one corner was a washstand, in front of the windows stood a dressing-table, and on either side of the bed was a small cupboard.

'It's a handsome room,' Andrew said to Mrs Beaumont.

'Some of my theatricals were married and this was the room I gave them,' she replied. 'Of course, there were those who would claim to be married when they weren't, but I wasn't having any of that.'

Sally's curiosity was piqued. 'How did you know which couples were married and which weren't?'

Mrs Beaumont preened. 'When you follow the lives of the

stars as closely as I do, you know these things. Besides,' she added in a down-to-earth tone, 'it's my job to know. This has always been a respectable house.'

When she left them to unpack their meagre belongings, Sally and Andrew looked at one another and chuckled.

'For a moment I felt as if we ought to show her our marriage certificate,' Andrew joked.

'Thank goodness the important papers survived,' Sally said seriously.

Their various certificates, insurance papers and so on, had all been kept in a stout tin box in the cupboard under the stairs, ready to be taken to the Anderson shelter. The box had survived the impact of the explosion, which would mean they wouldn't have the trouble of replacing their important documents.

The Henshaws had barely settled in when it was time to go out on duty again.

Mrs Henshaw was still in her WVS uniform from the previous night. 'I'll spend tonight helping people the way I've been helped today,' she said with a brisk nod.

Sally hugged Andrew. Then, unable to stop herself, she clung harder, whispering, 'Be safe.'

'You too,' he whispered back.

Sally and Betty set off together for the depot.

How quickly life could change – and how completely too. Last night, when Sally had been on duty on the depot roof, their house had been intact – or at least in her mind it had been. Not that she'd thought about it. You didn't, did you? You just assumed it. Even though she had seen the fires through her binoculars, she hadn't envisaged losing her home. She had worried about Mum and Dad and their house, but it had been her own that had been hit.

But she, her darling husband and his mother were all safe. In the end, that was all that mattered.

. . .

Sally seemed rather quiet that Monday night on the depot roof, and Betty could understand why. It wasn't the moment to say so but, as upset as she was on the Henshaw family's behalf, she couldn't help also feeling delighted to have them living with her at Star House, especially Sally. There was a special bond between her and Sally because they were working together both day and night. Moreover, Sally's approval of Betty's fledgling relationship with Eddie made Betty even fonder of her.

Not that Betty's relationship with Eddie could now be called fledgling, not now that they were unofficially engaged – or were they? Could you really be engaged if it had to be kept secret? It certainly didn't fit in with the dreams Betty had grown up with. She longed to confide in Sally, but she held her tongue, difficult as that was. If Eddie would go to Salford and ask Dad's permission, then all would be well... wouldn't it?

She and Sally left the depot at the end of their shift. The raids last night had been some way off, though not in Salford's direction. Betty's gratitude was tinged with guilt. If you or your loved ones were spared, it meant that somebody else's family hadn't been.

Mrs Henshaw arrived at Star House at the same time as the girls did, and Andrew wasn't far behind. Soon they were all seated in the dining room, with Mrs Beaumont, decked out in her glamorous wraparound pinny, serving honey-sweetened porridge followed by toast and home-made jam.

Mrs Henshaw wanted to help serve up and clear away, but Mrs Beaumont wouldn't hear of it.

'You're my guest, Mrs Henshaw. I'm a professional landlady.'

'Let yourself be looked after for once, Mum,' Andrew said with a smile.

It wasn't long before Betty, Sally and Andrew had to set off for work, Andrew in a second-hand suit courtesy of the WVS. Mrs Henshaw wasn't due at the WVS that day. Perhaps she would end up vying with Mrs Beaumont over who would do the honours and stand in the shopping queues that morning.

Lorna arrived at the depot a few minutes after Betty and Sally. Having started off not caring for Lorna in the slightest, Betty had thawed considerably towards her, especially since Lorna had confided her unhappy experience at the party. She might easily have kept that to herself, but she had chosen to share it and Betty respected her for that, as well as feeling closer to her. Fancy Lorna being the scandalous society girl! That judge had had a real go at her. The papers had been full of it – as Betty remembered only too well, because hadn't she read the articles in salvaged newspapers right here in the depot yard? She had lapped up the story as eagerly as anyone. She under-stood why people had been so outraged by the portrayal of Lorna as shallow and selfish at a time when everybody else in the country was doing their bit towards the war effort, but that didn't mean Lorna had deserved to be hounded out of her home to hide away in an unfamiliar place. Besides, Lorna wasn't a bad sort after all. True, she hadn't made a good start at the depot, but she had improved no end since then.

The girls got changed, opened up the premises and set about their work. They had barely got started before Mrs Lock-wood came swanning in. Betty suppressed a sigh.

'Good morning, girls,' said Mrs Lockwood. 'Mrs Henshaw, Miss Sadler has informed me of your family's unfortunate situa-tion. I'm sorry to hear of it.'

'Thank you,' said Sally.

'I've come here to relieve you of your duty so you can attend to matters. I'm sure you must have plenty to do.'

Sally looked first startled, then resolute. 'Thank you, but there's really no need. Everything is already sorted out.'

'Nonsense,' said Mrs Lockwood. 'You look exhausted.'

'I am rather tired,' Sally had to admit, 'but—'

'There you are, then,' Mrs Lockwood ploughed on, speaking over her. 'I cannot stand by and watch the depot falling behind because the girl Mr Merivale and Mr Pratt foolishly put in charge simply hasn't got the backbone to rise above her personal woes.'

'I never said—' Lorna began.

'I've as much backbone as the next person,' said Sally.

'Whether you have or you haven't is irrelevant, Mrs Henshaw,' Mrs Lockwood replied, 'because I have already telephoned Mr Merivale at the Town Hall to inform him of the new arrangements. I happen to know that you and your husband have been given a billet over in Wythenshawe.'

She made it sound like the other end of the earth but even Betty, with her limited knowledge of local geography, knew it was just a few miles away.

'It would be a difficult journey for you, Mrs Henshaw. It would take you two buses and, with all the diversions we face every day because of craters on the roads, it simply isn't feasible for you to continue working here. I know you are determined to do your bit so fear not. I will ensure a suitable post is offered to you near your new home. I can't say fairer than that.' Mrs Lockwood looked at Betty and Lorna, her grey eyes flinty. 'Why have you two stopped working, may I ask? Such a lax attitude won't do at all. You'll be required to pull your socks up now that I have taken over.'

'You can't do this,' fumed Sally.

Mrs Lockwood looked her up and down in a manner that reeked of condescension and self-satisfaction.

'I already have.'

CHAPTER TWENTY

It turned out that being hopping mad was a good antidote to the lingering effects of shock. Sally took the bus into the city centre to go to the Town Hall. She hoped she wouldn't see anybody she knew from when she used to work here. It would be just too awkward to have to explain her presence. She was obliged to wait for ages for Mr Merivale to be available, but she was determined not to budge until they had met face to face.

While she was waiting, Mr Pratt walked past her into Mr Merivale's office. Sally pictured Mr Merivale placing a call on the house-telephone and telling his colleague that she had set up camp outside his door. Mr Pratt was the other official who had jointly appointed her. The door shut behind him. Two minutes later it was opened by Mr Merivale, who called her inside. He was a broad-shouldered, straight-backed gentleman. Mr Pratt was paunchy with round cheeks, above which his eyes crinkled when he smiled. He wasn't smiling now.

Mr Merivale returned to his seat behind the desk as Sally entered the office. 'Please have a seat, Mrs Henshaw.'

Offering a polite greeting to both men, Sally sat down,

placing her handbag and her gas-mask box beside her feet. The two gentlemen also sat down.

'I'll come straight to the point,' said Mr Merivale, 'since we only have a few minutes. Mr Pratt and I are busy men and your appearance here is unexpected. Mrs Lockwood informed me earlier of your family's situation and I have just apprised Mr Pratt. Please accept our sympathy,' he said briskly. 'This must be very difficult for you, but many families, many workers, face exactly the same problem and manage to do so without collapsing in a heap.'

Sally could hardly believe her ears. 'Without *what*?'

'This is war, Mrs Henshaw,' said Mr Merivale, 'and everybody has to be strong, no matter what.'

Mr Pratt leaned forward. His manner was more kindly, but there was a firmness about him that said he wasn't going to be taken advantage of.

'According to Mrs Lockwood,' he said, 'you've taken this very much to heart.'

'Wouldn't you, if it was your house?'

'Mrs Lockwood was originally going to take over the depot from Mr Overton,' said Mr Pratt, 'so it makes sense to let her do so now. Salvage is essential to the war effort, as you are well aware, Mrs Henshaw, and we need someone we can rely on.'

'You can rely on me,' said Sally. 'I don't know what Mrs Lockwood has told you but—' She stopped herself from saying 'she's making it up.' She mustn't alienate these men by doing down Mrs Lockwood.

'Mrs Lockwood has suggested a clerical position for you in Wythenshawe,' said Mr Merivale. 'That is where you'll be living, so everything works out neatly.'

'I don't want to be sent to Wythenshawe,' said Sally. 'I want to stay at the depot in Chorlton.' Taking a breath, she adopted a steady voice. 'Contrary to what Mrs Lockwood might have suggested, I have not gone to pieces. Our house was hit the night before last, but I took no time off from the depot and all the daily work continued to the usual timetable. My family moved into our new digs yesterday evening – in Chorlton, not in Wythenshawe – and I spent last night on the depot roof in my capacity as fire-watcher – the third night in a row, I might add.'

The two men glanced at one another. A good sign?

'I am more than capable of coping without collapsing in a heap,' said Sally, looking Mr Merivale in the eye. 'Have I given satisfaction so far as manager?'

'You haven't been in the post very long,' Mr Pratt pointed out, 'but in fairness, yes, you've done well.'

'Then let me stay there,' said Sally. 'I won't let you down. Losing our home has given me an extra reason to work hard.'

'I have already agreed with Mrs Lockwood that she should take over,' said Mr Merivale.

Sally winced inwardly but then she tightened her fists in her lap. She wasn't going to give up.

'I think Mrs Lockwood has... overreacted.'

'That's a strong word,' said Mr Merivale. 'She is dedicated to the depot.'

'And she is concerned for your personal well-being,' Mr Pratt added.

Drat the pair of them. They were too wary, if not downright scared, of Mrs Lockwood to attach any criticism or blame to her, which meant Sally mustn't either.

'Exactly,' she said steadily. 'Gentlemen, you were the ones who appointed me and Mr Pratt has just acknowledged that I've done well so far. I know you value Mrs Lockwood's opinion – as do I,' she added through gritted teeth, 'but please don't lose faith in me. Mr Merivale has said that others who lose their homes simply get on with their lives and their jobs. Well, that's what I've done. My husband, his mother and I have all taken a deep breath and got on with it. I promise I won't let you down. I won't let my country down.'

Another look passed between the men.

'You have made a convincing argument,' said Mr Merivale, 'and perhaps we did act a trifle hastily.'

'But with the best possible intentions,' added Mr Pratt.

'Indeed. With the best possible intentions,' said Mr Merivale. 'Very well, Mrs Henshaw. We shall reinstate you.'

'Reinstate me?' Sally repeated. 'But I haven't left.'

'On paper you have,' said Mr Merivale. 'I will ask my secretary to attend to the matter.'

'And we'll have to speak to Mrs Lockwood,' said Mr Pratt.

Sally noted the *have to*. She was sure neither gentleman would be keen to do that. Mrs Lockwood wasn't going to be pleased and that was putting it mildly.

'She has kept watch over you since you were appointed,' said Mr Merivale. 'We shall ask her to continue with that, and perhaps to do it a little more closely.'

'But—' Sally started to object.

'If Mrs Lockwood is right and you can't cope,' said Mr Merivale, 'she can report the matter. But if you are in the right job, Mrs Henshaw, you have nothing to fear. Thank you for coming. Good morning.'

As Sally made her way back to the depot, she felt all churned up. She was shocked by how quickly Mrs Lockwood had moved against her, as well as angry and resentful. Because the matter was so closely tied to the loss of the Henshaws' house, she ended up on the verge of tears as she sat on the bus to Chorlton. She knew she would emerge from this experience all the more determined to prove herself, but just now she felt rattled and sore.

As she approached the depot, the paper-mill lorry was parked outside and the driver, Mr Craig, and his assistant, Mr Mack, were trundling sack-trolleys of bundles of waste paper to be loaded up, as were Lorna and Betty.

Sally pinned a smile on her face as she said hello and slipped through the gates. Betty broke off from what she was doing and hurried after her.

'How did it go?'

'Crisis averted,' said Sally. 'For now, anyway.'

'That's good,' said Betty.

Sally changed into her dungarees but she didn't join the others. After the upheaval she'd faced, she needed to be on her own. It might be a good time to look in some of the depot's empty rooms. When she had started working here in September, everything had been done outside but as the days had shortened and grown colder, she had gradually moved much of the salvage indoors. The trouble was, she had only opened up the rooms on the ground floor. If she'd thought things through more fully, she would have stored only bulkier and heavier things downstairs and used some of the upstairs rooms for the lightweight articles. As it was, downstairs now felt cluttered and it was high time for a proper sort-out.

Sally went around the upstairs rooms, checking them for size and noting how far they were from the stairs. Most of the rooms were unlocked but a couple weren't. It didn't matter. She had a master-key.

She unlocked a door – and stopped dead. The room contained – well, not salvage, that was for certain. There were some pieces of furniture, though not big pieces: chairs, side-tables, a copper hip-bath, a baby's cradle. Most of the items were small: candlesticks, trays, ornaments, clocks, pictures, fireside companions, even a wicker picnic basket. Sally flicked up its catches and opened the lid to reveal a set of plates, cutlery, condiment bottles and a spirit-lamp. Looking behind her, she removed the lids from some boxes, finding a flat box that, when she opened it, contained a set of fish-knives and -forks, nestling in a velvet bed. Another box contained a pair of fruit-spoons. On the shelves near the window was a stout cardboard box with a variety of china trinket boxes and little glass dishes, the type you would find on dressing-tables, as well as hand-mirrors and pretty perfume bottles with puffers to squeeze.

Sally's mouth dropped open and her shoulders sagged. Where on earth had all these things come from?

In the Star House dining room that evening, Betty inadvertently let the cat out of the bag about what Mrs Lockwood had done by asking Sally if she felt all right now. 'It was horrid but you coped really well. I hope you're not still upset.'

'What was horrid?' Mrs Henshaw asked at once.

Sally explained how close she had come to having a new job in Wythenshawe. 'But it turned out fine in the end,' she finished, not wanting to make a fuss. Truth be told, after what she had discovered upstairs in the depot, what had happened before that had faded from the forefront of her mind. 'Mr Merivale and Mr Pratt said I could stay where I am.'

'I should think so too,' Mrs Beaumont declared.

Even though she had been furious at the time, Sally played down the incident. She had other fish to fry now.

Alone with Andrew in their bedroom, she told him about the room with all the bits and bobs in it.

'It sounds a regular Aladdin's cave,' he remarked. 'What did you do?'

'First of all, I telephoned the Town Hall and got through to Mr Overton.'

'Did you tell him?'

'Not as such,' said Sally. 'I just asked if anybody had ever been allowed to store their belongings in the depot. He said no. The depot was set up just before the war started and he was in charge of it from day one, so he should know.'

'Then where did it all come from?' Andrew asked. 'I have to say it doesn't sound above board.'

'I agree,' said Sally. 'I can only think that one of the delivery drivers has been taking advantage. The thing is, if it was one clock and one set of fire-irons and one set of cutlery, I'd think that whoever was responsible was just storing their own things, which would be understandable given how hard it can be to find suitable storage accommodation these days, though obviously they should have asked for permission. But it isn't just one of each thing. It's several. It isn't just the things from one house. It's a number of different houses.'

'Theft,' Andrew said softly.

'I'm afraid so,' said Sally.

'I hate to say it but there are people who go thieving during air raids or soon afterwards. I've even heard of men posing as ARP wardens to gain access to bomb-damaged houses so they can take their pick of what's there.'

Sally shivered. 'To think that one of our delivery men might be involved in something like that. It's horrible.'

'It's better than thinking it's one of the girls you work with,' said Andrew.

'Oh, it's neither of them,' Sally said at once. 'I trust them both, especially Betty.'

'What are you going to do?' Andrew asked.

'I ought to report it to the police.'

Andrew smiled. 'Do I hear a *but* in there?'

'I didn't say it downstairs,' answered Sally, 'but, when Mr Merivale and Mr Pratt gave me my job back, it was on the understanding that Mrs Lockwood is going to keep a close watch over me.'

'She was doing that anyway, wasn't she?'

'Yes, but it's official now. Before, she did it off her own bat, but now Mr Merivale and Mr Pratt want her to do it.' Sally waited a moment to order her thoughts before she continued. 'I'm considering not telling the police about the stolen goods – or at least not telling them just yet. What if I keep watch and see what happens? If I can solve this mystery and unveil the wrongdoer, it will show the powers that be that I am more than capable of running the depot without being under Mrs Lockwood's thumb. What d'you think?'

When Lorna came upon Sally and Betty talking, they both fell silent as she approached. This used to happen sometimes when she was new because her being Mrs Lockwood's lodger had led the other two to draw certain conclusions. But as they had realised that Lorna was her own person and not Mrs Lockwood's devoted follower, these instances of stopping talking had ceased.

But this morning, when it happened again, Lorna knew why. She decided to take the bull by the horns.

'I want you both to know that when I'm at Mrs Lockwood's house, I wouldn't repeat anything you say here in the depot.'

'You can't blame us for feeling iffy,' said Betty, 'not after what Mrs Lockwood did yesterday.'

'What exactly did you say to her about my family being bombed out?' Sally asked bluntly.

'That you'd lost your home,' Lorna replied. 'What else was there to say? I didn't know any more than that.' Then the real question behind Sally's words clicked into place. 'Look, I can assure you that I didn't utter a word to suggest that you'd gone to pieces, if that's what you're thinking.'

'There was no need for you to mention anything at all,' Betty said with a trace of stubbornness.

But Lorna wasn't having that. 'It was perfectly reasonable to mention it, Sally being a mutual acquaintance. I thought – well, actually, I didn't think about it, but if I had, I would have expected it to make Mrs Lockwood be nicer to you, Sally.'

Sally's nod showed she accepted this. Lorna looked at the others, realising how important their friendship was to her. She truly liked them and wanted them to accept her.

'I don't want to feel like piggy-in-the-middle between you and Mrs Lockwood, Sally,' she stated. 'It's not my fault where I was billeted.'

She kept it to herself, but maybe it was time for her to look for fresh digs. It wouldn't be easy, though, because priority was given to the bombed-out and to families. Besides, there was the danger that, if she were to stick her head above the parapet, her true identity might be revealed, and she couldn't let that happen.

She changed the subject. 'Never mind where I go home to. You two are now billeted together.' She laughed. 'You work together, fire-watch together and now you live together.'

'With Sally's family,' Betty added.

'It couldn't be better,' said Sally. 'We're true friends. Betty was one of my bridesmaids and I'm married to the best man in the world.'

Sally's eyes sparkled. Lorna didn't begrudge her the happiness but she couldn't suppress a sudden pang of longing. She pinned a smile on her face.

Sally continued, 'My parents originally said I couldn't get married until I turned twenty-one – in which case I'd still be waiting. Fortunately for me, they changed their minds. I've never been happier in my life than I have been since I got married, even though we're at war.'

'What's your husband like?' Lorna asked.

'He's a real family man,' said Sally, eager to describe the love of her life. 'He's very caring towards his mother. He's going to be a wonderful dad one day. He's kind and thoughtful and a very good listener. By trade he's a carpenter and joiner, but then he went to college and trained to be a teacher. He feels strongly about doing the best he can for the boys he teaches.'

'He followed his heart,' said Betty.

'Yes, he did.' There was no need for Sally to say how proud she was, because it was there in the warm tone of her voice and the light in her eyes.

Lorna turned to Betty. 'How about you and your chap? You mentioned that you'll be taking him to meet your family.'

'It's very much on the cards,' Betty said eagerly, 'but Eddie wants us to be a couple for longer first so my dad will see how serious we are.'

'Wedding bells?' Lorna asked.

'It's early days,' Betty said demurely.

Belatedly Lorna saw her mistake. By instigating a conversation about Sally's husband and Betty's boyfriend, had she opened the door to questions about George? She was sure the others would be too polite and considerate to press her, but even so it felt better to move things along.

'Mr Atkinson seems a nice sort of fellow,' she remarked.

'Oh, he is,' Betty agreed at once. 'He's civil and kind and he knows ever such a lot about books and all kinds of things. He had a very good education but he never makes me feel that he's better than I am.'

'I've always found him likeable,' Sally agreed, 'and he's good at what he does. Speaking of which,' she added lightly, 'it's time we stopped gossiping and started being good at what we do.'

The conversation about men and relationships had left Betty feeling all the more anxious to pin Eddie down. She finally admitted to herself how fed up she was of making out to Mrs Beaumont and Lorna, and especially to Sally, that everything was wonderful when really and truly 'wonderful' would only be achieved when she took Eddie home to meet Dad and Grace. She appreciated that Eddie only meant to be respectful by wanting them to be a properly established couple before he met her father, but surely what mattered most was that Dad could see how much they cared for one another? After all, Sally's parents had begun by wanting her to wait until she came of age before she got married, but then they had changed their minds and she and Andrew had tied the knot less than three months after they had first met, which just showed how successful and serious a whirlwind romance could be.

That evening at Star House, Betty was in the sitting room with Mrs Beaumont when the doorbell rang.

Betty got up. 'I'll go.'

'I hope it isn't the ARP warden to say we've got a light showing.'

In the hallway Betty switched off the light before pulling aside the long door-curtain and opening the door.

'Eddie! I wasn't expecting you.' Her heart gave a happy leap. 'Come in.'

'Can you come out here? Pop your coat on, there's a good girl.'

The coat-stand was beside her. Betty slipped on her coat and stepped outside, pulling the door to.

'I haven't got long,' said Eddie. 'I promised my nan I'd spend this evening with her.'

Betty caught her breath. 'I'm dying to meet her.' She gazed up at Eddie's handsome face, waiting for the invitation.

'Sorry, love,' he said. 'You know I'd ask you over if I could. It hurts me that I can't, but until you've introduced me to your dad and made it official... That's the way round it ought to be, see? The fella has to meet the girl's family first, then she can meet his. That's the respectable way.'

Betty dropped her shoulders, then hitched them up again,

not wanting Eddie to see her disappointment and feel upset. She smiled bravely. 'What brings you here?'

'Can you let me into the depot again and—'

'I'm not sure,' she put in quickly, her heart sinking. 'You keep bringing things.'

'Maybe I want to take summat away this time.'

She brightened. 'Do you?'

'One or two bits, yes, but I've also got more stuff in need of temporary shelter. This is a good thing we're doing, Betty. Helping folk. Storing their precious belongings. I thought you'd have a better understanding of that by now.'

'Well, of course—'

'Good. So you'll help me out again? There never was a girl like you, Betty Hughes. You're a jewel. I can rely on you every time. What a lucky bloke I am. Don't ever change, will you?'

For once, Betty wasn't charmed. 'When do you want access to the depot?'

'Now,' he said.

'Now?' It came out almost as a squeak. 'I thought you meant tomorrow or the next evening.'

'I've got the van parked along the road,' Eddie told her.

Betty huffed a sigh but she couldn't say no. Letting Eddie use the room in the depot brought them closer together. It was a kind of war work and they were doing their bit together. That meant the world to her.

'Hang on,' she said. 'I'll fetch my keys.'

Soon they were hurrying up the road to where the van was waiting. As they approached, the engine started up.

'Leon's driving,' said Eddie.

Betty swallowed her disappointment. She'd thought it would be just her and Eddie. He opened the door for her and she slid along the bench-seat, nodding a greeting to Leon.

At the depot she unlocked the door in the fence for her and Eddie to go inside and unbolt the gates to open them for the van, then closed them again at once. Leon climbed out and threw open the doors at the rear of the vehicle. Betty was dismayed to see how many items there were, but it was too late to say anything.

She unlocked the building and hurried upstairs to open the room. The two men carried the bulkier things while she brought in some smaller boxes that didn't have lids, giving her the chance for a quick glance at a brass table-lamp with a silk shade, a pewter candlestick, a shallow wooden box with a carved lid, a photograph frame, a pair of book-ends, a china pot with a lid, a chubby little vase with flowers painted on it, some horse-brasses and a toby jug. She set the boxes down close to where the men had put some larger boxes and a few items of furniture, including a footstool with a tapestried top, a side-table with legs twisted like barley-sugar, a pair of ladder-back chairs and a dainty chest-of-drawers with a curved front.

Seeing the precious articles from bombed-out houses always boosted Betty's confidence in what she was helping Eddie to do. Leon's presence seemed like a good thing too, because he was helping Eddie out of gratitude for the way Eddie had helped his mum. They were both assisting Eddie in his endeavours to support desperate people who needed help in a way they had never needed it before.

As promised, Eddie removed a couple of items, though Betty didn't see what they were because he put them inside a box.

'The owners will be glad to have them back,' said Betty.

Eddie placed the box in the back of the van. Leon climbed into the front. As the van pulled out onto Beech Road, Eddie and Betty shut and bolted the gates before leaving the yard by the door in the fence.

Betty had expected Leon to drive away, but no. The van was waiting a little further along the road.

'I'm sorry, love,' said Eddie. 'Leon's giving me a lift home. My nan's waiting for me.'

Betty gave him her most brilliant smile. She wasn't going to let him down by being fed up.

'Off you go,' she said cheerfully. 'Have a nice evening. Tell your nan I can't wait to meet her.'

CHAPTER TWENTY-ONE

Since Tuesday, when she had found the household items hoarded in the locked room upstairs, Sally had been watching the collection drivers closely – which made it sound as if she'd been doing it for ages. Today was only Thursday, which meant she had been aware of the stash for just forty-eight hours, but it felt far longer than that. Yesterday, and again this morning, she had quietly removed herself from the yard each time a van arrived. Slipping upstairs, she'd entered the room across the passage and hidden inside, listening hard and watching through a crack in the door, but no matter how vigilant she was, she hadn't seen anything happen. Nobody had crept up the stairs. Nobody had entered the room containing all the goods.

Should she have gone to the police as soon as she knew? When she and Andrew had formed the plan for her to perform her own investigation, they had imagined the culprit being unveiled more or less immediately.

Sally had just spent twenty minutes in the empty room across the landing and she was cold and anxious. How many more days would this take? Feeling a need to have another look in the locked room, she took her key-ring from her pocket and inserted the master-key into the lock.

As she went inside, she frowned. Something was... different. But there couldn't be anything different, because she had been on watch across the passage each time a van had pulled up outside the depot. She told herself she was imagining it, but she knew she wasn't.

Then it hit her. There were more things here than before. That corner over there to the right had previously been empty but now it was occupied. Sally walked across, her footsteps sounding loud. She scanned what was on show. As well as some pieces of furniture, there were boxes. Some had lids, some didn't. She could see a pair of book-ends, some horse-brasses and a table-lamp with a shade. The sight of a pretty vase decorated with flowers brought a feeling of nostalgia: Mrs Henshaw had owned one just like it.

And then – and then – her insides turned to ice. A wooden cigarette-box with a carved pattern of swirls across the lid. One of a kind. Made by Andrew's late father.

For a few moments Sally battled with a feeling of light-headedness. Then she dropped to her knees and picked up the box. Placing it on the floor, she started removing other things. An ornamental plate – Mrs Henshaw's. A photograph frame. The picture had been removed but – oh, it had been of her and Andrew on their wedding day. Wrapped up in a piece of cloth was the Henshaws' bone-handled cutlery, along with a honey-spoon that had been a wedding gift to Sally and Andrew from one of the neighbours in Withington.

Sally remembered being pleased that the neighbours had given practical presents, including a pair of pillowcases, cotton reels with useful colours and a darning-mushroom. It was much better than being given fripperies.

'You wait,' Mum had said. 'If this war goes on as long as the last one, that honey-spoon will be a frippery and young couples will be grateful for a tin of tuna or a flour-sieve.'

Distress flooded through Sally. When she had found this stash two days ago she'd known these must be stolen goods, but she hadn't really confronted that knowledge, not properly. She confronted it now, though. Someone had looted bomb-damaged houses. A horrible sense of intrusion wound its way around her heart. Their home had been *invaded*. Not by Jerry, not by the enemy, but by someone who was home-grown. That made it worse.

She thought of the missing ration books, which Mrs Henshaw thought had been carried away by the blast, but that wasn't what had happened. They'd been pinched. Easy pickings for a dirty sneak-thief.

A huge ball of emotion welled up in her chest, a potent tangle of anger and pain. How was she going to break the news to Andrew and his mother? Mrs Henshaw would be deeply hurt.

All at once Sally couldn't bear to stay there a minute longer. She ached to grab all the Henshaw possessions and take them with her. She had to force herself to leave them behind. She locked up and went downstairs.

Outside, the van was leaving and Betty and Lorna were heading back towards the building. Sally called to them from the doorway.

'Could you come into my office, please? Both of you.'

Sally sat behind her desk, trying to be calm even though her thoughts and emotions were churning. Because they'd been using the office as their staffroom, there were already chairs in there for Betty and Lorna.

'Sit down,' Sally said as they entered.

'Has something happened?' Betty asked.

'You look serious,' Lorna added.

'You look upset,' said Betty.

'I'm both,' said Sally. 'I've got something important to tell you and then I'll take you upstairs so you can see for yourselves. Somebody – one of the drivers – is using the depot to store household items and small pieces of furniture. I found them locked away in one of the rooms.'

Lorna frowned, puzzled. Betty's creamy-smooth complexion paled.

'Do you understand what I'm saying?' asked Sally. 'These are stolen goods.'

'No, they're not!' Betty burst out. 'I promise they're not. They all belong to folk who have been bombed out.'

Sally and Lorna stared at her but she seemed too distracted to notice. Her fingers twined together and her blue eyes were over-bright.

'I can explain,' said Betty. 'Oh, I wish I'd never agreed to it, but Eddie said...' Her voice trailed away.

'Eddie said what?' Sally asked.

'I don't want to put the blame on him. This is just as much my doing. I wish I'd never said yes.'

'Stop rambling and tell us,' said Lorna.

'Those things upstairs aren't stolen,' said Betty. 'They belong to people who've lost their homes. You know how diffi-cult it is these days to find a storage place with any space to spare. So Eddie asked if he could help out some people by keeping their things here.' She directed a pained stare at Sally. 'He didn't want me to ask you in case you said no.'

Betty stopped but Sally didn't say anything. It was Eddie. Handsome, cheery Eddie whom Betty adored. Eddie!

Probably feeling forced into it by Sally's silence, Betty carried on. 'I'm so sorry, Sally. I know it was taking advantage, but honestly, there's no harm in it, and it's only temporary. I'll tell Eddie he's got to take everything away.'

Sally fought to maintain her composure. No harm? The

harm that had been inflicted on her own family boiled up inside her.

'Sally?' Lorna prompted. 'If Betty arranges for everything to be removed...?'

Sally gazed at Betty and her heart broke for her. Betty was such a lovely girl, kind, good-natured and without an ounce of guile. They had become dear friends and Sally had been happy and proud to have Betty as one of her bridesmaids.

'I just want to make things right,' Betty whispered.

'I'm sorry, Betty,' said Sally, 'but it isn't that simple. When I said the things upstairs had been stolen, I knew what I was talking about because some of them belong to my family.'

'No!' Lorna exclaimed.

Betty's mouth dropped open but no sound emerged.

'They must have been taken from our house at some point before the wardens came to check it was safe to enter,' said Sally. 'They might have been stolen during the night – during the raid itself.'

Betty found her voice. 'No,' she declared with surprising firmness. 'You're wrong. You're mistaken. There might be things up there that look like yours, but they're someone else's. They just came from the same shop. My mum got me a christening mug and the girl up the road had the exact same one because we're the same age and our mothers went to the same shop.'

'Andrew's father was a master cabinetmaker,' Sally said quietly. 'Everything he made was designed and built for a particular customer. When he made something for his own home, it was different to anything he sold. There's a cigarette-box upstairs that he made. I saw it every single day after I moved in with Andrew and his mother.'

'No...' breathed Betty.

'But that means that Eddie...' Lorna looked at Betty and let the sentence fade away.

'That's exactly what it means,' said Sally. 'I'm sorry, Betty, but you have to face up to this. I know how hard it must be.'

'There must be another explanation,' said Betty. 'There has to be.'

'Such as...?' asked Lorna.

'I don't know,' Betty burst out. 'Eddie has a friend. Leon Hargreaves – he helped bring things here. Maybe it's him. Yes, that's it. Eddie is busy helping people, not knowing his friend is really a thief.'

Lorna reached out and touched Betty's arm. 'Betty, sweetheart, listen to yourself. You're clutching at straws. The truth is, your chap is a bad lot.'

'But we're *engaged*,' wailed Betty. 'It's not official but...' A violent shiver rippled through her and she wrapped her arms round herself. 'He said all that just to make me – just because it was what I wanted to hear, didn't he?'

Sally came round the desk and hugged her friend. At first Betty went stiff but then she yielded, leaning against Sally and starting to sob.

Lorna stood up. 'I'll put the kettle on.'

Presently they were drinking tea, Betty spluttering a little.

'Do you think it was all lies, all those lovely things Eddie said to me?'

'We can't possibly know the answer to that,' Lorna said sensibly. 'Maybe some of it was true but it doesn't really matter if it was or not, not after the way he has led you into harbouring stolen goods.'

'I'll have to tell the police now,' Sally said soberly.

'I know.' Betty sounded utterly ground down.

'Wait a mo,' said Lorna. 'If you tell the police – and Betty is the one who gave the thieves access to the depot – well, it doesn't look good for her, does it?'

Sally groaned. The last thing she wanted was to land Betty

in trouble. Seeing how pale Betty looked now was all it took for her to make up her mind.

'The reason I didn't go to the police in the first place was so that I could do my own investigation and make myself look good at the Town Hall. That was going to be for my benefit. Now I want to do something for Betty's benefit. Before we get the police involved, we need to come up with a way of unmasking Eddie that will show Betty in a good light.'

To Betty the rest of the day felt like a dream. A dream? No, a nightmare. Eddie, who had made her heart beat faster simply by being nearby, was a thief. She had held out against Sally for as long as she could but, when Sally had mentioned the cigarette-box made by Andrew's father, Betty had known she had no choice but to believe her.

Sally had taken Lorna to see the stolen goods. Betty hadn't wanted to go but had found herself trailing in their wake. Maybe Sally would take another look at the cigarette-box and slap her forehead, exclaiming, 'How could I have been so stupid? This is nothing like our box.' But of course that hadn't happened.

No, it was all too real. Pain swamped Betty.

'I believed every word he said.'

'That's because you're so trusting,' said Sally.

'That's the wrong word,' said Betty. 'I'm stupid and gullible.'

Oh, and Eddie had traded on it right from the start. All those nice things he'd said hadn't been flattery. They'd been a load of flannel – and she'd fallen for it.

And she might have fallen for a lot more than his silver-tongued words as well. The memory of how he had done his best to tempt her into bed made her go hot and cold all over with shame. Thank goodness she had turned him down. If she hadn't, she would be damaged goods now. You heard about girls like that.

All Eddie had wanted all along was a way of getting into the depot. She could see that now. She remembered the air raid when they had sheltered in the depot's cellar and she had mentioned that plenty of the rooms were standing empty. If she hadn't told him that, would she ever have seen him again? Humiliation slowed her heart and squeezed her ribs. What a fool she had been.

Her heart, which had pitter-pattered so many times in happy anticipation since she'd become Eddie's girl, now felt sore and heavy. She kept sighing. It brought no relief, but it was as if her body simply couldn't stop doing it. Many times during that long afternoon and endless evening, Betty found herself drawing in a long breath, her chest slowly expanding as she did so. She held the air inside her for a long moment and then gradually released it in a soft, lingering breath.

She'd been a prize idiot. She had trusted Eddie implicitly and he had been using her all along.

She, Sally and Lorna had come up with a plan – well, she hadn't, not her personally. She had hardly been capable of thinking straight at that point. But the other two, after some discussion, had decided on what must happen next.

'No!' Betty had exclaimed. 'I'm not doing that. I can't,' she added wretchedly. 'I don't want to see him ever again.'

'You have to,' Lorna said gently. 'It's the only way. You must see that.'

Betty nodded miserably.

'It'll be worth it,' Sally promised. 'It will prove to the police that Eddie is a thief and your part in unmasking him will show that you're innocent.'

Betty made an effort to pull herself together. Sally was right.

'I'll nip across to the police station,' said Sally, 'and ask Sergeant Robbins to come here.'

'Shouldn't we go over there to talk to him?' Lorna asked.

'I think not,' Sally answered. 'If we go there, it looks like we're asking for help – which we are, of course – but if we invite Sergeant Robbins to come here, then we're taking the initiative. We've thought up a plan to collar Eddie and we've brought the sergeant here to discuss it. It will look better.'

The glance she sent Betty showed exactly what she meant. It would look better for Betty.

She hadn't met Sergeant Robbins before, though she knew him by sight. She looked at him with fresh eyes when he came to the depot. He was the same sort of age as Dad. Betty tried to decide if his brown eyes were kind. But even if they were kind now, they were bound to harden when he realised why he was here.

He listened attentively, then exclaimed, 'Eddie Markham!'

'Do you know of him?' Lorna asked.

'I'll say we do. He's been in and out of trouble all his life. Why do you imagine he isn't fighting for his country?'

'Flat feet,' Betty said at once.

'Flat feet, my eye,' scoffed Sergeant Robbins. 'I'm willing to bet he paid an unscrupulous doctor to write him a medical exemption so he could dodge being called up.'

Disgust and sorrow wrapped around one another inside Betty's stomach. She had believed every word that had come out of Eddie's mouth.

'There is another man involved as well,' said Sally. 'His name is Leon Hargreaves. That's right, isn't it?' She looked at Betty, who nodded.

The policeman frowned and shook his head. 'I don't know the name. He must be new to this game.' He gave Betty a stern look. 'What can you tell me about him?'

'Nothing. Only that he owns a van.'

'What type?'

'I don't know.' Betty was forced to admit. As soon as she'd learned it wasn't Eddie's, she had lost interest in it.

'What does this Leon Hargreaves look like?' asked Sergeant Robbins.

Betty floundered. 'Late twenties, early thirties. Well-built.'

'Hair colour? Eye colour?'

'I don't know. I only saw him a couple of times, both times in the blackout, and I was more worried about the depot being used than I was about what Eddie's mate looked like.' Something occurred to her. 'When Eddie brought the first lot of stuff here, he said it belonged to Leon's mum. If that was true, then maybe Leon helped Eddie afterwards out of gratitude. Maybe he isn't a thief at all.'

'You mean maybe he's innocent, the same as you?' asked Sergeant Robbins.

Betty looked at him quickly but his face didn't give away what he thought of that.

Sally showed the sergeant upstairs so he could see the stolen goods. When they came back down, the police officer's expression was set hard.

'There ought to be a special place in hell for villains who take advantage of the war,' he said. 'Looting is a horrible crime, coming as it does on top of people losing their homes.'

'Our plan is this,' Sally explained. 'This evening Miss Hughes will tell Eddie Markham that the room he is currently using is needed for another purpose and so he has got to move everything immediately. She'll say it has to be done tomorrow evening – Friday – because the room is needed on Saturday.'

'In a building with plenty of empty rooms, why would that room in particular be needed?' asked Sergeant Robbins, obviously believing he had found a fatal flaw.

'We've thought of that,' Lorna replied. 'Miss Hughes will say there's a backlog at the paper-mill and so we're going to store masses of waste paper, so you see, it won't be just that one room that is supposedly going to be required.'

Betty felt she ought to say something instead of sitting there looking like the idiot she knew herself to be. 'I'll say the waste paper is due to arrive on Saturday morning.'

'For the record,' said the sergeant, 'I am not at all pleased at the way you have taken this matter into your own hands. Having said that, it seems a good enough sort of plan.' He posed some further questions and then issued instructions. 'I cannot stress how important this is, Miss Hughes. When you let Markham into the depot tomorrow evening, you must hang back and let him take the lead. Hand the key to him. If he goes straight upstairs and unlocks that room, it will prove he knows the whereabouts of the stolen goods.'

An unexpected flash of anger scorched Betty. In that moment she hated Eddie. Wasn't it enough that he had broken her heart? But no, she now had to go through with this wretched charade as well. Not only that but she had to behave exactly as normal, exactly as Eddie would expect. Her skin crawled. She would have to let him kiss her if he felt like it, and she would have to kiss him back. For a moment she was overwhelmed by resentment and disgust.

But she would have to face it. It was the only way.

CHAPTER TWENTY-TWO

On Friday morning, heavy rain-clouds formed thick smears that clotted the low-lying grey skies. That just about summed up the way Betty felt.

Yesterday evening with Eddie had been horrible in all sorts of ways. She never wanted to set eyes on him again, but she had been obliged to let him hold her and kiss her even though his embrace had felt like a kind of violation. When she had got home, she'd run upstairs to her room and locked herself in. Sitting on her bed, she had rocked herself forwards and backwards, clutching her pillow tight and using it to muffle her heart-rending sobs. Sally had knocked softly and called to her but Betty had ignored her. She couldn't bear to be with anybody else just then. She couldn't even bear to be with herself.

Now here she was at the depot, desperate for today to be over but at the same time dreading what the evening would bring. Eddie had believed her story about the waste paper that was going to be stored here. Well, why wouldn't he? As far as he was concerned, she was the adoring twerp who would do anything he asked.

'Friday the thirteenth,' Lorna remarked. 'Very appropriate.'

'Don't make light of it,' snapped Betty.

'I wasn't and I apologise if it seemed that I was. I just want it to be finished so that you can start to put it behind you.'

'That's what we all want,' said Sally.

Betty closed her eyes. To have it all behind her: yes. She longed for that more than anything.

First of all, though, she had to get through the whole of today. It felt strange having to spend the time performing her duties as usual. She was back to feeling as if she was in a dream. Lorna and Sally hovered close by, keeping an eye on her, occasionally asking if she was all right.

'If you want to vanish into the office for a while and be on your own,' Sally offered, 'that's fine.'

'Thanks, but I'd rather keep busy.' Betty was touched by her friend's kindness. 'Time to think is the last thing I need.'

'For what it's worth,' said Lorna, 'being busy has helped me through the last few weeks – even though salvage work isn't my favourite thing,' she added with a rueful smile.

Glad to have her attention diverted from her own concerns, Betty asked, 'Do you still hate being here?'

'Actually, no,' said Lorna. 'I've got used to the job – and the company isn't bad either.'

Sally pretended to slap her arm. 'Less of your cheek, madam,' she teased.

The light-hearted moment gave Betty's spirits a boost, but nothing could make her feel better for long. A heavy weight had lodged itself inside her chest and she knew it wasn't going to go away until Eddie was removed from the premises in handcuffs.

In some ways the day dragged by, in others it simply flew. The one bright spot came when Samuel arrived unexpectedly with a box of books for salvage.

After he had greeted them, he explained, 'I d-decided not to let the shop's s-salvage pile grow to the extent that I needed to use a van to bring it here, like last time. One box at a time is much more manageable.'

'Bring the box and I'll show you where to put it,' said Sally.

When Samuel followed her, Betty longed to go with them. Samuel was a good friend and she yearned for the opportunity to lean on him, but it was safer to keep her distance.

When he came back, he said his goodbyes, smiling at the three of them. He had such a kind smile. Betty knew the smile wasn't for her alone, but even so it helped her. It steadied her.

At last it was time to lock up and go home.

'Good luck,' Lorna said quietly to Betty before they parted.

Betty nodded. Sergeant Robbins had tried to order Sally and Lorna to keep well away from the depot tonight but they had refused point-blank, insisting that Betty would need them once her ordeal was over. A disgruntled Sergeant Robbins had finally said that they could wait in the office with the light off as long as they got there before half past seven, well over an hour before Betty was due to admit Eddie.

At home in Star House, Sally sent Betty a glance across the table, encouraging her to eat. It was the last thing Betty felt like doing but she forced herself. Mrs Beaumont had already remarked that she looked peaky.

'Are you feeling quite the thing, Betty?'

'Yes, thank you,' she had replied, not meeting her landlady's eyes.

'She does look pale, doesn't she?' said Mrs Henshaw.

'Mum,' said Andrew, 'don't talk about Betty as if she's not here.'

'Sorry, dear,' said Mrs Henshaw. Betty was still getting the measure of Sally's mother-in-law. She looked stern sometimes – austere, Sally called it – but when she smiled, her features softened and showed her kindness.

At the end of the meal, there was the daily tug-of-war between Mrs Beaumont and Mrs Henshaw about clearing the table and doing the washing up. Mrs Henshaw was determined to help and Mrs Beaumont was equally determined to attend to all domestic matters herself. As she said, it was her job as landlady.

Not long afterwards Andrew went out to a training evening for all the light rescue squads.

'Does he know what's happening at the depot this evening?' Betty asked Sally.

'Yes. I wouldn't keep a secret from him. He's kicking himself because he had no choice but to go out tonight. Otherwise he would probably have insisted on hiding in the office with Lorna and me.'

'That wouldn't have pleased Sergeant Robbins,' said Betty.

Sally gave a sudden smile. 'Let's hope Lorna doesn't let it slip to Mrs Lockwood or she'll be in there as well.'

'She'd probably rugby-tackle Eddie to the ground,' said Betty.

Both girls giggled, then tears sprang into Betty's eyes, blurring her vision.

'I'm sorry this has happened to you,' Sally said gently. 'You were so happy and it's all come crashing down.'

Emotion built up inside Betty and she had to turn away. It was lovely of Sally to be so kind, but nothing would make Betty feel like less of a fool.

Presently it was time for Sally to set off for the depot.

'I've told Andrew's mother and Mrs Beaumont that I'm meeting a teacher to talk about school involvement in collecting salvage,' she said to Betty. 'Be brave. It'll soon be over.'

Betty felt as if her insides were quivering. She tried to fix her thoughts on afterwards, on Eddie being led away by the police and herself being free of this nightmare. But the sour taste of dread filled her mouth at the thought of having to live through the coming scene first.

. . .

As Betty opened the front door of Star House to him, Eddie
blew a stream of smoke over his shoulder and stubbed out his
cigarette on the wall, dropping the cigarette-end on Mrs Beaumont's garden path. Betty had put on her hat and coat, scarf and
gloves ages ago, wanting to be ready when he arrived. She
seized her handbag and her gas-mask box and slipped through
the door, pulling it shut behind her.

Turning, she found herself face to face with Eddie. She was
standing on the step, which brought her almost to his height.
When he angled his face to kiss her, she ducked away before
she could stop herself, then tried to hide it by darting
round him.

His laugh sounded surprised. 'That's not very friendly.'

'Not right in front of the door, Eddie.' From somewhere she
conjured up a voice that was half-chiding and half-loving. 'Not
on the step.'

'How about by the garden gate?'

He tried to catch her arm but she evaded him, scurrying
onto the pavement. She slid her hand through the crook of his
arm and started walking up Wilton Road.

'You know what they say. *Never kiss by the garden gate.
Love is blind but the neighbours ain't.* You've heard that one,
haven't you, Eddie?'

'Can't say I have.'

He didn't sound amused any longer and Betty knew that, if
he made another attempt, she would have to submit. She
desperately didn't want to have to kiss him again, not after last
night, not after the way it had made her feel.

'I'm sorry about having to move the things at the depot,' she
said.

'Yeah, so you said yesterday.'

'It's lucky I heard about the room being needed for the
paper. If I hadn't...'

'You're a good girl, Betty.' Warmth returned to Eddie's

voice. 'I don't know what I'd do without you. You're the best girl a bloke could have. There's a lot of folk with reason to be grateful to you. Me most of all.'

Alarm streaked through Betty. Was he about to reward her with a kiss? But he simply used his arm to press her hand against him as they carried on walking.

At the depot, Betty unlocked the door in the fence and then locked it behind them. She was tinglingly aware that, from now on, their every movement would be closely watched. She wanted to peer into the darkest corners of the yard but she had to behave exactly as normal.

She unlocked the front door to the building and pushed it open.

'Drat,' she said. 'I've got a stone in my shoe. Here, take these.' She thrust the key-ring at Eddie, holding up the correct key. 'You go ahead. I'll be there in a minute.'

Guided by torchlight, Eddie walked away, leaving Betty ready to slump against the door-frame in relief, but she couldn't afford any such luxury. She had been told to behave normally and that meant following Eddie up the stairs. He mustn't have any reason to become suspicious. As if he'd ever be suspicious of her! Stupid Betty, who hung on his every word.

She let him get halfway upstairs, then followed, calling out, 'I'm coming.'

Her mouth was dry as she started up the staircase. The air was cold but her skin felt colder.

As she reached the landing, she heard the click as Eddie unlocked the door. As he went inside, Sergeant Robbins emerged from the shadows near the top of the staircase, putting his finger to his lips before indicating with a movement of his chin that Betty should move in the opposite direction to keep out of the way. She was more than glad to do so.

After that things happened so quickly that, even though Betty was expecting it, it still alarmed her. One moment, the passage was still, dark and silent; the next, there were loud shouts, people everywhere with clattering footsteps, beams of torchlight darting hither and thither, the sounds of a scuffle, some crashes as stolen goods went flying.

Then Eddie was marched out of the room in handcuffs, flanked by a copper on either side, each of them gripping one of his elbows. Betty's heart thumped. She wanted to step forward so Eddie could see her and realise how she had tricked him, but a firm hand on her arm warned her not to move.

Sergeant Robbins stepped in front of Eddie. 'I'm placing you under arrest for theft, specifically for looting bomb-damaged properties. You'll find that the courts take a dim view of that. You are further accused of concealing stolen goods, and my investigations today also show that you have sold stolen goods. Take him over the road,' he ordered the two policemen.

Betty pressed a hand to her heart. It was over. Tears sprang into her eyes.

'Thank you, Miss Hughes,' said Sergeant Robbins. 'You've been very helpful.'

He extended a hand, indicating that she should precede him down the stairs. When they reached the bottom, Sally and Lorna appeared, smiles all over their faces, but before they could rush to hug Betty, Sergeant Robbins inserted himself between them and her.

'I'd like you to accompany me to the police station, Miss Hughes,' he said in a formal voice. His expression was formal too, with no sign of kindness or gratitude for the assistance she had provided. 'I'd like you to help me with my enquiries.'

'But I already told you everything I know,' Betty protested.

'Ah, but have you? You see, I know a thing or two about you, Miss Hughes. For instance, I know that you aren't averse to breaking the law yourself. I know all about the magistrate's fine you received for selling goods in defiance of the food rationing regulations.'

There was a gasp from close by and a quick glance showed Betty that Sally was pale and wide-eyed.

'I'm not placing you under arrest *at this stage*,' Sergeant Robbins said, putting meaningful emphasis on the final words, 'but if you decline to accompany me to the station for questioning, I will be obliged to arrest you. Which is it to be, Miss Hughes?'

The room was small and plain with no windows. There was a scuffed table in the middle with a wooden chair on either side. The air was stale with old tobacco. Betty had been left sitting here for what felt like ages. Dread rolled around in the depths of her stomach. What was going on? The whole point of the girls coming up with a plan to capture Eddie red-handed, and telling the police in advance, had been to show that Betty was the innocent party, but that didn't seem to have been the outcome at all. She wished she had never listened to Eddie.

And what about Dad? What if word got back to him that she had been taken to a police station because she was under suspicion? He would be heartbroken. So much for the wonderful new boyfriend Betty had been so anxious for him to meet.

Tears welled up but Betty forced them down, and not a moment too soon, because the door opened and in walked Sergeant Robbins followed by a constable. The sergeant sat down opposite Betty while the constable, having shut the door, stood beside it as if Betty might be expected to make a dash for freedom.

Sergeant Robbins fired some questions at her. Betty answered them honestly but he didn't give her any time to think.

'We were trying to help you,' she said desperately. 'We were the ones who came up with the idea of how to unmask Eddie.

We came to you with the plan. We told you all about what Eddie had done.'

Sergeant Robbins eyed her thoughtfully. 'Interesting use of the word "we". Are you implicating Mrs Henshaw and Miss Sadler in the thefts?'

Betty gawped at him for a moment. 'Of course not. You know I'm not.' Was he trying to trip her up on purpose?

'So it was just you and Eddie Markham.'

'It wasn't *me* at all,' Betty insisted. 'Eddie lied to me. I believed all those things came from bombed-out houses.'

'And you were right to believe it because that's exactly where they came from.'

'But I didn't know that they were stolen,' said Betty. 'Eddie told me he was helping people by providing storage.'

'And you believed him?'

Although she felt like curling up in a ball of shame, Betty lifted her chin. 'Yes, I did. He said a lot of things that I believed – including that we were going to get married.'

Was that a flash of sympathy that crossed the sergeant's face? Or contempt?

'You tell a convincing tale, Miss Hughes,' he said in a neutral voice.

Betty didn't dare feel relieved. She would save that for when she walked out of here a free woman.

'Do you want to do yourself a good turn, Miss Hughes?' asked the sergeant. 'You know all about what was kept at the depot—'

'Because Eddie lied to me about the things he wanted to store there,' Betty put in quickly.

'If you say so,' Sergeant Robbins said calmly. 'Where else did he store things for his friends and neighbours?'

'You what?' The question took Betty by surprise.

'Let's say for the sake of argument that he did indeed pull the wool over your eyes about his use of the salvage depot.

What I want to know is: where else has he got things tucked away?'

That had never crossed Betty's mind. Nor had it come up when she'd talked things over with Sally and Lorna.

'I don't know,' she said. 'Nowhere. Just the depot.'

'Are you sure about that?' the sergeant asked.

'Positive.'

'So he never took you anywhere else?'

'He took me to the pictures,' said Betty. 'He took me out dancing. He took me for walks.'

'Now then, don't get clever with me, miss.'

'I'm not,' said Betty. Then she remembered. 'The only other place he took me to was his nan's house in Fallowfield.'

'Oh aye?' Sergeant Robbins lifted an eyebrow at her. 'First off, Eddie Markham doesn't live in Fallowfield. And second, he doesn't have a nan. If he did, he'd have sold her. Isn't that right, Constable Collins?'

'Yes, sir,' agreed the young copper.

'But I went to their house,' Betty protested.

'So you're telling me that you visited the house Eddie Markham doesn't live in with the nan he hasn't got?'

Betty knew the sergeant was poking fun at her but she didn't care. All she could think was that Eddie had deceived her even more than she'd realised. The room where he'd been born. The very bed in which his mother had given birth. It was all a pack of lies. And that had been the occasion when he'd done his best to get her into bed. She felt ill.

'Can you provide the address?' Sergeant Robbins asked.

'I don't know it,' Betty whispered.

'Very convenient.'

'I'm telling the truth,' she said.

'How about the name of the road?'

'I don't know. It was dark – but there was a corner shop.'

'That's a big help,' Sergeant Robbins said drily, 'being as there's only one corner shop in the whole of Fallowfield.'

'We got off the bus outside the cinema,' said Betty, 'and then we went down a road on the left – not the first on the left; the second or maybe the third. This corner shop was a grocer's and it had a big display in the window but Eddie said all the boxes were empty.'

'I see,' said Sergeant Robbins.

If Betty had imagined him jumping up and dashing from the room in search of the shop, or even ordering the constable guarding the door to find it, she was disappointed.

'You have to admit your story sounds pretty vague, Miss Hughes,' said the sergeant.

Betty didn't know what to say to that.

'Eddie Markham, on the other hand,' the sergeant went on, 'has been specific about one or two things.'

'Has he given you information?' Betty sat up straighter. Oh, if Eddie had come clean, this ordeal would soon be over!

'Tell me about the debt you owe to your father, Miss Hughes.'

Betty felt as if cold water had been poured over her. 'How do you know about that?'

'You don't deny you owe your father a considerable sum.'

'It's the magistrate's fine,' Betty said resignedly. 'Not just the one I was given but the one my old boss, Mr Tucker, was given too.'

'Because of you selling food you had no business selling?'

'Mr Tucker had to pay both fines before we were allowed to leave the court. Then my father had to reimburse him. Mr Tucker's fine was my fault, so...'

'That must have been a lot of money,' said Sergeant Robbins.

'It was. My fine was two pounds and Mr Tucker's was five guineas.'

The young constable let out a whistle that he quickly cut off when Sergeant Robbins turned a stony face in his direction.

'Mr Tucker had kept back my week's wages to put towards the fine, but that still left six pounds for Dad to pay back to him.' Tears filled Betty's eyes. It was a huge sum for an ordinary working man to part with. Dad had had to plunder his savings.

'And now you have to pay it back to your father,' said Sergeant Robbins.

'I put by a bit each week. It'll take for ever but I'm going to pay it back, every penny.'

The sergeant nodded. 'Except that you got tired of it taking for ever, didn't you?'

Betty looked at him. 'What do you mean?'

'Eddie Markham says that it was your idea to use the depot. In fact, it was your idea to do the thieving. He says it was all your idea because it was going to clear your debt for you.'

Lorna knew it was up to her to take charge. She was every bit as stunned as Sally by the sight of Betty being carted off to the police station, but Sally's shock was all the deeper because she was the one who had told Sergeant Robbins about Betty being up before the magistrate.

'She made a mistake and that was her fault,' said Lorna after Sally had explained, 'but that doesn't make her a master criminal. Sergeant Robbins will see that.'

But all Sally could think about was her own part in it. 'If only I'd kept my mouth shut. There was no need for me to tell him but somehow my tongue ran away with me.'

'I expect he's good at getting people to tell him things,' said Lorna. 'It's part of his job.'

'Even so,' said Sally. 'As soon as I'd said it, I wished I hadn't.'

Lorna could see this conversation would go round in circles

if she didn't put a stop to it. 'We have to find a way to help Betty.'

'I think she might say she's had enough "help" from me.'

'I realise you feel bad,' said Lorna, 'but you have to set that aside for now. We have to concentrate on Betty.'

'We should go to the police station and ask to see her,' said Sally. 'No, we'll ask for Sergeant Robbins. He listened to us yesterday.'

'He humoured us yesterday,' Lorna said soberly. 'I don't think appealing to him is going to do any good. He wasn't best pleased with us yesterday for taking matters into our own hands and coming up with a plan, and I don't think he'd thank us for interrupting him now.'

'Then what should we do?' Sally asked.

'He's like my father,' said Lorna. 'Not on the surface. My father is loud and bombastic and Sergeant Robbins couldn't be more different. What they have in common is that they think women and girls need to be protected and looked after because we aren't clever enough to do things for ourselves.'

'My father is the same at heart,' said Sally. 'He lets my mum make the decisions but when he puts his foot down, that's it.'

'Sergeant Robbins isn't going to listen to us,' said Lorna, 'but he might listen to a man.'

'Andrew's out at a training event,' said Sally.

'It wasn't him I was thinking of,' said Lorna. 'It was Samuel Atkinson. He's a decent sort. I bet he'd help.'

'He's sweet on Betty,' said Sally. 'He asked me if I thought he stood a chance, but she'd started going out with Eddie.'

'There you are, then,' said Lorna, pleased. 'He's bound to help us. Let's go to his bookshop and bang on the door.'

'We'd better get a move on,' said Sally. 'He's an ARP warden. If he's on duty tonight, we need to catch him before he goes out.'

Lorna smiled at her. 'What are we waiting for?'

CHAPTER TWENTY-THREE

Betty had been left alone to stew in the windowless room for – she checked her wristwatch yet again – over an hour. Was Sergeant Robbins interviewing Eddie again? And was Eddie telling more lies about her? Betty's hands went clammy as fear rippled through her at the thought of how Eddie had turned on her. Would the police believe him rather than her? She wished she had never confided in him about the debt she was determined to repay.

And Dad – what would he make of all this? It was bad enough when she had been taken to the police station for questioning, but now Sergeant Robbins was treating her as Eddie's accomplice. Dad would be dreadfully upset. Betty didn't kid herself that he wouldn't get to hear about it. Even though Chorlton and Salford were some miles apart, word spread quickly on the police grapevine. Keeping in touch with other police stations was part of the job. Sergeant Robbins would want to know if Eddie's name was known in other places and it was inevitable that Betty's name would get passed around too.

Not that Dad would believe such a bad thing about her for a single moment. Of course he wouldn't. But then, he would never have believed that she would wrongly sell rationed butter... until she had done it. And goodness alone knew what Grace was going to say, what morsels of so-called concern she was going to drip into Dad's ear.

The door opened, jolting Betty from her reverie. She expected it to be Sergeant Robbins again, but instead in walked—

'Samuel!' she exclaimed, surprise jolting his first name out of her.

'Miss Hughes.'

He stopped on the other side of the table. He looked so concerned for her that she almost came to her feet, but Sergeant Robbins followed Samuel into the room, bringing her sharply to her senses.

'I wouldn't normally permit this,' said the sergeant, 'but Mr Atkinson has a solid reputation locally and he says you have worked at his shop.'

'Miss Hughes has been assisting with a branch of my w-war work,' said Samuel, 'and most c-competently, I might add.'

Sergeant Robbins raised an eyebrow but made no reply to this. All he said was, 'You can have two minutes.'

'Surely a little longer,' said Samuel.

'Two minutes,' said the sergeant and left the room.

'How did you know I was here?' Betty asked.

'Mrs Henshaw and Miss S-Sadler came to s-see me. They told me everything.'

Heat poured into Betty's cheeks. She hated to think of Samuel knowing what an idiot she had been. His good opinion had been important to her from the start.

'I c-came immediately,' said Samuel.

'Thank you,' said Betty. 'I can't tell you how much that means to me. Did you say Sally and Lorna came to see you? I wonder what made them do that – but I'm very glad they did.'

'S-so am I. They w-wanted to see you for themselves but they thought I'd s-stand a better chance.'

'And they were right,' Betty said gratefully.

Was he here just because the others had asked for his help? Betty couldn't come up with the right words to ask. Besides, what if the answer was 'Yes'?

The door opened again and Sergeant Robbins appeared.

Samuel leaned across the table. 'I w-want to help you, Miss Hughes.'

'Time's up,' said the sergeant. 'You must leave now, Mr Atkinson.'

'S-so soon?' asked Samuel.

Annoyance flickered across the sergeant's face, though it didn't show in his voice. 'I've already stretched a point by allowing you in at all.'

Samuel nodded. Looking at Betty, he held out his right hand and she slipped hers into it. His hand folded itself round hers as he shook it. Instead of letting go, he kept it in his firm, gentle grasp. 'Goodbye, Miss Hughes, but it's only goodbye f-for now. Please try not to be f-frightened. You have f-friends on your side. I promise I'll d-do everything I can to help.'

Betty struggled for the words to express her gratitude, but Sergeant Robbins made an impatient movement.

'I believe in you,' Samuel whispered as if they were the only two there, then he let go of her hand and left the room.

Betty had no time to dwell on his words, because Sergeant Robbins spoke the moment the door shut.

'I am now going to escort you home, Miss Hughes.'

'Home?' Betty flopped back in her seat in relief. 'You mean I'm free to go?'

'Not entirely,' said Sergeant Robbins. 'You aren't under arrest, Miss Hughes, but that does not mean I am no longer interested in you. I am placing you under a curfew, young lady. You may leave Star House to go to work at the salvage depot and for no other reason. After work, you must go straight home. The only other place you are allowed to be is the Anderson shelter in the event of an air raid. You're not allowed out in the evening. I've had you removed from fire-watching duty. If you attempt to leave Star House when you are not authorised to do so, and I find out – and I will – it will be added to your list of misdemeanours.'

'But I haven't done anything wrong,' Betty said in a dull voice. She felt two inches tall. It was as if the sergeant had taken her real self, her character, her good name, and battered them to a pulp.

'If you deviate from my instructions in the smallest degree,' Sergeant Robbins warned her, 'you'll find yourself in a police cell.'

Sergeant Robbins delivered Betty back to Star House. Would he knock on the door and pour out what he called her misde-meanours to her landlady? But he left her at the garden gate and watched her until she closed the front door behind her. No sooner had she taken off her outdoor things than the air-raid siren commenced its mournful wail.

'Quick, Betty,' said Mrs Beaumont, appearing in the hall-way. 'You need to get ready and scoot along to the depot to do your fire-watching. Where have you been? Sally set off twenty minutes ago.'

Betty's heart sank. Perhaps it would have been easier after all if Sergeant Robbins had come inside. Now she had to tell Mrs Beaumont everything. Even if she had felt like keeping it all to herself, she couldn't put Sally in the position of holding it back from Andrew and his mother. It was better for all sorts of reasons to tell the truth.

'I'm not going fire-watching,' she said. 'Let's get the house ready and go into the Andy, then I'll tell you what's happened.'

thief and nobody else. Secondly, if you believe the depot manager bears the ultimate responsibility, then which one of us are you referring to? You can't have it both ways. You can't flaunt your power and then heap the blame onto my shoulders.'

So saying, she left Mrs Lockwood opening and closing her mouth like a goldfish, and walked away with her head held high.

Lorna witnessed the confrontation between Sally and Mrs Lockwood, which took place when she was returning to work after her dinner-break. She had been just about to walk into the yard when she heard Mrs Lockwood's familiar carrying voice challenging Sally and she had tactfully stepped back from the doorway. Perhaps she ought to have withdrawn fully and made herself scarce so as not to listen in, but she couldn't resist a spot of earwigging. She wasn't being nosy as such but, ever since that day when the depot had been exceptionally busy and Mrs Lockwood had ridden roughshod over Sally and made her look small, Lorna's curiosity had been piqued as to the relationship between the two women.

She was glad Sally had given as good as she got. Even so, the confrontation was categorically none of her business, so she ran upstairs and waited by a window until Mrs Lockwood departed. Only then did she go down again.

Although it was cold, the day was dry. A consignment of damaged floorboards and other pieces of wood from bombed buildings had arrived a day or two ago and Sally rooted in the toolbox to find a couple of claw-hammers so they could prise out the nails.

While they were in the middle of this task, Mr Atkinson walked through the gates.

He raised his trilby to them. 'Good afternoon, ladies – though I have to s-say it d-doesn't feel all that good, not w-with the trouble that is hanging over Miss Hughes's head.'

'Thank you for going to see her at the police station yester-day,' Sally said warmly. 'When I saw her this morning, she said what a difference it had made. It really bucked her up.'

'That's good to hear,' said Mr Atkinson. 'I s-said I'd help her.'

'We all want to help her,' said Lorna, 'though it's difficult to see how.'

'I c-couldn't concentrate on my w-work this morning, so I shut the shop for the afternoon. I've just come here from St-Star House. Miss Hughes has told me everything she knows. Have the police s-said anything to you about this Leon Hargreaves fellow?'

Lorna and Sally looked at one another.

'No,' said Lorna. 'I don't think Sergeant Robbins had heard of him before this.'

'All we know about him is that he drives a van,' Sally added.

'And supposedly it was his mother's belongings that Eddie originally stored in the depot,' Lorna finished.

'It's easy to assume he's Eddie's accomplice,' said Sally, 'but it's also possible that he's a gullible friend.'

'Like Miss Hughes,' Lorna added.

'S-so we d-don't know anything about him, really,' said Mr Atkinson.

'We don't seem to know anything at all for certain,' Sally said gloomily, 'except that my family's possessions were stolen.'

'And that Eddie Markham is a rat,' said Lorna.

'There's one thing w-we do know,' said Mr Atkinson. 'Miss Hughes told me that Markham took her to a house in F-Fallow-field. She wasn't able to provide the address but she described the d-display in the window of the c-corner shop. The house was down that road.'

Sally made a hopeless gesture. 'How are we to find that corner shop?'

'She s-said they got off the bus outside a cinema and then

took the s-second or third turning on the left, and the shop was along there.'

'So it should be possible to find it,' said Lorna. 'What then?'

'I d-don't know,' Mr Atkinson admitted, 'but it's the only c-clue we have. I'm going there now.'

'Don't go yet,' said Sally. 'Wait for the depot to shut and the three of us will go together this evening. If there's anything to be found out, we'll do it together. One other thing,' she added. 'The three of us are doing this to help Miss Hughes – Betty – because we're her friends. I think that makes all of us friends too, so I'd like to dispense with the formalities and move to first-name terms – if you're happy with that, Mr Atkinson? Or Samuel, if I may?'

'S-Samuel. I'd like that,' he said shyly.

'That's settled, then,' said Sally. 'My name is Sally and this is Lorna.'

Lorna smiled at Samuel. 'It's good to have friends.'

Andrew wasn't happy about what Sally proposed to do, not because he thought her misguided but because he couldn't go with her. The local light rescue squads had taken on new recruits and Andrew was among those whose job it was to train them up. That was how he was due to spend that Saturday evening before his official duty commenced at ten o'clock.

'I'm not trying to talk you out of it,' he told Sally. 'I just wish I was free to come with you.'

Betty shed some tears when Sally explained what she and the others proposed to do.

'You're all so kind,' she said, trying not to sniff.

'It might not lead us anywhere,' Sally felt obliged to point out.

'I know,' said Betty, 'but the simple fact that you've tried to help me means everything. I just wish I could come too.'

'Don't even think of it,' Sally replied at once. 'You have to stay here and obey Sergeant Robbins's instructions.'

At last it was time to set off. Guided by the barely adequate light of her tissue-dimmed torch, Sally made her way to the bus stop where the three of them had agreed to meet. Presently they climbed aboard the Fallowfield bus.

'W-we need to get off outside the cinema,' Samuel told the elderly conductor.

Sally held her breath in case he asked, 'Which one?' but he said, 'I'll give you a shout when we get there. Don't worry. I won't let you miss it in the blackout.'

True to his word, he set them down at the correct stop and they walked along to the second road on the left. Down here they checked the displays in each of the corner shops, but couldn't find one that matched Betty's description. They doubled back and went down the next road on the left, and here they found what they were looking for.

'This must be it,' said Lorna as they all gazed through the criss-crossed anti-blast tape at the large variety of packets on show.

Sally savoured the moment, but her satisfaction was short-lived. 'We've found the shop and therefore the right road, but we have no idea which house Betty went to, so what now?'

'W-we go along the road,' said Samuel, 'and...'

'And?' Lorna prompted when he stopped.

'And hope,' he answered. 'It's all w-we can do.'

They started to walk past the long line of terraced houses. After every fourth one was a narrow covered walkway that must lead to the long passage that ran along the backs of all these houses and the backs of those in the adjacent road. When they got as far as the next corner, they halted.

'It's no use,' said Lorna. 'We came here with the best of intentions but the truth is we were never going to discover anything, were we?'

In silence they went back in the direction of the shop with the misleading display. Before they reached it, they heard the sound of an engine. Then dipped and shaded headlamps appeared, coming towards them. A few moments later a van passed them and pulled in at the kerb halfway down the road.

'Sw-witch off your torches,' Samuel whispered.

They peered intently into the darkness. Such was the depth of the blackout that Sally could barely see anything. She could make out the shape of the van only because she knew it was there. She heard a door open and shut – that must be the driver getting out. Then there were footsteps and another door opened.

'He must be getting something out of the back,' Lorna whispered.

After that, footsteps went towards one of the houses. There was a pause, then a door opened and closed.

'That has to be Leon Hargreaves,' said Lorna. 'Oh, please, it has to be.'

'W-we need the house number,' said Samuel.

'I'll go and look,' Sally volunteered. 'It'll be quieter if just one of us goes.'

A minute later, having nipped down to the house, she was back with her friends.

'What next?' she asked.

'I w-wonder what he took indoors,' said Samuel.

'A box of stolen goods,' said Lorna. 'It's got to be.'

'Whatever it was,' said Sally, 'we need to get back to Chorlton and give this address to Sergeant Robbins.'

'Let's have a look round the back f-first,' said Samuel.

At the first walkway they came to between the houses, they stopped and listened. They didn't want to bump into anybody. Then they hurried through to the passage that ran in between the two roads. At the rear of each house was a small yard enclosed by a brick wall. It was easy to find Leon Hargreaves's house because, even though the back-gate didn't have a number painted on it, others did.

They moved a short way along the passage to have a whispered conversation.

'Whatever he carried indoors, it could be the key to everything,' said Lorna. 'We need to be sure that he doesn't take it away again. Samuel, if you keep watch from here, I'll watch the front. Sally, go back to that corner shop and ask for the nearest police station – or stop an ARP warden or a WVS lady if you see one. The local police can telephone Sergeant Robbins. He'll tell them what he wants them to do.'

Sally sent up a swift prayer that Lorna's plan would work. If the police searched the house, and whatever Leon Hargreaves had taken indoors was indeed stolen – but then she realised that all that would achieve would be to prove that Hargreaves was a thief. It wouldn't prove that Betty wasn't involved.

All the same, it could bring the police a step closer to the truth, so she whispered, 'I'll be as quick as I can.'

But before she and Lorna could set off on their different errands, there was the sound of a door opening quietly and the three of them froze. There was no way of telling where the sound had come from. Then came footsteps – and then Leon Hargreaves's back-gate opened. Sally and the others pressed themselves against the brick wall.

More footsteps, then a pause in which the back-gate closed. A moment later Leon Hargreaves headed away from them along the passage.

'Did you s-see that?' asked Samuel. 'He's carrying a box. I'll go after him. You two f-fetch help.'

'No,' Lorna said firmly. 'We all stick together. It was one thing to split up when he was in the house but this is different.'

On cat-feet and keeping their distance, they followed Leon Hargreaves to the end of the passage, out into the street and round a couple of corners, ending up watching him vanish into the pitch-darkness blanketing a piece of waste-ground.

'Listen,' Samuel whispered. 'I think he's unfastening a padlock.'

A door-hinge squeaked and then the door shut.

'We have to do something,' said Lorna. 'Samuel – wait!'

But Samuel was striding across the waste-ground. The girls darted after him, stumbling on the uneven land. There was a shabby building, long and low. When he reached it, he glanced round.

'K-keep out of sight,' he ordered and, before they could prevent him, he thrust open the door and stepped into the door-way. 'Leon Hargreaves,' he said in a loud voice. 'Stop w-whatever you're up to. Put down what you're c-carrying. This is the police. The building is surrounded.'

There was an astonished silence. Then Leon Hargreaves spoke up.

'You're never the police.'

'I am a plain-clothes d-detective.'

'Nah. If there were others with you, they'd be swarming all over the place.'

Lorna quickly stepped towards a blacked-out window and banged on it, then did the same on another window. Sally followed suit on windows on the other side of the door.

'Alone, am I?' Samuel demanded. He must have shone his torch around because he then asked, 'What's all this s-stuff, then? I followed you because of what you're c-carrying, but now just look at all this. Your secret hoard, is it? Enjoy stealing f-from poor unfortunate families who've been bombed out, do you?'

'I don't know what you're going on about.'

'I think you do,' Samuel said in a voice of authority. 'This place looks f-full to the brim. Is this why you and Markham needed to use the s-salvage depot?'

Sally was so engrossed in listening that she was unaware of anybody close by until a hand slid across her mouth. As she began to struggle, a familiar voice whispered in her ear, 'Shh. It's Sergeant Robbins.' He let her go. 'We've been watching Leon Hargreaves's house all day and we've ended up following you. Stay out of the way while my men raid the building.'

'Wait,' Sally whispered urgently. 'Let Mr Atkinson finish – please.'

From the doorway Samuel said, 'You and Markham are both going to prison f-for this. The only question is: do you w-want a lighter sentence? A spot of cooperation c-could help you, but it has to be here and now.'

Silence. Then, 'How d'you mean?'

'There's the matter of whether Miss Hughes is involved,' said Samuel. 'Markham s-says she is. What do you say?'

'If I tell you, will it help me in court?'

All Samuel said was, 'I'm waiting.'

Finally Leon Hargreaves said, 'She's nowt to do with it. She's just a bit of fluff Eddie picked up.'

'That makes it his w-word against yours,' said Samuel.

'Hey, you said—'

'His word against yours,' Samuel repeated.

'I can prove it,' Leon Hargreaves said quickly. 'When did Eddie meet her? The end of October? Look around at all this stuff. It's been here way longer than that. We started looting in the summer. That shows she wasn't part of it.'

Then, as Sally sagged in relief, Sergeant Robbins shouted out the order and he and his men rushed towards the building.

CHAPTER TWENTY-FOUR

Betty wasn't just relieved. She was completely overwhelmed by what her friends had done for her. She was in Mrs Beaumont's sitting room with Sally and Lorna. Mrs Beaumont and Mrs Henshaw were there too. They had listened as avidly as Betty to the tale of what had happened and how Leon Hargreaves had been tricked into admitting that Betty wasn't and never had been an accomplice to the thieving.

'Samuel deserved the credit,' said Sally.

'Samuel?' queried Mrs Beaumont.

'Yes.' Mrs Henshaw's voice held a trace of stiffness. 'I was wondering the same thing.'

'This frightful business has brought us all together,' said Lorna. 'Samuel has shown himself to be the best sort of friend.'

'Where is he now?' asked Mrs Beaumont.

'On duty,' said Sally. 'He's an ARP warden.'

'Tell me again what he did,' said Betty. 'Did he really pretend to be a detective?'

'Yes,' said Lorna, 'and Leon Hargreaves fell for it. All he cared about was, as he thought, getting his own sentence reduced.'

'And Sergeant Robbins was outside listening to every word,' Sally added.

Although Betty nodded and smiled, this wasn't really what she wanted to hear. She didn't want to be told about Leon Hargreaves. What she hankered after was details about Samuel, the specifics of what he'd done and what he'd said, and had he been in any danger? She could now see Eddie for exactly what he was and she was ashamed to have been taken in by him. Dazzled by Eddie Markham, she hadn't been able to see what a good man was in front of her.

'What are you thinking about?' Sally asked her. 'You were miles away.'

'I'm impressed,' said Betty.

'By what Samuel did?' asked Sally.

'Yes, by his steady character and his willingness to get involved in clearing my name.'

'Impressed?' Lorna repeated with a knowing twinkle in her green eyes.

'Yes,' said Betty and then felt colour stain her cheeks as she realised what Lorna was really getting at. A picture of Samuel – his serious hazel eyes, his rather gangly appearance – appeared in Betty's mind's eye. Why had it taken her all this time to appreciate him?

On Sunday morning, when the others were getting ready to go to church, Betty put on her hat and coat too, but Mrs Beaumont took her aside.

'I don't think you should come with us, Betty. You should wait for Sergeant Robbins to lift your curfew.'

'But my name has been cleared,' said Betty.

'All the same I'd wait, if I were you. That'll show him you can be trusted to follow instructions.'

Betty conceded that her landlady was right. Sergeant

Robbins might now know that she definitely wasn't a thief, but he wouldn't have forgotten how she had come by the magistrate's fine. Sticking to the curfew until he told her otherwise was a small thing to do and, if it improved his opinion of her, then all the better.

Sergeant Robbins came to Star House while the others were out. Betty showed him into the sitting room.

'Your friends did you a great service yesterday,' said the sergeant.

'I know,' said Betty. 'They did the police a great service too, didn't they?'

'You could say that.' Sergeant Robbins smiled. 'We were watching Hargreaves in any case and would have followed him to the hideaway with the stolen goods, but it's because of your friends, and Mr Atkinson in particular, that your name was cleared so promptly. I'll need you to come to the police station to make a statement.'

'Now?' asked Betty.

'Tomorrow will do. I suggest that today you have a good think about what happened and generally get everything in order in your mind.'

'Does this mean you're releasing me from the curfew?'

'I'm pleased to tell you it does.'

Good. In that case, Betty knew precisely what she wanted to do with her freedom. After Sergeant Robbins had gone, she left a note for Mrs Beaumont and set off for Salford. It took a long time to get there because there were always fewer buses on a Sunday, not to mention a diversion caused by a crater in the road on the way out of Manchester towards Salford.

When she eventually arrived she went to the police station first, but Dad wasn't on duty, so she went home.

Grace answered the door. 'Oh – it's you! What are you doing here? Has your landlady slung you out? Only if she has, you can't come back here. I thought I made that clear yesterday.'

'I've come to see my dad,' said Betty.

She stared at Grace, who stared back.

'Who is it, Grace?' Dad called from the parlour.

Grace stepped aside, rolling her eyes as she let Betty into the house.

Betty didn't bother shedding her outdoor things but hurried straight into the parlour. She was anxious to see Dad, but she also wanted to get to him before Grace did.

He looked up as she entered, his habitually serious face softening into lines of delight at her unexpected appearance, immediately followed by worry. Standing up, he put his arms about her.

'Dad, I know what you've heard about me and it's not true,' Betty said immediately. 'I didn't do anything wrong – well, I did. I let Eddie use a room in the depot, and I should never have done that, but I thought he was helping folk who'd been bombed out.'

'Steady on,' said Dad. 'You're talking nineteen to the dozen. What I want to know is this...' He lifted her chin and looked into her eyes. 'Are you all right, Betty love? Is the trouble at an end?'

She nodded, swallowing a lump in her throat. Oh, how she loved her darling dad.

'Then come and sit down and tell me everything.' He drew her to the sofa and sat beside her, saying over his shoulder, 'Grace, put the kettle on, will you?'

Betty was still telling her story when Grace returned with a tray. She'd got to the part where her friends had followed Leon Hargreaves, who had ended up clearing her name.

'I was so worried about what you must have heard about me, Dad.'

'It gave me some difficult moments and I won't pretend otherwise,' said Dad, 'but all's well that ends well, eh?'

'Our biggest worry was for you, Betty,' said Grace.

Betty looked at her – and then she realised that Dad had no idea that Grave had descended on Chorlton-cum-Hardy yesterday afternoon and given her what for. Oh, the temptation to let him know the things Grace had said – but Betty would never upset her dad like that. All he wanted was for her and Grace to get along. Besides, Grace would probably talk her way out of it.

Then Grace, true to form, said brightly, 'Take your coat off, Betty, and hang it up. Then you must sit on the rug by the fire and drink your tea. It's a chilly day.'

Dad gave Betty a little push. 'Go on, love.'

Betty obeyed. When she sat on the hearthrug, Grace set Dad's tea on the table beside his armchair and he automatically moved back to his usual place. Betty felt a flare of resentment. Couldn't Grace let her sit with Dad just this once, when she'd been through a nasty ordeal?

'So the boyfriend turned out to be a bad lot,' said Grace.

Pain creased Betty's insides. Not because she had any lingering feelings for Eddie, because she definitely didn't, but because it hurt to be reminded. Aiming for a calm, steady voice, she said, 'Yes, I'm afraid he did.'

'Still, it's not as though you knew him all that long,' said Dad, obviously assuming that this meant Betty's feelings couldn't have run all that deep.

'It's all a great shame,' said Grace.

Was she commiserating? Or did she think it was a shame Betty was no longer heading towards matrimony and a home of her own?

On Monday Sally and Betty walked arm in arm down Beech Road to unlock the depot. Sally was delighted to have her friend by her side. As well as being pleased and relieved for Betty, she was still glowing with pride from the praise her beloved Andrew had heaped on her for her part in what had transpired.

'You're loyal and brave,' he had told her.

'It was really Samuel who pulled it off,' Sally replied.

But Andrew had been more interested in telling her what a marvel she was.

Now, as she and Betty arrived at the salvage depot, they found it already unlocked. Lorna appeared out of the dark and chilly December morning and gave Betty a hug.

'Welcome back,' she said.

Betty beamed. 'I can't tell you how good it feels to be here.'

'Go and get changed,' said Lorna. 'The daily sacks will be delivered any minute. I'll make a start on them.'

It was a busy morning. Even though it resembled any other Monday, it felt different because all three girls were aware of how close things had come to Betty still being under curfew.

Towards midday Sergeant Robbins turned up with some officers and asked for access to the room with the stolen goods.

'My men will be coming and going,' he said.

'What's happening about Eddie Markham and Leon Harg-reaves?' Lorna asked.

'They both appeared in court first thing this morning and they've been remanded in custody. That means they'll be kept in prison until they go on trial.'

'That's a relief,' said Betty.

'Would you care to come over to the police station now, Miss Hughes, to make your statement?'

Betty looked at Sally for permission.

'If you feel up to it,' said Sally.

'It would get it over with,' said Lorna.

'I am more interested in thoroughness and attention to detail than in getting it over with,' said Sergeant Robbins. Then he added with a smile, 'But it would put it behind you.'

'I was just thinking of Samuel,' Betty confessed. 'He really ought to get the credit, not me.'

'He doesn't want the credit,' Sally reminded her.

'Even if he did, he's not allowed to have it,' Lorna added cheerfully. 'Have you seen him since he went to see you in the police station?'

Betty shook her head. 'Apparently he came over to Star House yesterday afternoon, but I'd gone to Salford.'

Sally hesitated, then said, 'After the way I encouraged you to go out with Eddie, I don't know whether I should say this.'

'Say what?' Betty asked.

'Samuel is interested in you. Just after you started seeing Eddie, he asked me if I thought he stood a chance with you and I told him you were spoken for.'

The breath hitched in Betty's throat. Hope soared but she dragged it back down to earth. 'That doesn't mean he's still interested now. I was pretty gone on Eddie and never made a secret of it. That must have been very off-putting.'

'I don't know about that,' said Lorna. 'You didn't see how keen and determined he was to rush straight to the police station when you were being questioned.'

'Even so,' said Betty. She wanted to hope, but was scared of setting herself up for the worst disappointment of her life.

'Tell you what,' said Sally. 'Go to the bookshop. Get changed and take the rest of the afternoon off.'

'I couldn't—' Betty started to say.

'Don't argue with the boss,' said Lorna.

Betty looked from her to Sally. The muscles around her mouth twitched and a smile burst into life. So did something in her heart. She ran upstairs and changed into her own clothes and soon she was on her way.

When she reached Samuel's shop, she hesitated before opening the door. This mattered so much. After the madness of her relationship with Eddie, she knew now what a good and worthwhile man Samuel Atkinson was. She had known it all along, of course, but somehow the knowledge had stayed in her head instead of penetrating her heart.

The door opened, making her jump.

'W-why are you w-waiting outside in the cold?' Samuel asked.

'Silly me,' Betty murmured, ducking her head to hide her blushes as she hurried past him. Taking her courage in both hands, she turned in his direction. 'I hope—'

A craggy-faced man appeared from between a pair of book-cases. 'I can't find it, Mr Atkinson. Could you help me?'

'Of c-course.'

Betty would have liked to go through to the parlour-office to take off her coat, but it would feel like taking advantage, so instead she hovered, pretending to look at the books, while Samuel served his customer. He found the title the man was looking for and left him flicking through it.

To Betty he said quietly, 'I don't need your help here at present. Has there been a misunderstanding?'

'I'll take this, please,' said the customer.

He went to the counter. Samuel took his money and counted the change into his gloved hand. When the customer left, Betty followed him to the door, shut it behind him, turned the sign to CLOSED and shot the bolts. Then, her heart beating fast, she faced Samuel.

'Please can we talk?' she asked.

Was this a dreadful mistake? But the sight of him melted her heart. A couple of his natural curls had fought back against his hair-cream and bounced on top of his head. His loose-limbed frame seemed suddenly gawky and uncertain. Behind his glasses, his hazel eyes showed how unsure he felt.

Betty knew this was up to her. After her idiocy over Eddie, Samuel needed to know the new truth of her life and her heart, and she mustn't leave any room for doubt. After that it would be a question of whether he was still interested in her.

She remembered what Sally had once told her about herself and Andrew. When they had met, they'd both known very quickly that they were meant to be together for ever. But Betty's relationship with Eddie had well and truly put the mockers on that for her and Samuel.

'I'm not here to work on the donated books,' she said. 'I've come to see you. It's a – a personal visit. I want to start by thanking you again for everything you did at the weekend to help me. It was brave of you to confront Leon Hargreaves like that.'

'Anyone w-would have done the same,' said Samuel.

'No, they wouldn't,' said Betty. 'I can't think of anyone else who would have thought of pretending to be a detective to trick the truth out of Leon Hargreaves. It didn't just take courage. It took imagination and quick thinking. And – and you did it to help me.'

'You d-deserved it. You've w-worked hard for me. You've given me a lot of help.'

Oh, how Betty longed to ask whether he might have also had a more personal reason to help her, but it wouldn't be fair to put him on the spot. It wasn't his fault she had been blinded by Eddie.

Betty took the question she longed to ask and turned it into an honest declaration.

'The truth is that I hope, I very much hope, that there was a more personal reason for you to do what you did. I hope you like me, Samuel, because I like you.'

After a moment Samuel asked, 'What about Eddie Markham?'

'I've been a fool. Now, looking back, I don't know what I ever saw in him. Even when he did something that showed me he wasn't the man I thought he was, I still let him talk me round.

After that he pushed me into letting him use the depot. I knew it was wrong, but...'

'But you were d-dazzled,' said Samuel.

Betty took a step closer. 'I'm not dazzled now – and I'm not talking about Eddie. I never want to think about him again. What I mean is that I'm thinking clearly. When I look at you, I see clearly. You're a good man. You have integrity. You're a man to be proud of.'

'That sounds very d-dull,' said Samuel.

'If by "dull" you mean honest and hard-working and caring, then you're the dullest person I've ever met. I've come to my senses, Samuel. I know there has barely been any gap after Eddie, but I don't need a gap and I hope you don't either. I hope you can believe that the way I see you now, and the way I feel about you now, is real and true and lasting.'

Samuel stood very still. 'Lasting? D-do you mean that?'

Betty nodded. 'I promise.'

Samuel huffed out a breath. Behind the lenses of his spectacles, a light appeared in his hazel eyes. The effect of the shop's ceiling lamp – or maybe a glimmer of emotion?

Betty took a chance and stepped nearer.

'I'm sorry I didn't see you properly from the beginning. I wish I had. But things happened the way they happened and now I hope with all my heart that you can forget what a twit I was over Eddie.'

'You c-could never be a twit. You're a k-kind person with a loving heart and you were badly taken advantage of. Markham is a criminal and he knew exactly what he w-was doing. And now,' Samuel added, a smile appearing, 'let's stop talking about him. I'd much rather talk about us.'

Betty sighed. 'Us? Is there an us?'

'S-starting now, there is.'

. . .

Lorna went home from work wondering how things had gone with Betty and Samuel at the bookshop. Betty hadn't returned to the depot, which suggested the meeting had gone well. Lorna hoped so for Betty's sake. A deep pang almost carved her heart in two. She knew what it was to love – and she knew what it meant to lose that love. She hoped Samuel and Betty could find true happiness together. They were such lovely, decent people.

She let herself into the Lockwoods' house, noting, as she always did, the two umbrella-stands with their sturdy sticks, the hoe, the garden fork and the rake, put there so that, if push came to shove, the Lockwoods could engage Jerry in combat in the street. You couldn't fault their patriotism or their sheer determination to face whatever was thrown at them. Lorna quite liked Mr Lockwood, with his gentle manner and his warm chuckle, but she now entertained serious reservations concerning his wife. She was also aware that Mr Lockwood would always take the memsahib's side, no matter what.

Lorna saw matters differently now. To start with at the depot, she had found it hard to credit that Sally could be the manager when Mrs Lockwood cut a far more impressive figure. Since then she had come to value Sally's good points and she had also found herself on increasingly better terms with both Sally and Betty, and now they were her friends.

Lorna was especially impressed by the way Sally had, out of friendship and regard for Betty, let her take the credit for unmasking Eddie. She might easily have hogged all the glory for herself and made herself look good as the depot manager, which in turn would have been one in the eye for Mrs Lockwood, but instead she had stepped aside and put Betty first.

If there was one thing Lorna was now certain of, it was that she didn't wish to live with the Lockwoods any longer; but, with thousands homeless and bunking with relatives and friends for the foreseeable future, she had little hope of getting a new billet.

Now, glancing at the hall-table, she found a letter from

home was waiting for her and she was thrilled to see Mummy's
handwriting. She opened the envelope carefully so it could be
used again. It already had Great-Aunt Ida's writing on it,
neatly crossed out by Mummy before she wrote Lorna's
address.

Lorna's heart thumped as she read what her mother had
written.

*Because of the continued air raids in Manchester, Daddy says
you can go to the West Country. I will find you the best hotel I
can. All we want is for you to be safe.*

The West Country! A five-star hotel in Torquay or Corn-
wall, and the opportunity to sit out the war in comfort in the
company of the sort of people she was used to. People with
money and breeding, ladies with real pearls and gentlemen who
belonged to London clubs. Yes, there would still be rationing
and the blackout, but there wouldn't be as many air raids, if
indeed there were any at all. And best of all, no more salvage
work.

Lorna hugged the possibility to herself. It felt too precious
to share. Moreover, she was well aware that the news wouldn't
necessarily be greeted by others with pleasure on her behalf. It
was one thing to evacuate children and pregnant ladies to
places of safety, quite another for the well-heeled to evacuate
themselves. Lorna was going to have to be very careful how she
went about it if she decided to leave— if? Where had that *if*
sprung from?

The next morning she went to work as usual. It was strange
to think that her days at the depot were numbered. But the idea
of the West Country seemed less urgent now compared to
hearing what had happened between Betty and Samuel
yesterday.

One look at Betty told Lorna all she needed to know. Her

peaches-and-cream complexion glowed and her blue eyes were bright.

'Is it safe to assume you and Samuel will be a couple from now on?' Lorna asked.

Betty nodded, smiling happily, but then she looked serious. 'You don't think it's too soon after Eddie?'

'No, I don't,' Lorna said staunchly. 'If Samuel is the right man for you, then my advice is to grab him with both hands and hang on for dear life. Don't let anything or anyone come between you.' Realising she had spoken more forcefully than she'd meant to, she stopped.

After a moment Betty asked, 'Are you talking about me and Samuel or do you mean you and the man you were engaged to?'

Lorna stiffened, then she rallied, planting a smile on her lips. 'You, of course. I want things to go well for you. You deserve it.'

The three of them got on with their work. Later in the morning, a man entered the yard. Well into his fifties, he was well-made with broad shoulders and a square jaw. His cheeks were pitted and pockmarked. He had raised his hat in greeting, revealing a full head of silver hair.

'Good morning, ladies.'

Sally stepped forward. 'I'm Mrs Henshaw, the depot manager. Can I help you?'

But the man was looking past her. Something made Lorna's skin prickle as the man's gaze landed on Betty.

He smiled. 'No, thanks, Mrs Henshaw, I don't think you can.' He might be addressing Sally but his gaze was locked on Betty. 'But I believe this young lady can. Miss Betty Hughes?'

'Yes,' said Betty. 'What do you want?'

That was when the notebook appeared. 'I believe you have an interesting story to tell.'

'Are you a reporter?' Lorna demanded. She had no doubt that he was, but she asked the question out loud as a warning to her friends. This was a very different sort of situation to yesterday's with the men from the *Manchester Evening News*.

'Name of Geoff Baldwin,' said the man, 'and I'm a freelancer. That means I sell my stories to whoever will buy them. I'm not here to make life difficult for you, Miss Hughes, far from it. I've come to give you a fair hearing. You're the innocent party in all this.'

'How do you know about that?' Sally asked.

The *Evening News* piece wasn't going to appear until later today.

'A journalist never reveals his sources,' said Geoff Baldwin.

'He's got a friend at the police station,' Lorna said flatly.

Betty uttered a soft cry.

'Surely with all the air raids, there must be plenty for you to write about,' said Lorna.

Mr Baldwin ignored that. He focused on Betty. 'Come on, Miss Hughes.' His tone was wheedling but his eyes held triumph. 'Were you in love with Markham? Did he sweep you off your feet? Readers love a bit of romance. They'll be on your side.'

'Don't say a word, Betty,' Lorna cautioned her.

Mr Baldwin glared at Lorna. 'Don't listen to her, *Betty*. Listen to me. I can make you come out of this looking good. Everyone will be outraged on your behalf and mothers will warn their daughters to be careful who they go out with. I'm happy to write that story, but I can only do it with your cooperation. If you choose not to cooperate, well, who knows what I might be tempted to write?'

'Don't be afraid, Betty,' said Lorna. 'Mr Baldwin won't write a single word about you.'

'Oh aye?' sneered Mr Baldwin.

Lorna gave him back stare for stare. 'Because he'll be too busy writing about me.'

'Lorna!' Sally exclaimed.

'I've already been dragged through the newspapers once,' said Lorna. 'One more time isn't going to make much odds.'

'What d'you mean?' Mr Baldwin asked suspiciously.

'It's what I believe is known as a scoop, Mr Baldwin,' said Lorna. 'My story is a great deal more interesting than Miss Hughes's and I will grant you an interview. In return, you have to guarantee in writing to leave Miss Hughes alone. You can print whatever you want about me, though obviously,' she added, hiding sarcasm beneath a voice of honey, 'I hope you'll treat me with the sympathy and understanding you offered to show to Miss Hughes.'

'You'd do that for me?' breathed Betty.

'Yes,' Lorna answered simply. 'You're a good person, Betty, and you don't deserve the kind of publicity your story would bring. Mr Baldwin, there is one more condition. You mustn't divulge my whereabouts.'

'What's all this about?' asked the reporter. 'Who are you?'

Lorna ignored him. To Sally and Betty she said, 'I had the chance to move to the West Country but I'm not going. I've realised how much it means to me to be here, to do my bit and be with my friends, so I'm staying. I want to fight on the home front and I want to do it alongside the two of you.'

CHAPTER TWENTY-SIX

If Betty was understandably stunned by what Lorna was going to do for her, then she wasn't the only one. Sally was too. All she could do when Lorna calmly asked her permission to use the office for the interview was nod. When Lorna and the unpleasant Mr Baldwin had disappeared inside the building, Sally and Betty stared at one another.

'Well!' said Sally.

'I can hardly believe it,' said Betty.

'It's very generous of her,' said Sally, 'especially when you remember how she was hauled over the coals by the newspapers just a matter of weeks ago. I hope Mr Baldwin sticks to his side of the bargain and writes a sympathetic piece.'

'It's in his interests to,' said Betty. 'It will make what he writes different to what has been written before.'

'That's true,' Sally acknowledged. 'But will readers believe a sympathetic version after all the unkind reporting?'

'Samuel once told me that newspapers can put a slant on any story at all to make you see it the way they want you to,' said Betty. 'Mr Baldwin has already shown himself to be an expert in the art of manipulation.'

'Poor Lorna, putting herself through this,' said Sally. 'No matter how sympathetic the story is, it's still a huge intrusion into her private life.'

'And she's doing it for me,' said Betty with wonder in her voice. 'She hasn't worked here all that long and it's only very recently that we've all got along properly, and now here she is offering herself up on a plate to save me from adverse publicity.'

'It shows what she's made of,' said Sally. 'She's the sort who stands by her friends.'

'I think wartime has something to do with it as well,' said Betty. 'Everything feels more intense. Everything matters more.'

Sally nodded her agreement. 'Other people matter. Friend-ships matter. We all have to take care of one another.'

'First Lorna helped clear my name, and now this,' said Betty. 'I wish there was something I could do for her.'

An idea started to form in Sally's mind. 'Maybe there is. Maybe there's something we can both do.'

'What?' Betty asked eagerly.

'There's an empty single room at Star House,' said Sally, excitement growing. 'Why don't we ask Mrs Beaumont if Lorna can have it?'

'Yes.' Betty spoke softly but with emphasis. 'That would be perfect. Mrs Beaumont would much rather choose her own billetee than rely on the billeting officer to find her someone. She already knows Lorna and likes her.'

'I'll hold the fort here,' said Sally, knowing how much it would mean to Betty to be the one to ask Mrs Beaumont on Lorna's behalf. 'Why don't you cut along now while Lorna is occupied and ask Mrs Beaumont if she can move in?'

That evening, in Star House's cosy sitting room, Betty gazed in a mixture of delight and disbelief at the story, complete with the photograph of her perched on top of the pile of tyres, in the *Manchester Evening News*.

'You look very glamorous,' said Sally.

'And that headline is pretty flattering too,' said Lorna. She had come round for the evening to see her new billet.

Local Heroine Foils Looter

Betty was thrilled. It was impossible not to blush.

'Dad's going to be so proud,' she said.

'He's not the only one,' said Sally. 'So is Samuel.'

'Thank you,' Betty said to Sally. 'It was so good of you not to take the credit for yourself. I wouldn't have blamed you if you had.'

'I wanted you to have it,' said Sally.

'But you could probably have got Mrs Lockwood off your back,' Betty pointed out.

'And that would have been wonderful,' Sally admitted, 'but not as wonderful as doing this for my friend.'

'It's one of the best presents I've ever had,' said Betty.

'Just make sure you remember that when my birthday comes round,' teased Sally.

'Betty isn't the only one with reason to be grateful,' said Lorna. 'Thank you both for thinking of me and asking Mrs Beaumont if she'd let me come here.'

'The three of us will be living together as well as working together,' Betty said happily. 'I can't think of anything better.'

'Can't you?' asked Lorna with a smile. 'Not even being with Samuel?'

They laughed and Betty felt a flutter of anticipation. She glanced at the clock on the mantelpiece. She and Samuel were going out together this evening. It would be a truncated outing because both of them had to be on duty for ten o'clock.

It was time to get ready. Betty dressed with care, choosing

her cherry-red jumper. She had washed her hair earlier and Sally had helped her to put it in rollers to dry. Now Betty gently teased the rollers free. Her golden hair curled under at the back and she carefully brushed it away from her face, securing it in position with hairpins, adding a pretty comb on each side for show.

Soon after she went downstairs, a ring at the door had her flying to answer it. Although she felt like flinging the door wide, she remembered to open it just a crack for Samuel to slip through, bringing with him the scent of crisp air. Obeying regulations, Betty closed the door quickly and tugged the door-curtain across before she switched on the light, her heart drumming in her chest as she turned to face Samuel.

'Do we have to get straight off?' she asked. Eddie had always spirited her away quickly from Star House.

'Only if you want to,' Samuel answered. 'I thought it'd be nice to pop in and s-say how do.'

'I'd love that,' said Betty, helping him off with his overcoat. It was such a simple thing to do, yet it felt cosy and intimate. She popped his trilby on the shelf and he hung up his scarf and gas-mask box on one of the pegs.

Then he took a clean handkerchief from his jacket pocket and, removing his spectacles, buffed up the lenses. Not having his glasses on gave him a slightly vulnerable look. He had the kindest, most honest eyes Betty had ever seen. They made her feel content and at ease with the world.

She lifted her chin proudly as she led him into the sitting room. Andrew immediately stood up to shake hands.

'I've heard what you did for Betty,' he said. 'Good show.'

'She has some staunch friends,' said Mrs Beaumont.

'That's because she's worth c-caring about,' said Samuel.

Sally laughed. 'Don't, Samuel. You're making her blush.'

Betty, however, knew it wasn't a blush but a glow of delight at receiving Samuel's simple but sincere praise. He would never say anything he didn't mean. Betty would have admired and appreciated that in any case but, after the way she had been taken in by Eddie's smooth lies, Samuel's trustworthiness was something she valued all the more deeply. It made her feel safe. Proud, too, to know she was with such a good, decent man. She sighed happily at the thought of introducing him to Dad, knowing they would like and respect one another.

They chatted for a while, then Samuel glanced at Betty and she knew it was time for them to be going.

'Where are you off to?' asked Sally.

'Just for something to eat,' said Betty. She sounded as casual as she could, but really she couldn't wait to be seen in public with Samuel.

They said their goodbyes and went into the hallway to put on their outdoor things. Samuel wound his scarf round his neck and picked up the two gas-mask cases. Betty pulled on her gloves and reached for her handbag.

'Got everything?' she asked Samuel.

She switched off the light but, before she could pull aside the door-curtain, Samuel gently placed his hands on her shoulders and turned her to him, lowering his face to hers for the sweetest of kisses. Betty responded willingly. In Samuel's arms was where she wanted to be, now and always.

A LETTER FROM SUSANNA

Dear Reader,

Welcome to the second book in my Home Front Girls trilogy, *Courage for the Home Front Girls*. I hope you loved reading it and enjoyed meeting Lorna, the new girl at the salvage depot.

If you did enjoy the book, and want to keep up to date with all my latest releases, just sign up at the following link. Your email address will never be shared and you can unsubscribe at any time.

www.bookouture.com/susanna-bavin

Thank you for choosing to read *Courage for the Home Front Girls*. I would love to hear your thoughts on it in a review. These not only let authors receive your personal feedback but also help new readers to choose their next book and discover new authors. I hope you will also want to read my stand-alone sagas – *The Deserter's Daughter, A Respectable Woman, The Sewing Room Girl* and *The Poor Relation*.

I love hearing from my readers – you can get in touch on my Facebook page or through X. I hope you'll follow me on Facebook – and do please visit my website. My Welcome page is updated every week, usually on a Friday, and I blog once a week as well.

Much love, Susanna xx

KEEP IN TOUCH WITH SUSANNA

www.susannabavin.co.uk

 facebook.com/MaisieThomasAuthor
𝕏 x.com/SusannaBavin

ACKNOWLEDGMENTS

Many thanks to my agent, Camilla Shestopal, and my editor, Susannah Hamilton, for their support. Susannah is a marvel at bringing the best out of a book. I am also grateful to Hannah Snetsinger, who oversaw the process of preparing the book for publication; to Jacqui Lewis whose copy-editing gave the book additional polish; and to Nick Castle for the beautiful cover.

Thanks also to Jen Gilroy, Beverley Ann Hopper, Jane Cable, Cass Grafton, Kitty Wilson and Kirsten Hesketh.

PUBLISHING TEAM

Turning a manuscript into a book requires the efforts of many people. The publishing team at Bookouture would like to acknowledge everyone who contributed to this publication.

Commercial
Lauren Morrissette
Jil Thielen
Imogen Allport

Contracts
Peta Nightingale

Cover design
Nick Castle

Data and analysis
Mark Alder
Mohamed Bussuri

Editorial
Susannah Hamilton
Nadia Michael

Copyeditor
Jacqui Lewis

Milton Keynes UK
Ingram Content Group UK Ltd.
UKHW010740300424
441987UK00004B/228